Enjoy !

THE REFLEX

PART 1
FIRST BOOK IN THE REFLEX SERIES

MARIA DENISON

BALBOA.PRESS
A DIVISION OF HAY HOUSE

Balboa Press books may be ordered through booksellers or by contacting:

Balboa Press
A Division of Hay House
1663 Liberty Drive
Bloomington, IN 47403
www.balboapress.com
844-682-1282

Print information available on the last page.

Library of Congress Control Number: 2022908086
ISBN: 979-8-7652-2821-0 (sc)
ISBN: 979-8-7652-2823-4 (hc)
ISBN: 979-8-7652-2822-7 (e)

Balboa Press rev. date: 07/20/2022

CONTENTS

PROLOGUE

April 2014

THE LIGHTING IN THE ROOM is dim. Grime covers the floors and small kitchenette Cara has in her visual. The apartment looks like no one has lived in it for some time. The studio appears as if no one has updated it since its location in Berlin was called the German Democratic Republic. Everything seems at least 25 years old.

So, this is how it ends for her. She will experience a painful, tragic death at the hands of an older man, who resembles Albert Einstein, holding a gun to her head. She will die alone, and only God knows when her body will be found. Not how she ever pictured her death.

When Cara Bianco Andre was young, she never envisioned her mortality. She felt invincible. Taking chances with her life was the norm. It was the adrenalin rush she sought out. If ziplines and bungee jumping were around back then, she would have loved them. She settled on other ways to satisfy her needs.

At the moment, those needs no longer exist. They haven't made an appearance in years, closer to decades. Her adrenal glands pumping now have nowhere to go. She's on the verge of a full-blown panic attack. Her only thought before she dies is to somehow leave a message for her husband and children. They are her world.

Looking down she can see the puddle she left when she lost her bladder. She could try to fingerpaint a message to them with her pee. What would she say, though? "I am sorry I was an ass and got myself killed?" No, those can't be her last words. They are most definitely true, but something more emotional would be appropriate.

How about, "I love you three so much. I will watch over you forever, but please move on with your lives." No, Einstein holding the gun will notice her writing all that. Einstein. She could leave a clue about him. Something they can solve her murder with.

Wait, she doesn't know his name. "He looks like Einstein." No, that's not going to help them. Why has she never thought about her last words? Do most people? Maybe, not. Especially if you have no regrets about the life you have chosen and lived. She wouldn't change a thing, except for coming to Berlin.

Deciding it's now or never, she discreetly places one fingertip in the puddle and drags it out to spell, "sorry, love you."

Of course, Einstein notices, and says, "Eeewww, gross. It's bad enough I had to drag you in here covered in piss. Now you've got your hands in it? I am going to shoot you twice for that."

She might have let a little more of her bladder go after that.

CHAPTER 1

Four Days Earlier

CARA IS HAVING THE MOST sensual dream. She can feel full lips trailing softly down her exposed back. There is a sensation of warm fingertips following behind them. Her breathing speeds with her arousal and she smiles. It's been awhile since she's had an erotic dream, she intends to enjoy this one, but a sudden slap on her ass jolts her awake. "Ouch!"

"Get that fine ass up now. This is the third time I had to come in here to wake you, Cara." Her husband has lost his patience. Every morning it's the same routine. Nic has fed their children, packed their lunches and finally, struggled to get her out of bed. "You have ten minutes before driving them to school."

Wide-awake now, she whines, "No, I hate drop-off." She rolls to her side to get comfortable, again, just to torment him.

"Gotta catch a flight, remember?" He leans in to brush his lips across hers, waiting for her to murmur her appreciation. As soon as he hears her soft moan, he yanks her up out of bed, sets her down in front of him and commands, "Get ready, now!" and he walks out of the room.

Sighing audibly, Cara stalks around the king size bed. The bed is completely disheveled, evidence of a tantric evening. She picks up a pillow thrown by a hand painted armoire and tosses it back on the bed. Affectionately, she brushes her hand across the front of armoire. It's one of the first pieces of furniture she and her husband purchased.

Cara uses the toilet room, brushes her teeth quickly, and pulls on the yoga pants, sports bra and T-shirt she'd left lying across her vanity stool from the night before. She walks out of the bath, through the bedroom, and down the long hallway. Even the length of the hallway is exhausting for her at this hour of the morning.

When she reaches the kitchen, Nic is just grabbing his leather messenger bag and heading out the garage door. He abruptly stops, grabs Cara around the waist, and pulls her in for a long, sensual kiss. In the background they hear, "Stop that. It's disgusting!" They separate from their kiss with an audible pop and glare at their daughter.

Nic instructs her, "Mia, be nice to your mother today, please." Turning to Cara, he states, "I'm in and out of Detroit." He points to a to-go coffee on the counter for her as he waves and walks out.

Cara ignores her daughter in favor of a sip of that coffee, first. After she has several gulps, she inquires, "Is your brother ready?"

Mia scowls, a permanent gesture for her. "Is he ever? He's still in his room messing with his hair. Total fem."

Cara looks around her perfectly designed kitchen. The granite counters shine, despite the litter of breakfast plates and school lunch preparation discards. She sighs audibly for the second time this morning. Nic is the most amazingly attentive husband and father, but cleaning up after himself is not his thing.

She leans into the back stairwell, which only leads to the second floor of their home, and yells, "Max! Downstairs, now!" She grabs the two lunch sacks, her coffee and starts towards the garage exit, glancing back at her daughter. "I'll be in the car waiting."

Walking into the garage Cara suddenly realizes she's only wearing a T-shirt and the temperature must be 50 degrees. Hopefully she can make to school and back without incident. She climbs into her Audi Q5 and positions Mia's lunch on the floor of the front seat, and Max's in the middle of the back seat.

And this is how it's been done, every morning, for over a decade, since the twins have started school. She raises the garage door and starts the car, immediately turning on the seat warmers for both front seats. Mia will pose a fit if her seat isn't sufficiently heated when she arrives.

Now, she waits. Mia emerges first; frown on her face, ready for the day. She climbs into the front seat, struggles with her backpack and settles in without a word. Cara does not look at her, because making eye contact with one's almost sixteen year old daughter is, at any time, forbidden.

Max comes out within thirty seconds of his sister. He looks and is dressed like he's right off an ad for Abercrombie & Fitch. He is, by far, the most handsome boy at school. The problem is, he knows it.

Again, no one speaks as Cara pulls out of the garage. As they head out onto the open road, Cara breaks the silence. "So, what's the afterschool schedule today?" she asks sensitively.

Mia huffs out, "I don't know. I'll text you." Max doesn't answer. Cara looks in her rearview mirror and notices her son has his earbuds in. She waves a hand around between the two front seats until he notices.

He pulls one earbud out and grunts, "What?"

Cara inquires again, "What is the afterschool schedule today?"

"I have baseball practice after school."

"What time will you be done?"

"I don't know. I'll text you." Ditto.

This is as much conversation allowed until they arrive at school. Cara sips her coffee to keep herself busy. Mia continues to frown and Max bobs his head to music. Dealing with two teenagers can be more stress than any parent should endure first thing in the morning.

Cara is about to take the right turn, which will lead them to the High School drop-off oval. She's forced to slam on her brakes as another mom, with an obnoxiously large Lexus SUV, cuts her off by taking a left from the oncoming traffic. Cara tries for a deep, cleansing yoga breath.

Mia hears it, and immediately launches into the morning diatribe. "Don't even start Mom! I can't deal with the way you and Dad get so worked up every morning in the oval. Can't you be like all the other parents and just deal with it?"

Cara holds her tongue. She's really going to try to get through this without a word. Suddenly a car is headed right for her, going the opposite direction on the one-way entrance.

Now, all hell breaks loose. Cara loses it, as she usually does for morning drop-off. "What kind of assholes are these people? Since when is dropping your child off at school a frigging competitive sport? Why doesn't the school administration police this oval?" Before she can continue with her screaming rhetoric, a car pulls out of a parking spot, almost T-boning them. Cara lays on the horn to alert the moron that he has a rearview mirror; he should try looking at it occasionally.

Mia is fuming with embarrassment. "You're actually worse than Dad! Did you have to honk?"

Regaining her composure, Cara calmly states, "No, I guess I didn't. Would you have preferred he hit us?" She feels badly, but, sometimes, she needs to give her daughter some shit. Mia never censors anything coming out of her mouth. Cara's blood pressure has skyrocketed up 30 points and she's only halfway through.

They're making their way around the top corner of the oval, which is reminiscent of the final lap at Indy. Cars are ignoring the pleasant, wait your turn at the stop drop, and are instead, darting two, sometimes three wide, to get to the front doors. It's total chaos. Cara finally gets to the doors, by waiting her turn. She vows one of these days she is going for the checkered flag, and the win. Damn all these bitches to hell!

She pulls close to the curb for her children, who file out of the car without a single word. She knows to look in the backseat before Max closes his door. And yes, as usual, she yells, "Max, lunch." He leans back in for his sack and shuts the door. Cara still needs to negotiate an exit from the oval, but the worst is usually over by now.

As she gets close to the exit, her cell phone rings. Cara answers with her usual, "Hello, bitch."

"Yo, not THE bitch today." Her dearest friend corrects, "You should be hunting down the faked-boobed, blonde one that cut you off in the Lexus. I saw that."

"You know who she is?" Cara inquires with zeal.

"No, but I will make it a priority to find out…and then we will exact our revenge. You up for Starbucks?"

Looking down at herself, Cara answers, "Can't, not wearing a coat, underpants or shoes right now."

"You're my hero."

"Thanks Jinx. Coming from you that means a lot." Cara has conference calls with clients early, but, "Can meet you at 10:00? Also, need to hit Target. I promise to put on shoes, the panties are non-negotiable."

"OK, coffee, then wanna work out?"

She wants to decline the work out, but Jinx will guilt her into it anyway. Confirming, Cara hangs up.

Taking more deep breaths to decompress as she drives back home, Cara wonders how she could have survived living in Cleveland, of all places, without her good friend, Jinx. They were roommates for ten years when they worked in Washington, DC. Jinx left to take a new job in Cleveland. After several months, Cara arrived at her doorstep, beaten and battered; with nowhere she wanted to go after quitting her job. She was in a bad place, emotionally.

Her intention was to just hide in Cleveland while she licked her wounds, but then she met Nic. After that, Jinx became a critical element in her local support system. Without any family in the area, Cara's certain survival would have been tenuous, especially when the twins were young.

Pulling through the gate of her neighborhood, she passes all of the lovely homes and manicured lawns. She smiles, knowing it's such a privilege to live in a gated golf course community. As she turns onto her street, she slows to take in the side view of her home. It is truly magnificent, despite being a cliché, new house, it's their dream house. Nic had designed the home and Cara designed the interiors five years ago. The architecture blends classic English features with some Victorian touches, so it's not true to any one style, but it works.

Once in the kitchen, Cara glances at the clock. She has one hour to pick-up, clean the kitchen, make the beds, and start a load of laundry before her first client conference call. In advance of attempting any of that, though, she makes herself another cup of coffee. As she leans against the counter enjoying a fresh taste of java, she sees her reflection on the glass of the built-in microwave. Apparently, she forgot to run a brush through her hair this morning. She looks like a wild woman. "No wonder I don't have many friends here."

CHAPTER 2

CARA LOOKS IN THE MIRROR after brushing her thick, long hair. Giving up, she pulls it into a high ponytail. She leans closer to examine her hairline around her face. She spots quite a few gray hairs. Disgusted, she stalks out of the bathroom and stomps into the massive walk in closet. The closet is a thing of beauty. There are long rows of racks for clothes and shelves for shoes.

The right side of the closet is pristinely organized; clothes are color coordinated, as are shoes, by style and season. Every accessory is placed neatly in cubby holes or on hooks. Not a speck of dust can be seen. Then, there's the left side of the closet. Shoes are all over the floor. Clothes are haphazardly bulging from all of the racks. Dust bunnies are collected on the ground around the thrown belts, scarves and discarded socks. Cara kicks around all of the shoes on the left to find her sneakers, grabbing two mismatched socks off the floor, smelling them, and heading out of the room.

She pulls into the local Starbucks at 10:05; Jinx's car is already there. Cara added a pullover sweatshirt, the socks and sneakers to her original outfit, but otherwise that's all she's changed. As promised, no underwear.

When she steps out of her car, Cara hears, "Hey, slut, I'm sitting outside, and you're late."

Jinx has procured the premiere outside bistro table in front. "I'm only five minutes late, and you are the sluttier between the two of us."

Cocking her head, Jinx muses, "Is sluttier a word? Or is more slutty better use of the term?"

Cara wordlessly approaches the table, giving her friend a knowing smile to remind her she is well aware of all the men Jinx has slept with.

When they lived together, Cara would joke Jinx needed a revolving door on her bedroom, and a deli counter numbered ticket dispenser by said door.

Interpreting Cara's contemptuous smile, Jinx offers, "You get laid a hell of a lot more than I do now."

"Only because your husband is gone for weeks at a time and you're left with your electronic boyfriends." Cara quips while she takes a seat. Jinx's husband, Jake, travels all over the world, and is sometimes away for as long as a month. His location and purpose for the trip is never offered, despite Cara's incessant probing. "Speaking of, when is Jack Reacher due back from his latest secret adventure?"

"JAKE," Jinx emphasizes his name, "Is on his way home today. And, you know he hates that you guys call him Jack Reacher."

They know, but they do it anyway. Cara has the whole gang calling him that. Jake is huge, mean and mysterious. He's a big bastard with a heart of gold. Not that most people will ever see his heart. "Jake gets pissed off because he thinks we're comparing him to Tom Cruise who played Reacher in the movie. Poor choice, by the way. The real fictional Reacher is totally your husband. Get him to read a book."

Rolling her eyes, Jinx quips, "Real fictional? Oxymoron, you moron."

"Whatever." Cara smirks while she mentally calculates how long Jake has been MIA, "Hey, you want I take Elijah this weekend so you can get hot and heavy with your hot and heavy?"

"You calling my husband heavy?" Jinx asks with feigned indignation.

Cara laughs. Jake is six foot six and 270 pounds. He's a hot gorilla. He would make anyone piss their pants if they got caught alone in a dark alley with him. "He's seriously scary in a hot, BIG way. He's Jack Reacher."

Jinx huffs loudly knowing she is going to lose this Reacher fight on her husband's behalf. Deciding on counter maneuvers, she throws out, "And you should be the last person to talk about hot husbands. Nic is prettier than you."

"So true." Cara nods in agreement as her head lowers involuntarily.

"Don't start that inferiority thing with me today. I didn't bring my Freud hat." Jinx pushes a grande skinny latte in front of Cara. "You're late, so it might be cold."

"Five minutes!" What is it with Jinx and time? "You're a horrific housekeeper and cook. Your disorganized and yet, completely anal about money and time."

Throwing her head back in frustration, Jinx accuses, "You mean like how you home cook everything, and keep the perfectly clean house, but your side of the closet looks like a cyclone hit it, and Nic's side looks like he was in the military?"

A snort bursts from Cara, "Funny, I was just noticing that before I came over here." How can a man be so compulsive about his property and possessions, but can't seem to get a mug from the counter into the dishwasher-even into the sink for God's sake. Cara is all about the appearance of organization. If the public walking into your home can't see it, then it doesn't count. Must be something she inherited from her mother. "Next time bring the Freud hat so we can explore that."

Before Jinx can comment, Cara adds, "Have any intel on the blonde with the Lexus yet? Because bitch is going down."

"No, but why were you there? Nic out of town? Man's a saint for taking them every morning." Jinx looks to Cara waiting for a confirmation of Nic's sainthood status.

Cara bows her head while placing her hands in prayer. "Day trip for him."

"Are you here this week? Or are you off to the East Coast? And why is it always East?"

She and Nic own a design and construction firm. Cara starts to spew her schedule explaining she has jobs sites in construction in Boston, Philly, Syracuse and NYC. She has new projects just commencing in Greensboro and DC. As a native East coaster, Cara has more familiarity with the region, and she and Nic try to take advantage of that with her getting the bulk of work in that area. Mostly though, their work is client based. "Some clients respond better to Nic, and some to me."

"You mean do they want to work with the hot guy or the hot girl?" Jinx asks with piercing eyes.

"Of course." Cara confirms too quickly. Well, it used to work that way but Nic has aged better than she has. Although her husband still believes she's beautiful, lately it's become harder to feel that way. Maybe if Nic had a dad bod and receding hairline it would help.

Jinx interrupts her self-castigation with, "Will you take Eli this weekend?"

"Sure. Does he have any place he needs to be other than hanging around my house as usual?" Eli is very close to Max, but he's Mia's best friend. He is always at Cara's house. She suspects because he's fed better and more often there. "How are things with Elijah and the other boys at school going?"

Eli's freshman year was tainted when he became the object of bullies. Naturally shy and very reserved, Eli keeps to himself. Cara's daughter, Mia, has many of the same qualities in school, but is very vocal and forthright at home. That introverted personality in girls, though, doesn't elicit the torment like Eli has endured. Cara gives Jinx her admiration for having the resilience to work through it. She is quite sure neither she nor Nic would be patient and composed if either of their children were bullied.

Jinx sighs before responding, "He's become much taller than the other boys this year. They appear to have backed off, recently. Eli still struggles with making friends, though."

Cara tries to formulate an appropriate response. Mia is closer to Eli than she is to any of her girlfriends. She isn't sure if it's because they've always been together since birth, or if it's really because they're so alike. "Mia and Eli are two peas in a pod."

Nodding Jinx adds, "Strange how your daughter and my son are closer than your daughter and her twin are."

It would be strange, but it's hard to compare Max to anyone when it comes to peas in a pod. That boy is on an entirely different level. Every student at the high school wants to BE him or DATE him. He's royalty and only a sophomore.

"Are the senior girls still calling him all the time?" Jinx asks.

"Yes, and it stresses me out completely." Mia is a shy, reserved and a normal, sullen, disgruntled teenager with braces, acne and body issues, but Maximillian Andre is an anomaly. He's so excessively confident, she worries he's going to fall off the fifty-story pedestal he's on and really hurt himself. Elijah and Mia can look forward to things only getting better, but Max has it all. What happens if he falters?

Cara composes herself for a moment and sips some more lukewarm latte. She and Nic agree, despite Mia's apparent constant distress, it's Max they worry more about. But then, they both feel guilty for saying that, because Max is in no pain whatsoever and Mia is anguished. Cara finally adds, "Just be thankful you have an only child. This two kid thing sucks."

Jinx and Cara have been through, seen and experienced more than most people. As much as they both thought they could handle children with the same grace and perseverance they endured with all else, the kids threw them off track. Children change everything. Suddenly, fear for their safety, concern for their well being, and a general anxiety they had never experienced consumed them. Neither woman wanted to get pregnant, again.

"Enough about the kids. Thinking of them is ruining my caffeine high." Jinx scoffs.

Cara confirms, "Here, here." Before adding, "Do you mind if I get a new latte? This one is cold."

"You were late!" Jinx shouts out for all to hear. She stands and places her hand out to Cara. "You buy, I fly." Cara reaches into her pullover pocket and contributes a twenty-dollar bill. Jinx does her best strut out of the chair to walk inside.

She uses the alone time to start stretching her legs and arms. Apparently, they are supposed to work out at some point this morning.

Jinx suddenly appears with two cups and a huge smile on her face, "Cara, you need to get in there, NOW. They're playing your song!" She barely gets the last part of the sentence out of mouth before dissolving into giggles.

Cara jumps up and quickly paces into the store. She is assaulted, immediately, by Duran Duran's The Reflex playing, what sounds like, too loudly, through the store's speakers. She wants to laugh at Jinx's humor, but for some reason she has a strange feeling, an ominous, prophetic sensation. She walks back out to Jinx, who's still giggling, and asks very seriously, "Don't you think that's weird? The Reflex playing in a Starbucks?"

Jinx composes herself. "It isn't normal Starbuck's Musak, but maybe it's 80's day. Which speaking of, 10:30 Zumba is 80's today. Want to hit that?"

Cara releases the tension from her body. "Sure. Let's head out. I'll drive and then we can go to Target all sweaty after."

Cara and Jinx's favorite thing is run monotonous chores together. It makes life's annoying and boring to do list so much more entertaining. Because both of them work from home when they're not traveling, they spend time together, often.

They get to Zumba with seconds to spare and go to the back of the class. This is their requisite place in the class. Not because they don't want to be seen, but because they can watch everyone else from the back and make fun of them. To them, it's more enjoyable than the dancing, and it keeps them focused, otherwise they would both give up and walk out.

When class is over, Jinx asks, "To Target?" as she wipes the sweat off her face with her arm.

The TP supply at the Andre home is running perilously low, and Cara wouldn't want a bathroom mutiny at the house. "In and out quickly, though." She needs to get some work done before the incessant pick me up texts start from her lovely children.

Target, of course, is very busy and very red. Always. So. Painfully. Red. Cara grabs a cart and starts down the main aisle at warp speed. Jinx grabs her cart, and heads perpendicular, but with the same haste. Cara yells to Jinx over her shoulder, "First one checked out and paid, wins."

Cara rushes to paper products first, and then works her way back through the grocery aisles to Health and Beauty. She spots Jinx, and covertly gets past the aisle unseen.

Feeling victorious, she rushes towards the check-out lanes looking for the win. She no sooner gets in line when she catches Jinx in her peripheral vision. She spins to see Jinx angling which lane to go for; the one with the mom and two small children but only a half full cart, or the lane with the older couple and a full cart. Cara calls out to her, "Tough one Jinx. The kiddies can slow you down, but the age can, too." She yells this so all of the parties can hear her, but no one understands or pays attention.

Just then the woman in front of Cara packs her bags into her cart and starts away. She expediently places all of her items on the belt. "I have the win in the bag, full pun intended," she yells out to Jinx over her shoulder.

"Oh, Cara…think again.".

Cara stops dropping items on the belt to turn and see Jinx has had an unexpected reversal of fortune. Target has opened a new lane, and Jinx is already throwing her items at the cashier. "Curse you," Cara shouts, returning her attention to the beltway and her cashier.

With only a few items left deep within the cart, Cara reaches to the bottom on her tippy toes when a sound assaults her. She freezes, unconcerned with her current competition, and listens. It can't be? Again? She grabs the remaining items, throws them on the belt and call out to Jinx. "Um, Ellie?"

"You haven't won yet, don't gloat!"

"No, El?" The distress in Cara's voice plus the use of her real name versus her nickname has Jinx cease all her movement. She turns towards Cara. Slowly, Cara's head tilts up towards the ceiling of the store. It takes Jinx a couple of seconds to comprehend what the concern is. Then, she hears it. Playing rather loudly over the speakers in Target is Duran Duran's The Reflex.

Jinx turns back to the cashier, swipes her Target credit card through, grabs her bags, throws them in the cart, and rushes to Cara's lane. "I win."

Cara is still frozen in place listening to the song. She doesn't move until the cashier interrupts her thoughts, "Ma'am, form of payment, please." She swipes her card while Jinx loads her bags into the cart. Neither of them speaks until they exit the store.

Silently stretching out the tension, Cara finally looks at Jinx when they arrive at the back of her car. "You don't think that's weird? That we would hear The Reflex, twice, within hours, at two places that are unlikely venues for that type of music?" She pops the trunk and Jinx starts loading her purchases to the left side.

When she's done, she turns to Cara. "I don't know if I would call it weird…maybe coincidental." Cara slowly unloads her bags into the right side of the trunk. She's moving too slowly, and Jinx helps her. Once the cart is clear, she reaches over and softly places her hand on Cara's arm. "It's probably in the Musak loop today. You're over thinking this, Cara."

"You know there is no such thing as a coincidence." Cara whispers.

Jinx firms her grip on Cara's arm to the point of pain. "Yes, Cara, there is. Get Connor Reed out of your head and calm the fuck down!"

Cara can't react to her friend's reprimand. She's standing expressionless and motionless like she's zoned out. She does this, occasionally, and everyone who knows her well has grown accustomed to it. Cara wigs out and looks like she's paying attention to some conversation in her imagination instead of the real world. At least that's what it's always felt like to Cara. It's a fugue state. Jinx calls it her 'seizures.'

Wrapping her arm around her, Jinx tries, "Listen, I'll do some investigating and see what both stores use for their background music if it makes you feel better. Okay?"

Cara can finally take a deep breath and come back to reality. "Thank-you. I know I'm just being paranoid, but I really don't hear that song often... hardly ever."

"Is it in your ITunes library?"

This question finally gets a smile from Cara, "Of course," she responds matter-of-factly.

CHAPTER 3

THANKFULLY, THE REST OF CARA'S afternoon proceeds as normal. Shower, hair, dress, emails, return calls, and then the texts begin. 'Pick me up', 'Drop me off', and the 'Pick me up, again.' Somewhere in between all of that 'picking', she manages to get a pot roast into the oven. It should be ready by 6:30, which is when, if she glances at everyone's schedule, that's color coded on her smartphone calendar, her family can eat together. Trying to eat dinner together is something Cara is always striving for. It's silly in this day and age, but it's how she was raised in her family.

Her parents are immigrants from Italy, specifically, Sicily. Food is Love, and eating together is loving together. It seems such a small price to pay, a little bit of your time to share a meal as a family. Of course, her twins hardly speak during most meals, but occasionally, they do all talk, and Cara feels those moments are enough to continue cooking and serving them. Tonight's dinner is not one of them.

Nic comes home by five o'clock and goes directly to his office on the lower level. No greetings or salutations. Cara knows this means some client is waiting for information by the end of the day. He has the 'run to the office and cut it close' look in his eyes. Cara waves at him as she pulls in the garage with Max.

Max is on the phone next to her, with a girl. He gestures his mother out of the car looking for privacy. Cara complies, heading into the house to set the kitchen table for dinner. She wouldn't dare ask her children to set the table. They don't do anything around the house as far as chores are concerned. This is a routine source of conflict between her and Nic. It's not that either disagrees the twins should have chores; they disagree on to how to make it happen.

Some methods worked better on Max, others worked better on Mia, but ultimately everything failed. Both kids are incredibly well behaved and every teacher has said, 'Pleasure to have in class.' They get great grades and both are in Honors level classes or AP level classes, so school is never an issue. They're both gifted musicians; Mia playing in the school's Philharmonic and Max, opting out of band because of sports, but still practicing music in his downtime. They even have great singing voices; Max choosing to sing in public more often than Mia, but both kids are just as talented.

Before Cara can continue her thoughts, Nic enters the kitchen. She looks down at the kitchen table and realizes she has been on autopilot; setting it and putting out the meal, complete with drinks during her mind hiatus…or seizure.

Nic pulls her back into his arms, "Cara mia, I'm so sorry for dashing in the house earlier. I needed to adjust a quote before six o'clock. I think I made it."

Since their first night together, Nic has always called her, cara mia. He says it with Italian accent, and it's a great play on words as it means 'my sweetheart' in Italian. Her birth name is Caralina, but she has gone by Cara, pronounced Car ra, since infancy. Nic speaks Italian, fluently. He speaks several languages fluently.

Cara tilts her head back to kiss him on the neck. "I figured by the look on your face you were bee lining it to your office for something. No worries. How was Detroit?"

Drawing her firmly against him, he quips, "It was Detroit. Still makes Cleveland look like grandeur."

"Don't let them hear you say that." She admonishes.

Nic releases her and walks over to the bottom of the back staircase and yells up, "Max! Mia! DINNER!" then, he looks begrudgingly at her. "That's my only regret when we designed this house. I regret we didn't install an intercom system. Of course, I don't think we knew they would come to hide in their rooms as teenagers."

"And hide they do." She muses.

They sit down at their usual spots at the table and serve themselves dinner and discuss work. Halfway through Nic and Cara's meal, Max and Mia come down in unison. Max is wearing nothing but board shorts and looks like a bathing suit model. Mia is wearing a camisole and skintight yoga shorts. Whatever they wore to school comes off the moment they get home, thrown to the floor, and they are mostly naked for the rest of the night, even in winter.

They sit and start to serve themselves. They both like Cara's pot roast, hence neither has any dinner choice complaint this evening. Mia keeps her head down and eats. Nic and Cara know better than to look directly at her. They keep their eyes averted. Full of life Max shovels food into his mouth all while smiling as if it's the best thing he's ever tasted.

When Nic and Cara are finished with their meal, Nic makes his usual attempt at conversation. "Anything interesting to report? How was school?" Mia grunts and Max stares at him and continues smiling. No discernable words come from their mouths, though.

Undeterred, Cara makes her attempt, "How's the homework coming? Need any help? Or anything from us?" Again, a grunt from Mia, and Max continues to grin. It can be unnerving, but Cara continues, "Okay, you've been warned. No ten o'clock 'I needs' from either one of you, understand?" They both nod affirmative.

Cara says this every evening at dinner, and she's getting better at really making good on it, but if she had a dollar for every time she hears, 'Mom, I need…' between 10 and 11 PM.

Mia stands from the table first, attempting to walk away empty handed. Nic narrows his eyes at her and scolds, "Pick up your dish and cup, and place them in the sink, please." She reluctantly complies. Nic follows his daughter with his stare as she ascends the back steps. Despite Cara's constant advice to ignore the flippant attitude, she knows he really wants to smack Mia sometimes. He catches Max standing and walking away in his peripheral vision. "Max!"

Max turns back to his father, clueless. "What?"

Nic repeats, "Dishes. Sink!" Max complies and promptly leaves.

Cara can't stifle the giggle. "They are oblivious."

Nic gets up from the table with his dish. "If they weren't cute and smart, I would sell them on EBay."

Without another word, he leaves and heads towards the front stairwell that leads up to the second story of the house or down to the lower level of the house. Nic's office is on the lower level. That level is finished to several rooms. There's a very large, working office for Nic, a soundproof music room, a theater room, a billiards room with full kitchen and bar, a work-out room, and a bedroom and bath for their, sometime live-in child care provider, Sasha. Nic spends most evenings downstairs in his office or in the music room. The twins share his talent for music. Even Sasha has the musical gift.

Cara cleans up dinner, before she heads to her office. This office is the showplace work area. This is Cara's sanctuary, as much as any woman can find a place in her home where no one disturbs her. Plopping down in her chair, she awakens the screen and decides Facebook needs a visit. Seeing a post from her sister with a new picture of her young nephew, she makes a funny comment. After getting caught up on social media, she pulls up her mail and composes several work related emails. She checks the time. 10:00 PM.

Her Pavlovian response is anxiety, but for some reason she's feeling vulnerable as well. Getting up, she decides to head downstairs. She doesn't hang much on the lower level. Except for working out, not much appeals to her down there. She heads towards Nic's office. He's at his computer typing, and his TV is tuned to a basketball game. He's glancing at it and typing, simultaneously.

It's so infrequent she's downstairs, Nic can sense his wife in the hall outside his office. Without even looking up for a visual, he calls out, "Are you spying on me, cara mia?"

"I'm not very good at it if I was."

"What's up? You hardly ever come down here."

"I don't know. Maybe I was thinking of hiding down here during the bewitching hour."

Nic glances at his clock. He waves her into his office and motions to the plush chair in front of his desk. His office is twice the size of Cara's. Along one wall there are long tables set up with construction documents and files. The other wall has his TV, large marker boards with project calendars, notes and schedules all over them. It looks like the construction version of a war room. Cara sits and stares at the TV.

Nic studies her for a moment before asking, "Something bothering you?" Deciding too late that was a loaded question, he gives up and adds, "Do we need to talk?" He winces after he says this expecting Cara to launch into one of her 'we need to talk' moments.

Cara smiles at him, "No. No talking. Can I just sit here, quietly?"

He snaps his head up to her, astonished. "Can you? I mean, are you capable of sitting quietly?"

Scowling, she narrows her eyes at him. "Keep that up and we will be 'talking'. Really, I just want to sit here. Will that bother you?"

"Um, no, I guess," as he goes back to typing. After about a minute he stops and looks at her. She has stretched her legs out in front of her and is watching the game. She really is sitting quietly. It's unnerving. There must be something wrong. "Okay, that's enough. Tell me what's going on."

Snapping her head towards him, Cara states, "Nothing is going on. Am I bothering you down here?"

Nic needs to proceed with caution here. "You're not bothering me, baby, it's just…I'm sensing something more. Like you NEED something."

"Maybe I just NEED to sit quietly in close proximity to you, and that's all."

"You miss me." He states with surety.

"It's possible." She retorts.

Nic smirks and gets up, walking over to her. He straddles her, placing his weight on his knees to each side of her hips. Her head falls back against the chair and her content sigh whistles through her lips as she admires him. "Love that beautiful face and those gorgeous ocean blue eyes of yours."

Undeterred by her flattery, he tries one more time, "Tell me what you need, please?"

Cara licks her lips, and places her hands seductively on his hips. "Like I said, I don't need anything but…I'm starting to want something." With that, she subtly shifts her hands towards the front of his jeans.

Nic grabs her wrists and places them on his chest while he scoots down further on her lap. He slowly leans in and brushes his lips against hers. She murmurs her pleasure as always. He places gentle kisses on her chin, and follows her jawline, until he reaches her ear. He whispers with baited breath, "I'll make you a deal. Make sure the monsters are to bed, and meet me in the bedroom so I can finish what you started here."

She obviously isn't fooled by the grim slant her mouth takes. She kisses his neck. "I AM bothering you sitting quietly down here."

He still has her wrists in his hands. Moving them down to feel his arousal stretching out his jeans, he retorts, "You are not bothering me, but you are a…distraction."

"Ha!" Cara chokes out as she pushes him off. Her finger pointed in his face, she declares, "I will meet you in the bedroom in thirty minutes. Do not make me wait." She storms out of his office. He watches her fine ass wiggle away and he giggles. After all these years, he still loves the Tom and Jerry games they play with each other.

CHAPTER 4

WHEN CARA FINALLY GETS TO sleep, she's exhausted and completely sated. It's well past one o'clock in the morning and Nic is snoring softly while wrapped around her. She pulls away, gently, without waking him. She repositions her head as far from his, so the snoring doesn't prevent her from sleeping. Next thing she knows, her hair is being pulled. She murmurs, half asleep, "No, Nic, not again."

"No again, baby. It's morning. Time to get up." He yanks the covers off her.

"How are you so chipper?" She huffs out.

"I got laid by a hot babe last night, how can I not be chipper?" He purrs over his shoulder as he walks out of the bedroom.

Cara glares at him. He gets laid All. The. Time. And it's annoying to have a husband that's such a morning person.

She enters the kitchen sporting a clean pair of yoga pants and a clean T-shirt, still no shoes or underpants. Nic hands her an omelet and a cup of coffee as she passes him. She stops dead in her tracks to see her two children dressed and ready for school. She quickly looks at the kitchen clock, thinking they must be running late, but they still have ten minutes to spare before they leave. Looking at the twins, she narrows her eyes at them. "What gives?"

"We forgot we need you to fill out some forms due today to go on the field trip to Chicago." Mia states, without remorse, before backing away from her mother.

Mia and Max hand her what appears like ten pages of paperwork to fill out. Trying to stay calm, she glances, again, at the clock and says while waving the paperwork in her hands, "You want me to complete this in 10 minutes?" She looks to Nic for explanation but he just shrugs. She turns back to her children, unable to contain her frustrations, and screams, "How long have you had these?!"

Mia doesn't answer her mother directly but pleads, "But we need these today..."

Cara shouts back at her, "But you can't get what you need now!"

And then Cara hears it, the humming. She spins to glare at her husband. He's humming the Joe Jackson song You Can't Get What You Want 'Till You Know What You Want.

Max laughs out loud and starts singing to Nic's humming. After a couple verses, Nic joins him and the two of them are harmonizing.

Nic grabs Cara by the hips to start grinding her to the harmony. He's trying to diffuse the situation, and knows his wife is on the verge of going postal. He takes her body and shimmies while Max air guitars and hums the instrumental portion. They begin to all out dirty dance to Max's full out next chorus of the song, all while Mia stares at the three of them in horror.

Mia finally breaks their revelry, "Okay, I get it. NOW STOP!"

Nic laughs at his daughter, "I'm sorry, Mia, and I swear I wasn't humming aloud."

"Dad, you always say that, but we always hear you."

"You two have hearing like your mother. No one but she has ever accused me of the humming thing."

"God, Dad, we can totally hear it! Maybe everyone else is just deaf. And I'm so glad I could add a song to the soundtrack of your life this morning."

That's what they call his little humming tic. The Soundtrack of His Life. Cara believes it's a coping mechanism he developed as a child. When he gets emotional, he plays a song in his head. Usually, it's somehow related to the current condition of his life. At first, when they were dating, it was peculiar, but then it became a game of 'Name that Tune' for her. He found it embarrassing she could hear the humming, make a connection to the song, and what he was feeling emotionally. He's tried to control it, but he can't, and he swears no one had ever noticed it before.

21

Knowing their daughter is upset, and deciding she has suffered enough, Cara tells both kids she will complete the paperwork and deliver it, if they apologize for screwing up, and make amends by cleaning their rooms for a 6:00 PM inspection. "Capice?" She adds.

Nic grabs the lunch sacks. He doesn't want to be involved in this. As he's walking out the door he calls out, "I'll be in the car."

●●●

When Nic returns from drop-off hell, Cara is slouched over the kitchen table with her head on the paperwork. "Baby, good job this morning. I know that was hard."

Cara doesn't lift her head for a visual, but groans out, "It was draining. And my coffee is cold."

Nic taps her head. She glances up to see he has placed a nice large cup of hot, double D coffee in front of her. He leans in to place a kiss on her head. "Here, fresh coffee. Your welcome and no, I'm not helping you with the papers. They stressed me out this morning. I'm going for a run."

She takes a gulp of her favorite coffee from Dunkin Donuts, impressed and appreciative her husband battled the crowds at the store on his way home for her. "Thanks, and please keep your shirt on during your jog." Nic quirks his head at her, as if he doesn't understand. She narrows her eyes at him. This timeslot isn't on his normal run schedule. "The neighborhood ladies will be sad if they miss Nic Andre go by bare-chested."

An hour later, Cara finally completes the five pack form, in duplicate, for each child, with the same information she has provided the school hundreds of times before, when her cell phone rings. "Hey Jinxie, what up?"

"Starbucks in ten minutes?"

"I have to stop at the school office. Make it fifteen minutes and you have a deal."

"That means twenty minutes to me. Deal."

Twenty minutes to the second, Cara pulls into Starbucks. Damn that Jinx and her time line accuracy!

Jinx is sitting at the same table from the previous morning with two cups in front of her. As Cara approaches, she says, "Let me guess, they gave you the Chicago papers this morning?"

"Bingo."

"Did you go all thermonuclear?"

"Bingo, again."

"Well, welcome to Hump day, two more days and we can rest. Before you ask, no, I didn't get any details on the music yet from Starbucks or Target."

Cara is about to respond when she sees Jinx's eyes go wide at something beyond her visual. An audible sigh escapes Jinx's lips. Cara knows what's coming up behind her. She leans into Jinx and commands, "Say nothing." She turns slowly to see Nic running towards them, of course with his shirt off and tucked into the waistband of his shorts. Damn him.

He approaches them while slowing down. "Ladies," he greets as he pulls his shirt out of his waistband and slowly wipes sweat from his chest; drawing attention to every sculpted muscle and beautiful line on it. Cara notices all the women outside are gawking. In her peripheral vision, she can see the women inside pressing their faces against the glass. It's a Magic Mike moment and Nic is clueless.

Now Nic has his arms over his head, reaching for the sweat on his back, and there's a collective gasp around them. His broad shoulders and chest appearing even more defined with his arms extended. Cara wants to offer to wipe the sweat for him, just to stake claim on her man, but she knows that's not in her nature. Let the ladies enjoy. "Nic, you want me to run in and get you a drink."

"No, I can do it." Nic says, while waving at her to stay seated.

"Put your shirt on, please, before you go inside. You promised, earlier."

He leans down and grabs the back of her head, wrapping her pony-tailed hair around his hand. He yanks her mouth to his with a nice smooch. There's even tongue involved. He breaks the kiss and whispers, "I never promised."

Hum, maybe Nic isn't as clueless as she thought. Bastard.

Jinx can't contain her enjoyment of the scene anymore, and she blurts, "Nic, nice show."

"I aim to please my fans," He retorts while brandishing a killer smile.

Cara grunts. "Shirt on, now!" He snickers and puts on his shirt while walking into Starbucks, making sure to stretch every muscle in the process. "And he wonders where Max gets it?"

Jinx giggles while nodding in agreement. "Sorry, I know it bothers you they all ogle him, but you have to admit, it's pretty funny. They're all in there now, fawning all over him." She continues to giggle. "You have to concede, they don't admire my Jake like that." She says pointing to the inside of the store where Nic is.

"I told you yesterday, Reacher is just as hot, but he's too scary. The women admire-but from a safe distance!" Cara laughs out. "Speaking of, is he back tonight?"

Shaking her head sadly, Jinx responds, "No, he texted this morning to say he missed the last flight out and will be back tomorrow night."

"Can you tell me where Jack is trying to get home from?"

Before Jinx can answer, Nic comes back outside with a coffee cup in hand and interrupts, "Reacher's coming home?" He takes the seat between the women.

Jinx loses it. "You guys need to stop with that nickname! Wait, you get a coffee already?"

Nic shrugs. "They had my regular waiting for me. The barista said she saw me outside."

"Of course they did," Jinx mumbles to Nic. She informs them of Jake's arrival and when, but continues to refuse to offer up much more.

Nic stands and announces, "I'm done." He motions to Cara for the car keys. "I'm hitching a ride home."

Cara is confused. She looks at Jinx, and then glares at her husband. "But I just got here."

Jinx stands; having already decided their little party is over. She mimes texting to Cara and picks up her coffee cup. Tossing her car keys to Nic, Cara asks her, "Same time tomorrow, then?"

Jinx calls over to confirm, "Sure."

CHAPTER 5

A COUPLE OF HOURS LATER, Cara is showered, dressed and settled in with her computer in her office. She keeps two email addresses. One is on a completely secure server and is used for business contacts only. The other is a Gmail address she utilizes for online shopping and all her social media accounts, basically the junk mailbox. Because it's mostly retail sales emails, she checks it, at best, once a day. After completely a call with a client, she downloads all of her Gmail. Skimming through it, Cara mostly hits delete, but stops when she sees something catch her eye. The heading of the email says Duran Duran Tickets.

Before she can stop herself, she clicks on the email. It opens and immediately The Reflex is playing through the computer speakers. Cara unconsciously pushes off the keyboard so hard, the back of her chair hits her desk with a slam. Her next reaction is to lean forward and click off the sound.

She stares numbly at the screen, sucking in air to keep breathing. Stay calm. Assess, calculate, formulate, and react. She focuses her eyes to read the screen. It's an email from a Duran Duran fan club announcing new tour dates and ticket sales. The email looks legit on the surface, but there is no such thing as a coincidence. Graphics on the email are sharp. There are lots of details on the shows, which ones have been added, and when the tickets will go on sale on Ticketmaster. Is Duran Duran even touring?

Suddenly, Cara is startled right out of her chair by her phone's text message alert. Holy Shit, get it together. She picks up her phone to see it's from Mia looking for a pick-up at 2:30. Cara texts her back asking why she can't make the bus at 2:30? Her answer is, 'carrying too much stuff'. She gives up and tells her daughter 'fine.' Although, the only thing worse than drop-off at the oval, is pick-up at the oval right at 2:30 when school gets out. She would sooner be water boarded. As if Mia has a moment of clarity she texts, 'Sorry mom, but I can use the extra time to clean my room. Thx'. Did her daughter just show a. appreciation and b. manipulation skills? Impressive.

Cara decides she should do her own investigating on this email. She clips and pastes the return email address and Google's it. The fan club is real, but she needs to do some additional scrutinizing to get an email address verification. She checks the Duran Duran site and, yes, they are touring, and yes, these are new tour dates. The Ticketmaster information is accurate as well.

She's feeling better. It's just a coincidence. But she's never signed up to be a fan of the band on any website. Info sold from ITunes? Apple must sell preferences and contact info to other marketers. Even the local grocery store sells your preferences.

Just then, Cara can hear Nic walking up the stairs from the lower level. She quickly closes out of the Google screens, with all its tabs opened to the various searches, and then drags the original email into a folder. She makes sure her speakers are manually turned off when Nic walks into the room.

"Hey, what's up?"

Before Cara can answer him, he launches into something he needs her do for their company. Nic does this often. He comes to visit her when he requires assistance. Otherwise, out of sight, out of mind.

As he drones on while handing her several pieces of paper, Cara glances at her clock. Great. More paperwork today. When he's finished she tells him, "I can do what I can before I leave to get Mia for a 2:30 pick-up."

"You're going to do a 2:30 pick up? Have you lost your mind?"

"Don't try to agitate me, Nic. I'll work on your shit until I have to leave, then after I come back with Mia, I need to do my own work, you understand?"

"Deal, and thank you for reviewing that contract." He walks out and Cara realizes where Mia gets her manipulation skills.

She needs to take some deep breaths and compartmentalize this song obsession. She's lashing out, unprovoked.

Making an effort to clear her desk, she takes those deep, cleansing breaths and lays out Nic's papers. She gets them all completed, emails request for info on any open items in the contract she doesn't like, or wants to see added or deleted, grabs her phone and her handbag, and heads to the car for Defensive Driving 101.

Successfully negotiating the Oval, Cara drives Mia home; neither saying much in the car to one another. No sooner does Cara pull into their driveway, a text message comes through from Max. 'I need to be picked up now.'

"No!" She practically pushes Mia out of the car and pulls back out of the driveway. This is ridiculous. How the hell does she ever get anything done? She's just reaching the main road when her phone rings. Not wanting her car's Bluetooth to pick up, Cara grabs her phone and answers; knowing it's Max waiting for a response to his text. Just as her hand slides across the bottom of the phone, she sees the call says, 'Unknown'. But it's too late. The call connects...and Duran Duran's The Reflex is blaring through her phone.

Cara throws her phone down on the passenger seat, yanks the wheel hard to the left, and pulls into the corner CVS. She isn't parked, she isn't moving; she's just in the middle of the entrance lane staring wild-eyed at her phone while the music continues to play. There's finally a loud toot of a horn behind her to snap her out of her daze. She robotically pulls through CVS to the next plaza, circles around to the back of the building by the loading docks, out of sight from the main traffic flow. The music abruptly stops, and the line goes dead.

Putting her head down on the steering wheel, she lets it rest there. After a couple of minutes, she picks up her phone and texts Nic with shaky hands. 'Have serious work emergency. Caught between home and school, please pick up Max for me. On hold for building official, now. Thx'.

She waits for confirmation from Nic. When he offers to run and get Max, she sits back, tries to calm down and think. Suddenly, she picks up her phone, finds her favorites and hits 'call'.

She can picture somewhere in a Pentagon conference room a cell phone shrills to life. A very handsome man, in his late forties, casually gets up and walks away from the conference table. He steps outside into the hallway with his phone and answers. "C, what's up, sweetheart? You hardly ever call during business hours, you just pester the shit out of me with texts."

"I need to clock in." Cara says firmly.

"Come again?"

"You heard me. I need to clock in. I'm booking a flight for tomorrow morning. I'll send you my itinerary when it's confirmed. Please provide standard protocol. I'll send you an email with all the details and my concerns to your secure address."

"I'll make sure I'm available for you." He promises.

"Please, do not reschedule any of your commitments for me. I can work with anyone there." Cara scolds.

"You let me worry about that, sweetheart. See you tomorrow morning." And with that, he ends the call.

When Cara finally returns home, she is composed. She heads down to Nic's office. "It's bad, Nic."

"What happened?"

Cara explains she's had a fiasco on her DC project. There was some obscure reference to the building as a historical landmark. The local architect never caught it. Of course the building officials practically fell over themselves to deliver a cease and desist on the construction. Whole project fell apart she tells him.

"Did we hire the contractor and or architect?" Nic asks very concerned.

She explains this is her bank job and the Owner contracts directly with the GC and the design team. She gets paid to project manage. They have no legal exposure, but she is still responsible for fixing the mess. "Client is in a meltdown. He wants me there to meet him tomorrow morning."

"Sorry, baby. Anything I can do to help?"

"Cover for me here tomorrow?" Cara lets out a huge grunt as she walks out of Nic's office looking defeated. That total lie went well.

CHAPTER 6

THE FOLLOWING MORNING CARA IS up by five o'clock to shower and dress. She replays the previous evening through her mind. She had kept her composure throughout the night's activities. Before dinner, she had her flight booked to Dulles. At six, the twins' rooms both passed a hardcore inspection, although Cara did find some candy wrappers under Mia's bed. She got off with a warning. Dinner was served promptly after. Kitchen clean-up was done by eight o'clock, and then early to bed, before Nic, by ten o'clock. Cara let Jinx know her construction emergency and bailed on their coffee date. She packed her carry-on bag, found her folders on the DC project, to keep with her cover, and placed them, with her IPad in her Longchamp tote.

While she's blowing out her hair, Nic appears into the bathroom, naked, as usual. He begins to rub his morning wood against her butt, playfully, while she stands in front of the mirror. Cara shuts the hair dryer off and turns to him. "Nothing is happening for you this morning, my love. I still have to choose a killer outfit and get out of here to make my flight."

"Wear the brown suede boots with the wedge heels. I love your legs when you wear those." He offers.

Surprised by his comment, Cara leans into him with a one-arm hug while still holding the hair dryer. "Thanks, babe, that helps me decide. Although, I'm shocked."

Nic eyes her warily. "You're shocked I want you to look your best to knock them dead on the jobsite? I understand sex sells. Or are you shocked that I wouldn't mind you wearing the boots for Reed? Are you seeing him while you're there?"

Cara lets him go from the hug and places a soft kiss on his lips. "There it is…I was wondering when you were going to ask." Nic looks at her imploring. "If I have to spend the night, Reed is in town and we agreed to meet for a late dinner and stay at his place."

"So you may not see him?"

"He's in meetings all day, and has an early professional dinner to attend. Only if I have to spend the night." She confirms, once again.

"Send him my love," Nic delivers with sarcasm.

"I will be sure to do that."

Cara pulls an outfit together utilizing the boots Nic suggested. She grabs her Burberry trench coat and heads out the door by six, missing the kids' wake up time. At the airport, she gets TSA Precheck on her boarding pass, so the boots can stay on, as will her coat. She arrives to the gate to hear her name called for a complimentary first class upgrade. So far, this is going well. Once on the plane, she's seated next to a man close in age to her, but only steals occasional glances, and makes no attempt at conversation. Things are going even better.

Upon landing at Dulles, Cara makes her way through to ground transportation. She recognizes her contact, immediately, and walks towards him. The young man wearing a dark suit gives her the once over and says, "Ma'am, follow me," as he takes her carry-on bag from her.

They walk outside to a curbside waiting limousine. The man with her bag opens the door for her to enter, then stows her bag in the trunk before getting into the front passenger seat. The driver hurriedly pulls away. The privacy screen between the two gentlemen in the front and Cara is left open. No one speaks for the thirty-minute ride. Cara texts her husband to say she has landed safely. She puts her phone away and stares out the window for the ride there, her thoughts and memories swirling. They managed to get through two checkpoints, and Cara wasn't even paying attention.

Before she can process and assimilate a building she doesn't recognize, she sees the lone figure standing with his hands in the pockets of his suit pants. His classic good looks evident even with the Ray Ban Aviators he's sporting. She can see his hard jawline, perfect nose and defined, full lips. The dark blue suit is cut to mold every muscle on his body. His hair is still full, cut short in a trendy style, but mostly gray now. His face is impassive, showing no expression until the limo pulls right up in front of him.

Connor Mitchell Reed, Jr. is a man of tremendous power and position, the current Director of the CIA, and Cara's best friend. He opens the limo doors and drags her out into a huge hug. "C, I've missed you so much." Pulling her away from his body, he slams a kiss on her lips while he dips her.

She pushes at him. "Stop that!" He's causing a scene on purpose to make trouble. With the legacy of scandal his position has incited over the last few years from its former occupants, she'd think he would want to be more discreet on property.

Gently slapping his chest, she notices his suit when she touches it. "You're wearing Tom Ford? I'm pleased you're adhering to my fashion advice. You look extremely handsome...and dashing."

"Thanks and you don't look bad yourself." He assesses while slowly perusing her from head to toe.

"Please, I'm so nervous. I changed my clothes six times this morning."

"Nervous?" Reed mocks.

"I haven't been on these hallowed steps in seventeen years. Although... I've never been on these steps." She points to the front doors. "Is this the new George Bush Center?"

"Yup. I figured I would walk you through here, first. It's the long way to my office, but I thought you would enjoy it." Reed takes her arm to place it around his as he strolls into the building. He bypasses security with her and hands her an ID badge. She notices the badge has her picture and the name 'Chase Bennett' on it. Reed is rambling on about construction costs and delays with the new Center. He points out interesting items in the lobby, and talks about additional square footage and facilities.

Normally, Cara would enjoy any conversation concerning the building of the new Center, but she hasn't heard a word Reed has said. She can only notice how all the employees are staring at him with her. Reed drags her through secure door after secure door, until she has no idea where she is within the framework of the site anymore. They finally reach an elevator and take it up to the seventh floor.

The exit the elevator and start walking through a bullpen of workstations, all grey, and all in need of refurbishment. The low din of work suddenly ceases while all the employees cast slight glances towards them. She's trying not to look in anyone's direction, but her nerves are getting the better of her. She notices they're not really watching Reed, but watching her. She whispers, "Why are they all staring?"

"Well, it's possible, it may have leaked that Chase Bennett is back for a visit." Reed tells her with a devilish grin.

"So?"

"So?" He chuckles softly, "Sweetheart, you're a legend around here."

"A legend? You make me sound like some old, medieval witch."

A broad smile appears on his face. "Witch wasn't the word I was thinking of, but let's go with that."

On an inhale Cara whispers, "You know the rules. If I'm a bitch, you're a prick." She pinches his side for good measure.

He yelps before adding, "Seriously, C, there are some people still here from your time, and others who have heard all the stories. Stories and legends built the walls here at Langley. You, of all people, should know about legends?" Reed raises an eyebrow as he says this and chuckles, again.

"Nimrod."

Reed laughs a little louder. She has managed to sling her three favorite insults at him, already, and she's been in the building for less than ten minutes. Another involuntary chuckle escapes his throat. Cara is the only person in his life who would ever dare to put him in his place. His staff is probably in shock over seeing a smile on his face. Let alone if they could hear the conversation at the moment. Reed would never get any respect again.

Reed waves his security fob through another secure door and they enter a quiet hallway, walking past several conference rooms. Towards the end of the hallway, through yet another secure door, they continue into the Executive area and his fairly plush office. He closes the door, after signaling to his Admin he's not to be disturbed.

After pulling the chair out in front of his desk for her to sit, Reed gets seated. For a few moments neither one of them speaks. Suddenly, he is a young man again. He's an idealist who thought he could make a difference. He's someone who was going to impact the world with the gorgeous woman sitting across from him. In some ways, they did achieve success. Together. But that was a long time ago. Realizing he's been holding his breath, his exhales, "Memories."

Cara snorts and ruins his nostalgia. "Memories? In this office?" She waves her arm around. "This office is incredible. My only memories involve you sitting behind a metal desk, circa World War II, in a shithole of an office."

He can't resist baiting her. "To think I keep an office like this at the Pentagon, as well. But this one is my favorite, and I will always be the most comfortable here."

Her eyes are wide and shiny, and entirely on him. "God, Reed, I don't know what to say. The reality of THIS." Again, her arm encompasses the room. "It blows me away." She pauses, "I'm so proud of you."

He doesn't acknowledge her admiration. He's not entirely comfortable doing so. Instead, he gets right to the issue. "Let me see your phone." She pulls her phone from her handbag and slides it across his desk to him. As he picks it up, the tone indicating a text message goes off. Reed reads it and relays Mia needs to be picked up from school at three.

"Jesus, those kids never listen. Text her back and tell her to text her father, I'm in DC."

Shrugging at her usual demands of him, he texts back and immediately there's a response. "She asked is DC a new grocery store? And where will you be parked at 3:00?"

"Give me the damn phone, damn kid," as she leans across the desk, reaches for the phone but not before flicking him in the head. He doesn't understand the beating. He hasn't done anything wrong…yet.

"C, remind me why we're best friends again?" She doesn't respond but continues typing on her phone. He leans in to see the text. It says, 'DC, District of Columbia, as in six hours away. Text your father for a ride. And NO, I won't text him for you! Stop bothering me, I'm WORKING!' She gently places the phone back in his hand and grins at him. Maybe, it wasn't such a good idea allowing her back into the building. His eyes glance up to make sure the blinds on his window facing his Admin are shut. "You do realize I run this entire facility now?"

"And you do that all by yourself?" She mocks.

Bitch. He wants to say fuck you but he can't. She makes a valid point.

Not only does he have an amazing staff, he texts and talks to her about all of his issues on a regular basis.

She interrupts his internal dialog with, "And why are we making this about you? This is about ME, today. Can you put away your narcissism for a morning, please, and let me take center stage?"

Now she's just trying to bait him. Bitch, again. He doesn't dignify the dig with a retort. Instead, he pops the SIM card out of her phone. He opens his top desk drawer, pulls out a file and a new SIM card. After placing the new SIM into her phone, he gets up and takes the original out to his Admin.

When he comes back in, he sits, and opens the file he pulled. Reed pushes three separate sheets in front of Cara. "You are correct. This is about you." He details their investigation so far. Both the Starbucks and Target music systems were tampered with. The email is from an unknown IP address. Not a legitimate Fan Club email. "None of this type of hacking is difficult, but it proves the music you heard was not a coincidence, and the email is a plant."

Cara can only sit there with a blank stare. She doesn't want to show Reed any signs of panic, but for some reason, she can feel the anxiety growing within her. Same anxiety she's had for days now. Something is wrong, possibly very wrong. She's repeating the mantra Reed had taught her so many years ago in her head. Capture and contain, capture and contain. She needs to get her emotions under control, and she certainly doesn't want Reed to see her unbalanced if she's going to solve this mystery her way.

She focuses on her breathing and continues, "So, we know that someone knows who I am... or who I was...whatever, someone knows I am the Reflex."

Reed's using his calming voice, "It would appear that way, my sweetheart."

He details the intel on the music and email before admitting he took the liberty to start investigating all of her known adversaries, and honestly, most of them are either dead or legit now. Of the ones who have gone on to normal lives, he can't see how they could've made the connection between

Chase Bennett, the Reflex, and Cara Andre. More importantly, he doesn't feel a motive from any of them.

He pulls a fourth sheet of paper from the file and lays it out in front of her. "Here's the list of anyone you tangled with who's still alive."

Cara looks at the list quickly. It's a short list. "Six people left...that's it?"

"Sweetheart, you removed the other threats."

Cara examines the names more closely before addressing the list. "Well, I'm sure you know I'm Facebook friends with Javier and Lucien... well...I'm friends with their alter egos living here in the States or abroad. They're not a threat."

"Yeah, about that, do you think that's wise? Facebook, Instagram, and Twitter? Posting pictures?" Reed gets his disapproving face on while he says this.

"Connor, first of all, I use all of the tightest security settings on the sites. I really try to monitor pictures of myself. Besides, it would have been far too suspicious if I didn't participate in social media. My God, what would my family and friends think of me? A middle-aged mom not using social media? Talk about red flags." She waves her hand at him dismissively. She's not fooling him with the cavalier attitude. Her eyes reflect her concern and worry.

Giving up, Reed exhales, "I will push this argument with you over social media for another time. So, it leaves the other four names on the list, and I don't feel their current situations warrant further investigation." They're all doing well financially, and there's no motive he can find to come after her in this manner. If they wanted to hurt her, they would've just found Cara in Ohio and killed her. That would be more in keeping with their profiles.

"I agree. So where does this leave us? One of the supposed 'dead' threats?" She asks.

"It's possible, one of the dead is still living, faked a death. But even that list is short, and again, they would've had to make the connection between Chase and Cara." He assures her there's no record of Cara Bianco or Cara Andre anywhere within the government's systems. When she left, and forfeited any pensions or payments, he wiped her file closed. Only her ten years of service there is on file...on file as 'Chase Bennett'. No known whereabouts. It appears like Chase ceased to exist after 2000.

"And no record of Cara Bianco?"

"Not here at Langley. Cara Bianco worked for World Bank from 1989 until 1999. All of the precautions I took for you are still in place. Solid." Reed confirms.

Before Cara can ask her next question, Reed's intercom comes through with a call. He picks up. "Agent Carter, what do you have for me?" He listens for a couple of minutes with a slight frown forming on his lips. "Bring me the details and thank-you." Reed hangs up and reaches for the short list sheet of the living threats. He glances at it, and places it back in front of her, again. "We were able to triangulate the call you received yesterday to cell towers in the area of Berlin, Germany."

Cara's brows rise as she looks down at the short list. "Olaf Stein."

"He and his company's headquarters are based there." Cara methodically stands up and turns towards the door. Reed moves with quick steps to intercept her. Grabbing her by the elbow he stops, "Where are you going?"

"To Berlin to visit Olaf."

"It's not that simple."

"Of course it is."

What's left of Reed's patience is gone. He grabs both of her arms and drags her back to her chair, pushing her in it with some force. Standing with his legs slightly apart, directly in front of her, Reed leans in and places his hands on the top of the chair back. He moves fully in, his face only inches from hers, and slowly whispers, "You. Are. Not. Going. Anywhere."

Cara sets her jaw and stares directly and defiantly into Reed's eyes. They remain locked in their match of silent wills for at least a full minute before she lets her gaze soften. She reaches for his wrists and slides her hands gently up Reed's arms until they're on his shoulders. She lifts her right hand and threads her fingers into the back of his hair. She pulls his head in closer, so their noses are touching.

Licking her lips slowly, "I got a bad feeling about this, Connor, and time is critical. Please."

Reed lets out a long sigh. Bringing his lips to the corner of her mouth, he brushes a light kiss before resting his forehead against hers. He leaves them in this position. Then suddenly, he grabs Cara by the back of her neck as he drops to his knees in front of the chair, pulling her forward with the motion.

He looks into her eyes again, "No time for me to get some recon done?" She shakes her head and Reed bites through clenched teeth, "Damn it, C! You and that fucking intuition of yours. You know I can't discount it, but I've got a bad feeling about this."

Cara just continues to stare into Reed's eyes willing him to concede. Before either of them can speak, there's a knock on the door. Reed releases her, quickly straightens, steps several feet away, leans back on his desk, crossing his arms and legs before commanding, "Come in, Carter."

A young, tall, very muscular, darker skinned man enters the office. Reed uncrosses his legs, pulls away from his desk, and strides towards his visitor.

Carter speaks first, "Sir, I'm sorry to disturb you, but I have the information you requested."

Reed puts his left hand out for the file Carter's holding. After Carter places the file in his hand, Reed seems to hesitate before thrusting his right hand out to Carter looking to shake hands. Carter is caught off guard for a moment before he places his own right hand into Reed's.

The Director conveys, "Thank-you for getting me this so quickly."

Carter is speechless by Reed's gratitude. He pulls the young man forward a bit with his hand before releasing it. Clasping Carter's shoulder in a fatherly way, Reed guides him deeper into the office.

Cara watches this exchange and realizes Reed is going to make introductions. She stands and faces the young man. Reed releases Carter's shoulder when he's a few feet from her. There's a moment of uncomfortable silence while Reed attempts to compose his introduction. He finally inhales softly and releases, "Agent William Carter, I would like to introduce to...Agent Chase Bennett. You will be accompanying her to Berlin within the hour."

CHAPTER 7

CARA, CARTER AND REED WALK quickly out of the building and back to the same waiting limo and driver. Reed opens the door himself before the driver can do it. The man knows to rush over and get back in the driver's seat. As soon as everyone is settled inside, Reed tells the driver to head towards the air base. Closing the privacy window between the front and back seat, he turns his focus to Carter and Cara. He reiterates their mission objectives.

They are to visit Olaf Stein tomorrow morning, first thing. They've hacked into his schedule, and Olaf will be in his office by 7:00 AM to prepare for a meeting. After initial contact, they convene back at the designated meeting place and do nothing else. Reed will complete his scheduled meeting this afternoon with the Joint Chiefs, attend the White House dinner tonight, and then take his Gulfstream to meet them.

Cara interrupts him to the noticeable shock of Carter, "Reed, it's crazy for you to cancel your schedule for this. You don't need to meet us in Berlin. You have Carter babysitting me…that's enough!"

Reed continues, ignoring Cara as if she hasn't spoken. "Carter, you have your service weapon and a Glock 43 9mm for Agent Bennett like I requested?"

"Yes, Sir."

"Under most circumstances, you are NOT to give her a gun. Only dire situations, and I'm holding you responsible for Agent Bennett."

"Life or death only, Sir."

Cara is now outright scowling. Again, she interrupts Reed, "That's ridiculous, why can't I have a gun?"

This time Reed deigns it to acknowledge her interruption and glares at her while saying, "You can't be trusted to follow orders when you're armed." Turning towards Carter he warns, "She is very cunning, Carter. Don't underestimate her."

For the first time since she met him, Carter shows some personality. He slowly turns to look at her with a wry smile on his face. While flexing his muscles and still smiling at her, Carter drawls, "Sir, there will be no trouble from Ms. Bennett."

Cara flips her head back at Carter with steel in her eyes, "First, that's Agent Bennett to you, and second, how can you be so sure I won't be trouble?"

"Ma'am, I have never met a woman I couldn't handle."

"Really? Out of what…the two of three you've had so far? What are you like, 19 years old?" Cara spits out.

"I'm 27, Special Forces trained. I've seen action in Afghanistan and I've been with the Agency for three years. AND…a gentleman never talks about how many women he has 'had'." Carter responds unfazed by Cara.

"Huh." Is all she can utter.

Reed injects, "I see you two will get along fine. We're here. I have you both on a military transport. I'm sorry for the lack of better in flight accommodations, but this was the quickest. Carter, do you mind giving Agent Bennett and me a moment, please?" Carter grabs his bag and Cara's and exits the limo shutting the door behind him.

Reed immediately pulls Cara into a bear hug. He doesn't speak. He just buries his face into her hair inhaling her scent. There's an anxiety creeping through his blood.

She has been his greatest agent, his dearest and best friend, but he hasn't sent her on a mission without him in a very long time. He has always had full faith in her. For the first time, he feels that faith wavering. While still embracing her, he gazes over at the transport plane. Every bone in his body wants to get on that plane with her. But, a last minute cancellation of his schedule today, would be too suspicious. He can cover their trip, and use of the cargo transport, but he can't use his plane to fly to Berlin after cancelling his commitments this afternoon at the eleventh hour. That would send a red flag. He has a strong intuition; he needs to keep all of this under the radar, for now.

His lips to her ear, he whispers, "Please be careful. I'm worried to death right now. Please do as I say and only talk to Olaf…and don't hurt Carter…he's a great agent…but I know you," pulling away from their hug to look her in the eyes, "You were and are a very dangerous woman, C, impulsive and arrogant…please wait for me before you pursue any leads. Please, promise."

Cara gives him her duh face. "Stop whining. It doesn't become you. Besides, it's like riding a bike, right? I'll be fine. And you know I've never listened to you. If I feel time is ticking, I won't be detained."

Reed leans down and places a gentle kiss on her forehead, "Carter will stop you."

As she starts for the door, Cara turns towards him and quips, "I'd like to see him try."

"That mouth…what I can do with that mouth…" He calls out.

Cara smiles, blows him a kiss, shuts the door and heads for the transport.

Carter sleeps the whole time on the plane. Cara can't imagine how. It's noisy, bumpy and entirely uncivilized. How did she ever travel this way? Of course she was a young woman the last time Cara was strapped into a stripped down cargo plane. This is an Airbus, but it doesn't resemble any Airbus commercial flights. Doesn't ride like one, either. Is this the plane, or are the pilots flying crazy? Must be the pilots.

She's feeling very shrill and needs to get a grip. She starts inspecting the seat. No padding and hard as a rock. The seat doesn't recline. It resembles the plastic seat on a city bus. She's harnessed in, so everything she's wearing will be a wrinkled mess. Still eyeballing the seat, she mumbles, "Hemorrhoid Makers."

She understands she should try to sleep, but examining the surroundings, she can't comprehend how. It takes her half a Xanax at home to get to sleep on a $3000 mattress. When did that change, anyways? Oh, yes, when the kids came! That's when she started worrying about everything…and never sleeping well again…unless it's drug induced. She trained to sleep anywhere when she could get some like all members of the military. Guess that training disappears once you have children.

40

Her thoughts fall to her family. She has to call Nic when she lands to tell him she'll need to stay in DC an extra night. She hopes he won't get suspicious. He's never happy when she is near Reed, anyways. Their relationship with each other, Reed and Nic, is tenuous at best; really more antagonistic than tenuous if she's being honest. Neither man is overly sensitive. It's just not a good set up. Hostility is inevitable.

Cara won't give either man up, though. After over 16 years of marriage, she hoped Nic would learn to accept Reed in her life. Nic did get slightly better about it, year after year, but it was marginal at best. Reed, on the other hand, kept waiting, year after year, for the other shoe to drop. He kept waiting to pick up the pieces of her broken marriage. Of course the marriage didn't break, and she still considers Reed her best friend and Nic, the best husband, ever.

She and Reed don't see each other nearly as much as they used to. Their timing hasn't always been the best. When Reed had time, she had twin babies. Now that the twins are older and pay Cara no attention, Reed is a very powerful and very busy man. She misses him like crazy, sometimes.

For the decade Cara was at the Agency, Reed was her handler. Their relationship was much more than managerial, though. He was her protector, trainer, confidante, partner, back up anytime he could, and mostly her truest best friend. He was Cara's White Knight. No one, including Nic, knows her better than Reed. They have been thick as thieves for 25 years.

They met in college and Reed dragged Cara to the Agency after she graduated jobless. The existing close friendship between them affected their relationship at the office. Most of her colleagues didn't like Cara. They always felt Reed gave her preferential treatment. Of course, Reed never gave a shit what anyone else who worked for him thought. He, also, did not give Cara any slack. If anything, he was much harder on her than the rest of his team. Reed expected so much more from her. And because he was her friend, she worked harder to achieve his expectations.

Before Cara's thoughts can drift any further, the pilot comes on to announce their descent into Berlin. Carter wakes up and smiles devilishly at her. She stares back at him with regret. She was so wrapped up inside her mind having a seizure, she neglected to play some sort of prank on him. It would've been standard practice for the situation. Maybe, she is getting too old for this.

There is a town car waiting for Carter and Cara on the runway at the Tegel airport near Berlin. How Reed managed to let them land at the commercial air field, as well as avoid the concourse and customs, is truly amazing. The man can make miracles happen. He never ceases to totally impress. As they enter the car, a large, wrapped package is waiting on the seat. The card is addressed to 'C'. They get comfortable in their seats and Cara places the package on her lap.

She opens the card, and reads, 'Sweetheart, because I knew you would break into the local Olaf store tonight, I decided to save you the thrill. Enjoy. Love Reed.' Cara laughs out loud. He knows her well. She had planned to ditch Carter at the hotel and break into the Olaf store.

Carter peeks at the card and looks confused. Cara explains while she opens the package, "It's from Director Reed. He knew I wouldn't go see Olaf Stein later without wearing something from Olaf."

"Why do you have to wear Olaf to see this man?" Carter asks, clueless.

She attempts an explanation he'll comprehend. "One does not go to visit an old friend without wearing his clothes, especially when you want to gain his good graces."

"You mean this guy Olaf Stein we're seeing later is the same Olaf from the fashion house?"

She snaps. "Did you get no intel at all? Forget intel, do you have no fashion knowledge whatsoever? Of course it's the same Olaf!" Cara thinks for a moment before continuing, "And 'we' aren't seeing Olaf later, I am seeing him. You're waiting outside."

She pulls the lid off the box just then to reveal the most beautiful cashmere coat she has ever seen. It's an off white color with no collar but wide lapels. It's classic Olaf. Beneath the coat are the most amazing stiletto heeled, black suede, over the knee boots.

Cara is touching the coat and boots with great reverence, almost in a trance, when Carter startles her. "You're stroking that coat and boots like a cock. You're kinda turning me on, Agent Bennett."

"Nice mouth. You implied you were a gentleman. Could have fooled me with that comment. I'm a married woman. I would appreciate if you kept your trash talk to yourself." Cara scolds.

Carter scuffs out, "You're married? Poor sap."

"What? Why would you say that?"

"Darling, you…with Director Reed? Not cool."

Cara is about to protest, but stops herself. What does this infantile moron know? He's no different from all of the others she and Reed have endured during her tenure at the Agency. Everyone assumed she was fucking Reed for special favors and treatment. She was hurt at first, but then it became easier to go with it. Most everyone grew resolved to the fact she and Reed were a couple. After the first few years, people even became bored with their perceived relationship. Seemed simplest to ignore the conjecture.

Cara turns her head away from Carter and decides to remain silent for the rest of the ride. She refuses to let Agent Carter judge her any further. Again, her thoughts drift as they begin to drive into the city proper, Berlin.

Her first time here was just after the wall came down. Things were crazy and chaotic, but even then, the city burned with an energy she'd never felt before outside of New York City. It was raw, and edgy, but determined and focused. There was so much to sort out and accomplish, but no one seemed daunted by the task. Maybe, it's a tribute to the Germans and their ability to look forward, or possibly to Berlin itself to continue to thrive despite being in the crosshairs of historical malice for most of the 20th century. It's not surprising Berlin would become the thriving business and cultural scene it is today, in just twenty-five years.

Olaf Stein must have felt it, too, because he chose Berlin to start his immensely successful clothing company. Olaf Designs are to Berlin what Burberry is to London. He branched out to a men's line, shoes, handbags, even domestics for the home in the last decade, and all of the new lines have been profitable. Olaf wasn't lucky either; he is an extremely talented designer. He's a subtle bridge between the outrageous looks of a Gaultier and the sophistication of Prada. Olaf's biggest attraction, though, are his creations have an extra sensory feel about them. They look beautiful for sure, but they all 'feel' beautiful. Sometimes, depending on shipping and store conditions, they even smell beautiful. So, consequently, when someone wears his designs, they are beautiful. It's a unique approach to design that really hadn't been done before. It was brilliant.

The fashion community snuffed at him, initially, but sales told the real story. Women loved them. Olaf struggled to get supply to meet demand at first, and women were paying a premium to get their hands on an original Olaf. That initial hysteria propelled him to the forefront of fashion in only his first two years in business. His house of fashion is presently considered one of the best in the world.

Of course, for almost 20 years, Olaf Stein has been referred to as 'Olaf', a single name icon up there with Cher, Madonna and Sting. Cara shouldn't be surprised Carter didn't know who Olaf Stein is. Then again, Olaf has spent considerable effort to conceal his last name. He has, also, spent significant energy obscuring his appearance. The media refer to him as a recluse because he's camera shy and refuses to be photographed often. His only appearances in public are at the end of his runway shows. Then he emerges, wearing his latest sunglass design, and he is always sporting a baldhead and full beard. Of course, the mystery of Olaf has only added to his appeal.

Cara smiles to herself. She has enjoyed following Olaf's career. Partly because she loves fashion; which is by no means evident on a day to day basis in her yoga pants and T-shirts, but it was her secret favorite part of the job at the Agency. Cara loved when she was allowed to prep for a covert mission with an expense account that included designer wear. She never could've afforded the wardrobe she wore on her salary. Best part was Reed would allow her to retain all of the shoes and clothes after the mission. He would write them off as 'collateral damage', although, sometimes, they really were destroyed. She had to promise Reed she would never jeopardize a mission to save her Louboutins from the mud. She did try to, though, always.

When she left the CIA and Virginia, the only things Cara packed were her designer swag. Pity most of it didn't fit ever again after two years. Having twins does that to a woman. Her feet swelled to three sizes bigger towards the end of the pregnancy, and she gained 60 pounds. Luckily, her children were close to 6 pounds each, and very healthy at birth, but Cara's body never recovered, completely. She lost most of the weight, but her hips and stomach have never been able to get back to the size four she once was. Even Cara's feet refused to go back to her original size eight. She ended up consigning most of her swag.

Since then, Cara hasn't had the money to purchase too many designer pieces. She and Nic have always tried to take what they've earned and re-invest in the business. They were fortunate to have had enough capital between the two of them to start the business 17 years ago.

Instead of taking any kind of pension from the government, Cara opted to be bought out. So she received a lump sum in cash when she left. She isn't entirely sure where Nic's money came from, but he had more than she did, and she was thrilled he could hold up his end.

Cara's mind starts to focus on her eminent mission. It's been over twenty years since she last saw Olaf Stein.

CHAPTER 8

OLAF AND CARA FIRST MET staring down the end of a Heckler and Koch P7 semi-automatic pistol in a back alley during 1994 Paris Fashion Week. Olaf Stein was an East German born KGB agent that fell off their grid, and was considered having gone rogue. He had a penchant for Paris, especially during Fashion Week, and Cara was tasked to find him and determine his loyalties. Of course they weren't referred to as the KGB by then, but the SVR. Reed used to joke it was like the Russians put lipstick and make-up on an ugly girl. It was still the same management and methods at the SVR as always; the poor girl was still butt ugly.

The Russians were not totally forthright in their concern for Olaf's allegiance, but it was made clear to the CIA, there were open questions. Reed thought it was possible Olaf could be waiting to make contact with the US, or he could be just another cover in an effort to bring down the CIA.

1994 was a particularly painful time for the CIA. The Aldrich Ames scandal was in full bloom and all hell had broken loose at Langley. Reed, and every Team Leader or Section Head, was nose deep in shit and bureaucracy; spending all their time digging up answers for the brass and the Deputy Director. Cara was Reed's best agent. Apparently, she was the Agency's best chance to determine Olaf's intentions.

Cara has this weirdly uncanny ability to decipher people. She's always assumed it's what made her effective at her job. She can sense danger and unrest. She can even sense apathy and disinterest. She has spoken at great length with some Navy Seals and Special Ops guys who say they can actually feel the prickles on the backs of their necks when danger is near.

They've told her they have come to rely on that sensation as much as all of their training. Reed found her talent to predict people fascinating, and initially called it her special intuition. After he met Cara's family, though, he started to call it her extreme judgments.

It's true. She hails from a severely judgmental family. They will pass verdict on anyone within two minutes of meeting them. That's it, done, to hell with judge and jury. Once the verdict is in, there is no changing it, either. Funny thing is…they're mostly accurate. It was hell making new friends, and forget dating. She and her sister were so traumatized by 'told you so' bad dates; they eventually stopped dating all together. Sure, there was one night hook ups as Cara got older, just to get some sort of relief, but she never took them past that.

And as she got older, the judgments became starker. Cara knew a guy wasn't for her the moment she met him. Her body could be screaming 'sleep with him' but her head was screaming 'loser'. Occasionally, Cara would let her body win. It wasn't until she met Nic that for the first time mind and body seemed to be in agreement, intense, total agreement. And at that moment, nothing could have scared her more.

Cara is shaken out of her thoughts when the town car pulls into the Hotel De Rome. "Wow," she says in almost a whisper.

"What's up?" Carter asks.

"Reed didn't spare any expense; this place is 5-star. This is the hotel to be seen at in Berlin. I'm just surprised he chose somewhere so public."

"Place to be seen?"

"There are dozens of places one should be seen while in Berlin. The city is an amazing mecca of cultural experiences." She chides him as he grabs their bags and heads into the hotel.

They approach the desk where Carter checks them into their rooms. Cara would have been more involved with that process, but she was not informed on what arrangements Reed made. She could let Agent Carter wear the pants for now. She does decide to find her phone and turn it back on. As it's starting up, she glances at the time. It's 5:00 AM Berlin time, which means 11:00 PM in Ohio.

Just then, her phone registers a missed call from Nic and texts from Max. The texts are, of course, for pick-ups. But the call from Nic must have come while she was in flight. Following Carter to their rooms, she clutches her tote and the box with the coat and boots, while he carries their bags. They're on the 5th floor in connecting rooms.

After thoroughly checking Cara's rooms for God knows what, Carter turns to her and hands her the key, "I will pick you up at 6:30 AM to head over to Olaf's building."

"K, bye."

Carter leaves and she immediately dials Nic's cell phone. It goes right into voicemail. She leaves a quick message saying she hopes to be home by late tomorrow night and she misses him. She tries texting him, next. No response. Suddenly concerned she makes some contact with her family, she decides to call Sasha, Nic's brother, and their sometimes live in Manny. Sasha answers immediately.

"Sash, I'm sorry to call so late, but I was trying to get ahold of Nic and my phone went dead earlier at dinner. What's up?"

"Yeah, he was trying to call you. Something came up with his Cincy job and he had to get down there. I'm here with the kids." Sasha smoothly replies. No inflection in his voice, as usual.

"How are my precious little ones?"

"Driving me nuts as usual." Still no inflection.

"You love it. Do they miss me?"

"Cara, they don't even know you're gone. Mia just called out for you to sign some form she needs for school tomorrow. I didn't bother to remind her, again, that her parents have left the building."

"So you forged my signature and hopefully yelled at her to go to bed?"

"Obviously." Total deadpan.

Cara hears a slight knock on the connecting door. She walks over and opens it to see Carter standing there in just his pants, barefoot and bare-chested. She motions to him with one finger to wait. "Sasha, hang on one minute, I have another call coming in." She mutes her call and says to Carter, pointing to his lack of clothing and intrusion, "What the hell, Agent?"

Carter gives a smirk and responds while he flexes his biceps, "I decided I shouldn't trust you. I need you to keep your connecting door open a crack until 6:30. I don't want you slipping out."

"Fine, I need to get back to my call." Turning towards her phone, she unmutes it while Carter stands there and listens. "Sasha? Sorry about that.

Apparently a few people were looking for me while my phone was dead. Do you know when Nic is coming back?"

"If all goes well, he should be back by tomorrow night, but it could be a couple of days. How about you, still scheduled for tomorrow?"

"No, that's why I'm calling." Cara gives him some bullshit about her DC project.

"Sorry, Princess, sometimes we need to work a little harder for our money, right? Are you with Reed and staying at his place while you're there?"

An involuntary sigh escapes Cara's throat. Sasha can be as suspicious and hostile about Reed as Nic. Not only does she have to constantly deal with Nic's jealousy of her relationship with Reed, but she must consume Sasha's judgment of it, too.

"Yes, Sasha, I had a late dinner with Reed tonight. He just left, though, on a trip abroad, so I'm by myself at his place." Cara makes a face at Carter after the 'by myself' part and starts closing her side of the connecting door. Carter places his foot in the jamb to prevent her from shutting it.

Cara continues to speak into the phone turning her back on Carter. "Do you have the twins' schedule for Friday? I assume Nic left you their schedule for tomorrow?"

"Good with tomorrow, can you forward Friday? Are all kids this busy all the time? It gives me a headache." Sasha adds with only minimal inflection.

"I don't know about other children. I try not to notice because I'm afraid of what I might learn. It could lead to disappointment with my own. I feel ignorance is truly bliss when it comes to parenting. You know that."

"Wise words to live by, Vizzini."

Sasha has his share of pet names for Cara. Most of them come from the movie <u>Princess Bride</u>. His favorite is Vizzini; the overly confident but ultimately flawed Sicilian thief. Sasha has managed to get most of their friends and family to refer to her as Vizzini as well. It bothered her at first, to be compared to a short, balding man, but any attention from Sasha is a bonus. He's a man of few words and fewer emotions. Which speaking of… this is the longest conversation she's had with him on the phone, ever. Strange.

"Very funny, Sasha. Please make sure my children are to bed. And please tell Nic I'll try him midday tomorrow, but to text me if he needs me. Thanks and love ya."

"Will do, um…and…take care, Cara." Odd. Sasha never fumbles his words.

Cara ends the call while Carter steps into her room. She places her hand up to stop him from coming in any further. "What do you want Carter? I need to get into the shower and get dressed."

"Is Sasha your nanny? Is she hot?"

Cara pauses before she answers, not wanting to correct him. "Yes, nanny, and yes, hot…in an untraditional way."

Carter heads back into his room, but slowly. He begins to shut her door before turning and stating with great thought, "It must be interesting at your house; that's all I'm going to say."

CHAPTER 9

CARTER IS PROMPTLY AT THE connecting door at 6:30 AM. He knocks, even though the door is technically not closed, but Cara gives him credit for being considerate. Carter is wearing black slacks and a cream colored silk collared shirt. Cara has spent extra time on her hair. She straightens it, and parts it to one side so it sweeps over one eye. She's wearing a gray silk shell with a grey lace push up bra underneath.

Normally, her D cup breasts are not treated to any additional support, but for today, she wants to call attention to them. The shell is button front, and she keeps some of the buttons undone. Her breasts and lacy bra are slightly visible, even if she doesn't bend forward. She has on a black pencil skirt and the black suede Olaf Boots with no hose.

Carter is pretty much trying to not look at her breasts. She ignores his lecherous stare and does her own groping. She slowly moves her eyes down from Carter's face to take in the way his silk shirt clings against his biceps and pecs. She can see the outline of his nipples in the fabric. The shirt doesn't tailor at his waist, but is loosely gathered at his waistband. She continues her assessment down to his groin and notices the area is loose as well; nothing is visible behind the zipper. She looks back up to Carter's face to find him staring at her, nervously.

With one finger, she signals him closer to her. He hesitates a moment, but obeys. She continues to motion him forward until he's only a foot from her. Deliberately, and with great thought, she raises her arms to unbutton his shirt.

After she gets one button undone, Carter grabs her wrist. "Agent Bennett...umm...I'm not comfortable with this."

Cara pulls her wrist from his hand and trying to mock him replies, "Ummm…Agent Carter…what is it you think 'this' is?"

Carter fumbles out, "I think you have enough men in your life already."

Cara drops her arms to her sides and very sternly asks, "Agent Carter, is this your first covert op?"

He quickly and vehemently responds, "No."

"Are you sure of that?"

"Yes!"

"Ok, I'm going to dummy this down for you. We do not have an appointment to see Olaf this morning. You know that, right?" He nods. "All we know is Olaf will be in his office at 7:00 AM." The throaty sigh emerges from Cara's mouth as she studies Carter. "We need to walk-in, in plain sight, Carter. Do you know what that means, my young Padawan?"

"Is this a test?" Carter chokes out.

"What the hell do you kids call this nowadays? We're going to grift, con or scam our way into his office this morning." Carter nods like he's following. Earlier, she said he wasn't going to be a part of this. She had an alternate plan, but now that Cara sees him in silk, she has a better plan. "Now let me fix you up – and NO, this isn't a play for your body, so calm the fuck down."

Proceeding back to unbuttoning three more buttons, she moves on to rolling up his sleeves until the shirt bunches around his biceps. She looks down at his crotch. "Where's your dick?"

"What!?" Carter fumes.

"Your dick, your cock, where are you hiding it?" She inquires, calmly.

"Oh my God, I have it positioned appropriately!"

"Well, un-position it and give me a bulge, please."

With great reluctance, Carter reaches into his pants and yanks his dick front and center. He pulls his hand out of his pants. "Like that?"

Cara studies the bulge with a critical eye. "Take your pants off and give them to me."

"What?!" Again, with the fuming.

"Oh, for God's sake, just do it. We're running out of time here!"

Carter quickly unbuckles his belt, unzips his pants and pulls them off. He throws them to Cara, who catches them with one hand as she heads towards her luggage. She pulls out a small stapler type device and uses it to pull in the inseam on the butt section of his pants.

Carter's face finally registers clarity and he sighs, "You're making my pants tighter, so my bulge will show more. You're primping me. Why didn't you just say so to begin with?"

"I don't know? I guess I never met a man that…" She doesn't finish her thought as she hands him back his pants.

Once he has the pants back on, she has her hands in front of his crotch trying to will his dick into the right position without touching it. Finally, she gives up and requests, "Move him to the left two inches, please." Again, Carter is rummaging around in his briefs. Satisfied with the cock placement, Cara continues by pulling his shirt so it's all gathered at his back. She reaches into his pants and staples the shirt to his waistband. She pulls away from him, re-assessing her efforts. She looks up and smiles, "Now, we're ready to go."

"No, we are not. Where am I supposed to conceal a weapon in this outfit?" Carter's fuming some more.

"You won't need one."

"I'm not going without a weapon." Hands on his hips.

"My handbag, put them in my handbag, Carter."

"Doesn't that break Director Reed's number one cardinal rule?" He asks, believing he's found a loophole.

"No, because YOU will carry my handbag."

"Argh!!"

Cara grabs her purse and gives to him, motioning with her hand to hurry up. He reluctantly takes her bag back to his room and places both weapons inside of it while Cara grabs the Olaf coat and walks into the hotel hallway, shutting the door to the her room behind her. He sprints to his door and walks out while Cara is striding for the elevator.

They get through the hotel lobby and the same town car and driver are waiting for them in the pick-up and drop-off circle. Before they step into the car, Cara reaches for Carter to stop him, "You're going to have some difficulty sitting with the staples I placed in your pants. You might want to try and keep your torso as straight as possible; in other words, no bending at the waist."

"You have got to be kidding me!" Carter shouts, gesticulating wildly with his arms.

With a straight face Cara responds, "No, I'm serious. You wouldn't want to, you know, pop one of your nuts," as she gets into the town car.

Cara watches, trying to keep her straight face, as Carter struggles to get into the car without bending. He ends up inside, with his ass lifted about two feet from the back seat, and his legs stretched out in front of him. The bulge in his pants is front and center for all to see through the side window. She reaches into her coat pocket, removes her phone and takes a picture of him, trying to get his whole body in the photo. Carter reacts shocked and attempts to grab at her phone, but Cara has the leverage, because her ass is on the car seat. She giggles.

"You did all of this on purpose!" Carter spits out.

"No, no, I didn't, I swear, but I couldn't help getting the money shot of you."

Carter clenches his teeth and gets right in her face. "I am going to kill you!"

Cara just laughs at him, reminding him the Director did warn him about her. "Did you underestimate me because I'm a middle-aged woman? Tell me, my young Padawan, because we are only getting started."

Carter chooses not to speak. He faces forward and is using some breathing technique to apparently calm down. When he's finally under control, he turns to her and asks politely, "Are you going to tell me what the plan is now?"

"I don't have a plan." She shrugs.

All control gone, Carter spits out, "What?!" as he loses leverage and topples into her.

"You say 'what' a lot." Deciding she has tortured him long enough, Cara takes pity and attempts to explain. When utilizing the covert grift like they're doing, the gameplan must be fluid. They don't know what they are going to encounter when they try to get in. They can make assumptions, but they have to be prepared to improvise. That's what this all comes down to, improvisation. And with any great improv, tools are critical. Pointing to her breasts, Cara details how she is purposely showing as much of them as possible. She's wearing the Olaf coat and boots to blend in, and has Carter posing as a male model. But, he's look can alter, quickly, into a businessman or bodyguard, should the gameplan need to change.

Waving her arm over both of them, Cara states, "See, we are fluid. You don't need to worry, just let me lead and react appropriately. Try to go with the flow and things will work out fine."

Starting to look a little less angry, Carter asks her, "Have you ever done this before?"

"For over 25 years, darling, 25 years." Cara drones.

CHAPTER 10

THEY ARRIVE IN FRONT OF the building at 6:53 AM. Cara notes the time and knows she has seven minutes to get upstairs. She does a quick assessment of the street, building, and block, and then marches into the lobby. The lobby guards are behind a centered circular reception desk, but there's no turnstile type security systems blocking the elevators. The high security must be on the Olaf floors.

She grabs Carter by the arm and says loudly, as they waltz right past the sign in guards, "Beeile dich! Wir brauchen, um in mein Büro für die Sitzung zu erhalten." She can see one of the guards glancing at them, but doesn't intercede. The elevator arrives and she pushes the button for the 17th floor, which is their best intel for the floor with Olaf's office on it. When the elevator closes, Cara glances at Carter; his chest is stationary. "Carter, breathe."

"What did you say in German?"

"I said we needed to get to my office before the meeting. You want them to think we belong in the building. Show confidence and no one questions it. But now, it may get trickier. Remember, 'go with it' is the motto."

The doors open and they are immediately hit with two guards and a receptionist. Cara's peripheral vision can see two secure doors leading from the lobby, one on the right and one on the left. Deciding she needs better than a 50/50 chance, she does some quick mental calculations of the building layout she studied from Google Earth. She pulls Carter completely out of the elevator and drags him towards the door on the left. The guards watch her, but don't attempt to stop her. She gets to the door and pulls it open, but it doesn't budge. She tries with evident frustration again.

At this point, one of the guards walks over and says, "Braucht man eine Sicherheitskarte?"

Cara answers roughly and quickly, with a full New York City accent, "What? Karte? Do you speak English? My German is horrendous. I don't have my Karte on me. Open this door, this instant! Don't you know who I am? I need to show Olaf this boy for the Vanity Fair shoot. He must approve him. We have a 9:30 flight to New York we have to be on. You know Olaf must personally approve substitutions! Schnell, Schnell!"

Cara peeks at the clock above the receptionist and screeches, "OH MY GAWD! It's 6:58! We have two minutes to get to Olaf! Diese tür öffnen!"

The guard quickly glances at the other guard who just shrugs back as does the receptionist. The man sporting a hip holster with a weapon tucked inside, swipes his fob over the reader and the door unclicks. Cara grabs the handle, shoving Carter through the door, before reaching out and pulling the guard into a hug while pressing her breasts into his chest. "Danke," she adds before sliding through the door as it closes.

Carter is shaking his head. "Fucking unbelievable. You got more of that?"

Cara places her hand in his and quickens their pace through the offices. Her assumption is, based on the architecture of the building; Olaf would have his office at the very end of this section. It would afford him the largest number of windows, and the best views of the city. She can only hope she's correct.

As they near the end of the floor, she's rewarded with what looks like Olaf's office. Cara leans in and whispers some direction to Carter. She approaches the Admin still holding Carter's hand. "We're here for Olaf to approve this model for substitution. I'm sorry we're late; I hope he's still available."

The administrative assistant, who is a man in his early forties with a full head of dark hair and a wiry thin body, looks over Carter with scrutiny. He doesn't even glance in Cara's direction. He asks Carter, "What's this about, sugar?"

Carter lets go of Cara's hand and folds his arms across his chest, causing all kinds of muscles to ripple and stretch. He looks right into the man's eyes and sighs out, "I'm supposed to be approved by Olaf for the shoot in New York. Does he want to see me with my clothes on or off?"

The Admin's mouth forms a perfect 'O'. Carter practically purrs while dropping his hands into his pockets to draw attention to his nicely cached junk, "I have to catch the 9:30 this morning to New York if he approves, just two minutes, pretty pleeeeeaaaase?"

The Admin immediately gets up and grabs Carter by the hand to escort him to Olaf's door. He turns the handle, leading Carter through the door, while discreetly slipping his business card in Carter's pants pocket.

The Admin announces, "Olaf, I need a quick substitution approval," while still holding Carter's hand and dragging him center court of the office.

The office is at least 40 feet by 30 feet. It's entirely white with black lacquered wood flooring. An all glass desk, with surrounding built-in glass counters behind it, sits at one end. The upholstered furniture is black leather, including sofa and four plush chairs. The only splash of color is the crazy geometric rug centered in the room with mostly reds and purples in it. There are windows on three sides of the office, and the view is sweeping.

Olaf is a handsome man with a shiny bald head and a full beard of mostly salt and pepper hair; kept short allowing for just enough coverage to conceal his jawline. His eyes are a piercing teal color.

Olaf lets a smile form on his lips while he addresses Carter. "What's your name, beautiful?"

But before Carter can answer, Cara walks into the office and states, "His name is Carter, Agent William Carter." She has the Glock in her hands and it's aimed right at Olaf.

Carter immediately places the Admin in a headlock, securing him. Olaf can only stare at Cara. He doesn't react to the fact there's a gun trained on him. He slowly stands and continues to gaze, motionless, at her. Olaf isn't a small man. He must be at least six foot and 220 pounds of what looks like muscle.

Olaf finally speaks, and it comes out a whisper, "Chase?" Cara lowers the gun as she nods affirmative to him.

Olaf, still whispering, asks, "What are you doing here?"

Cara has the Glock pointed down to the ground now. She walks towards Carter, still keeping her eyes trained on Olaf, and she responds in a whisper back, "I was hoping you could tell me." She hands her gun to Carter requesting he take his new friend outside and makes sure she and Olaf get some privacy.

Carter leans into Cara while they're both still watching Olaf. "I don't think that's a good idea."

"I didn't ask you."

Carter looks at the gun in his hand, obviously shocked she was able to get the weapon out of her handbag in the confusion.

"Leave us, Carter...please," she pleads. Carter releases the Admin from his hold, but guides him by the shoulders out the door and closes it behind himself.

"I think Tomas was enjoying the choke hold Agent Carter had on him." Olaf muses.

Cara gives Olaf a big smile, raising her hands and taking off the coat, slowly, so he can see she is unarmed.

"Do you think that I think you would hurt me?" He questions.

She gives him her most honest face. "I would never hurt you, but I'm possibly thinking you want to hurt me."

"Hurt you? Darling, I spent two years paying people to find you!" As he speaks, he cautiously approaches her.

Cara is frozen to her spot. "Find me? When? Why?"

"Why? Because look around you, Chase. All of this," his arms encompassing the room, "This is all because of you." After that declaration Olaf grabs Cara in a bear hug, lifting her up off her feet, and swinging her around in a circle.

Cara begins to laugh and enjoy the spinning, but then she stops him, and while still in the embrace, she looks into his face. "I don't understand?"

Olaf places his hands on each side of Cara's face and turns very serious. "When I couldn't find you, or get any information on you, I thought you were dead and my heart broke." Olaf can still see the confusion on her face. He grabs her hand and leads her to the sofa in his office and sits her down, getting comfortable next to her. "Remember Paris?"

Nodding, Cara affirms, "Of course I remember Paris. First, we almost killed each other, and then we almost got our asses shot off, together."

"Yes, fun times. What were your orders?"

"I was to locate, determine and destroy, if necessary."

"No, not that part. The part about what Reed told you for the first time ever." Olaf is getting more animated now.

Reed had ordered Cara to seduce Olaf, even if it meant bedding him. Olaf had the reputation for being a Lothario. Seductions were his MO, and he could extract all kinds of intel from women while he made love to them. Reed believed it may be the only way Cara could determine Olaf's loyalties. It wasn't in the initial script for the mission, but Reed altered it at the last minute. She wanted to argue with Reed, but she was too hurt to find the energy. Cara had never actually fucked anyone during the course of her work. Seduced and teased, yes, but Reed never allowed her, or any of his female agents to sleep with someone. "I was so stressed out about the mission scope. I forgot I told you about that."

Olaf laughs. "Do you remember approaching me at the Hermes after party?"

Chase came onto to him wearing a dark blue YSL dress and carrying a Hermes evening bag. She threw herself at him in an obvious attempt to flirt. Olaf surmised she was the American agent they called, Reflex. He knew she was sent to determine his allegiance. He was enjoying her transparency, and decided he would let the evening play out. Chase dragged him back to her hotel room. Olaf willingly went, figuring it was as good a place as any to kill her. He purposely resisted all of her advances and was amused by her evident frustration.

Olaf was on the bed with Chase on top of him in only her undergarments, when she reached into her handbag to produce her Glock, and pointed it right at her own head. With a lunatic calm, she told him, "Just admit you're gay, and confess you want to be left alone to have a real life, and I won't kill myself."

He stared at her for the longest time before pulling the gun away from her head, and placing it on the nightstand. He started to cry. He had no idea how he couldn't pass her gaydar. He never had any woman suspect his sexual preference. He ended up confessing everything to her. How he didn't want to live that life and lie anymore, and just wanted to have the freedom to explore his passions.

"It was as simple as that. One statement, threatened by you, and my world jerked, tumbled and righted itself." Olaf delivers with no inflection as he contemplates that evening so long ago.

Chase places her hand on his cheek. "I felt heartbroken for you. I never meant to upset you. I'm so sorry for that."

"I was so empty…Do you remember what we did after that?"

"If I recall correctly, we got very drunk and talked about clothes, and designers, and your love of all of it." They spoke about the brutality of their jobs, and how they both wanted out, but how it's difficult to walk away. How it would be harder for him because the SVR would want to insure his silence.

"Do you remember what you suggested?" He questions her.

"Um, I was pretty drunk…"

Chase recommended Olaf should let his superiors know he was gay. He could use it to insure his silence. Tit for Tat, she said. They would be embarrassed if it got out, and he would be embarrassed if it got out. It was too simple, but it did get Olaf thinking she might be on to something. Maybe, he did have some leverage.

"Is that what you ended up doing?" Chase asks amazed her drunken advice was intelligent.

"A more complicated version of it, and I got some inside assistance, but, yes, it is."

"I don't want the details." She gives him a look of understanding. Many former SVR agents got out of their service without an extermination order pending on their heads. Money, bribes, and more money were involved. "As far as I'm concerned, it's none of my business. Every agent deserves a life after what we have all done for our countries. No judgments from me on the topic."

Wondering, Olaf has to ask, "Did you get your life, Chase? Did you get to fall madly in love, have babies, and live happily ever after?"

Chase sucks in a breath when he says this. "Is that what I told you I wanted that night?"

"Yes, you were, how do you say it in English…emphatic." Olaf can see she appears distressed. "Have I upset you?"

"No, it gives me chills to think I don't remember telling you and yet, that's exactly what I got." She looks into his eyes and continues, "I did get my happily ever after, that's why I'm here."

"Darling, I don't think you understand, I owe you my life." If it wasn't for Chase that night in Paris, he's sure he would not have survived long enough to come to terms with all of it. He was a hunted man. He may have figured it all out eventually, but he didn't have an eventually. Her intervention and timing was cosmic. Olaf takes both of her hands in his and turns into her on the couch, "Tell me why you've come to see me."

Chase spills everything to him. She summarizes her life since leaving the Agency. Shows him pictures of her family and talks about her company. She tells him about the song at Starbucks and Target, the email, and the ultimate cell phone call from the unknown number somewhere within Berlin.

While she's speaking, he calls Tomas to bring Carter back in with coffee and breakfast. After they eat, Olaf studies Carter, disgusted by what Chase must have done to his outfit. "Go with Tomas and have him get you dressed appropriately, please."

Carter looks imploringly at Chase to intercede on his behalf. She waves him out of the office. He leaves with Tomas, but not before turning back to her with a steely glare.

Olaf waits until Carter is gone to turn to her, "So, you came to me because of the lead on the call?"

"Reed and I didn't think you were involved, but being based in Berlin, we thought you would still have your pulse on some of the nefarious activity in the area." She turns to look at his wonderful view of Berlin in deep thought for a moment before adding, "We have all left our pasts behind, but the past has a way of staying only a few steps behind."

"Why didn't you just phone me?" He has to question. Breaking into his building and office seems a bit extreme.

"You know we left each other in Paris years ago under…how can I put this…duress? I had to see you to be sure there weren't any hard feelings." Chase makes a concerned face.

Clarity dawns on him. "Oh, you mean because you shot me?"

"Um, yeah."

Again, he laughs. "Chase, my darling, I understand why you did it, and it was brilliant. Wait, should I be calling you 'Cara' from now on?"

"Please, call me Cara. We're going to be friends, yes?" Looking more relieved.

"Good friends, I hope. We didn't have a choice years ago in the alley, did we?"

Olaf and Cara headed to a small, local bar after her suicide attempt in her hotel room in Paris. They talked, and laughed, and got categorically plastered for hours. When they emerged from the bar, stumbling into an alley, they came face to face with the Ukrainian Agent, Lucien Romanov. His weapon pointed right at Olaf's heart.

Olaf knew Romanov wasn't there to chat. He was there to kill him. His own gun in a holster on his back, there was no way he was going to get to it in his drunken stupor. Before he could panic, Olaf could see another weapon at his temple. Cara had her Glock out and pressed to his head. He could barely stand, and was completely confused on how Cara could even have her weapon out. She was already screaming at Romanov, while Olaf was still processing his options.

Cara was screeching, "He's mine! I found him, first! Back off!" It was obvious Romanov wasn't going to take her seriously. He drew closer, and the next thing Olaf knew, Cara lowered her weapon and shot him in the foot. Nice, clean shot directly through it. Olaf dropped to the ground in agony, but the movement made Romanov's gun waver, and Cara shot it right out of his hand, next.

"I heard Romanov screaming, and I did what any trained agent would've done…I got up and ran away as quickly as my shot foot would take me!" Olaf laughs out. He can hardly speak to finally ask what he's always wanted to know. "What happened to you after that?"

Trying to speak through her laughter, Cara tries, "I was so drunk! I was aiming for Romanov's arm but made a direct hit to his gun, instead! YOU ran away and I was left watching poor Lucien Romanov writhing on the ground holding his wrist. Then my eyes focused and I realized I shot a good portion of Lucien's middle finger off. I felt terrible. I started frantically looking all over the ground for his finger – and I found it!"

Olaf lets out a loud exhale realizing he was holding his breath. "Why on earth did you want his finger?"

"Duh. I grabbed what was left of his weapon. Ran back into the bar for a bag of ice. I placed his finger in the bag, and then hailed a cab. I sent him to the hospital with a bar napkin wrapped tightly around the stump of his middle finger, and the bag of ice with said middle finger in it. I apologized, profusely."

Such compassion for a foe? Olaf doesn't understand why she would bother. Before he can inquire, she rambles, "I told Lucien, before the cab could whisk him away, you weren't a threat to US or the Russians, and to please leave you alone. If he failed to do that, I would tell everyone a girl shot his finger off."

He must be staring blankly at her because Cara quips, "What can I say? I was drunk."

He must ask, "You didn't kill him?"

"No! Why would I do that? He wasn't a threat to me anymore. And I felt badly I might have destroyed his career. I mean how was he going to handle a weapon without a finger in the future?"

Olaf has only had his own personal encounter with the Agent known as the Reflex, and that confrontation lead to freedom, growth, success, and a life worth living. He had heard she was fair and just, but, "Do you know what happened to Rominov?"

"About six months after the incident, I received a letter at Langley from Lucien. It would've been cryptic to anyone intercepting it, but I understood its meaning. He was thanking me for my mercy that night. He left his job, changed his name and found more rewarding employment."

While she is back at her phone, she tells him, "Lucien and I have kept in touch. He has a wife, family and a lucrative career." Then, the pictures come out again. There stands the man who almost ended his life with two beautiful little girls clinging to him while his lovely wife watches in adoration.

Olaf is holding the phone with shaky hands. That night led to both Lucien and him getting out…and all because they crossed paths with Agent Bennett. Looking back up at her he realizes she doesn't truly understand the magnitude of what she did. He whispers, "You're our angel."

She scoffs. "No, more like the devil with the blue dress on."

"Wait! That's a great idea for a collection! 'Devil with the Blue Dress'. Again, you inspire me!" His mind is already picturing wicked manipulations of blue silks, chiffons and lace.

Snapping her fingers in his face, she brings him out of his preoccupation. "Earth to Olaf, back to my concerns, please. Do you know who may be hunting me after all these years, or have you ever heard rumblings of revenge?"

"I haven't heard anything, ever. I told you after I made my deal with my superiors, and I got out, I started the Olaf line." With his initial success, Olaf paid some former colleagues to look for Agent Bennett. He felt he owed her in some way. She was no longer employed with the Agency, and penetrating the US government files produced nothing at all. His people worked on some leads, but they all led to a dead end. However Cara got out, she did it perfectly. Chase Bennett was dead; and there were no clues to a new alias. Olaf gave up looking. He hasn't heard anything about the Reflex in the years since.

She digests his information before asking, "And these folks you paid to find me? Could they have betrayed you and known of my whereabouts?"

"Absolutely not." His Security team has been with him since the late 90's. He has full trust in them. Security here at the building isn't severe. He doesn't feel he needs personal protection. He can still defend himself. As a designer, though, he worries more about corporate espionage and systems hacking. The design department is highly monitored with the latest and best technology.

Olaf pauses to study her for a moment while he connects the dots. "My personal contacts list was hacked into from my laptop Outlook account, about three months ago. At the time, we presumed it was benign, but what's interesting is…we traced the IP to here in Berlin."

Her eyes light up. "I'm starting to think this can be related."

"It's possible they were looking to see if I had a contact for you." The address they came up with was in the Prenzlauer Berg section of the city. It's a very bohemian area, so they didn't bother to do much investigating. "We figured it was just a fledging, young designer, or someone looking to get info on a celebrity I outfitted."

Carter is making his way back into the office while Olaf is at his desk searching for the address. He is dressed to kill in a beautifully cut dark gray suit, black shirt and no tie. He opens his jacket to reveal a black snakeskin shoulder holster with his weapon tucked inside. Looking at Olaf, and pointing at the holster, Carter bows his head. "I LOVE it. It's my favorite design of yours. Thank-you."

Olaf snickers, "I see Tomas let you have one my special designs. We reserve those for my security team and me. You must have made a special impression on Tomas for him to give you one."

Carter smiles and raises his eyebrows, "Maybe I did."

Olaf grins back while he slowly checks out Carter's body fitted inside one of his designer suits, "Well, Agent Carter, if you ever want to do any modeling on the side, give me a call."

Cara huffs out, "Please don't compliment him. His head is big enough as it is."

Olaf stands up and comes around his desk towards Carter, stopping when he's next to Cara. He addresses his comment to Cara, but is staring at Carter, "From here, seems Agent Carter's head is just right to me." Of course he isn't looking at Carter above the shoulders when he says it. Carter flushes crimson and looks down at his pants. When he does, Olaf slips the paper with the address into Cara's skirt pocket.

Cara diffuses the discomfort by announcing, "On that note, we should be going." She leans in to give him a big hug and whispers a 'thank-you' in his ear.

But before she can pull away, he freezes. "Wait, I need to send you with some of my designs! You can't leave here empty-handed, I forbid it. Tomas, when's my next meeting?"

"9:30, I cancelled your earlier ones." Tomas absently answers while still admiring Carter.

Olaf looks at his watch and announces with glee, "That gives me 15 minutes to raid the closets for her."

He grabs Cara's hand, pulling her out of his office while she protests. "Olaf, look at me, nothing in your samples are going to fit my frumpy, middle-age ass."

"Stop being so modest! You're still a total knock-out...for a girl that is." And with that, Carter stops at Tomas' desk, picks up a bag of additional clothes that he received, and Cara's handbag, and they follow him.

Olaf returns to his office with only seconds to spare before his 9:30 conference call with his London team. He's feeling elated Chase, or Cara, was back in his life and he had managed to find her a few great articles of clothing and some wonderful bags and shoes. He can't contain his happiness. He shuts the door of his office, quickly, and strides to his desk;

his mind on the unexpected great morning he's had so far. It's this mental distraction that prevents him from noticing the tall, big man hidden in the shadows at the far corner of his office. The man slowly emerges pointing a Beretta M9 with a laser sight aimed at Olaf's forehead.

Olaf freezes when he recognizes the man with the gun. He speaks carefully, while raising his hands. "I guess it's finally my turn to meet the Divine. Welcome to my office, Dark Angel of Death."

CHAPTER 11

THE TOWN CAR PICKS UP Carter and Cara as they make their way back to the hotel with their care packages from Olaf. She starts to calculate the math in her head. It's 9:30 in Berlin. The best Reed's going to do for time is a noon arrival. She needs to decide if she's going to wait for Reed to go checkout the address in the Prenzlauer Berg, bring Carter in on the new intel, or get rid of Carter and go by herself.

Problem is, Cara has no particular aversion to Carter coming with her to check it out, but she thinks he won't go against Reed's orders to stay and do nothing until he arrives. That means she'll lose 2 ½ hours. She could be there and back, having completed investigating the lead, in much less time. She can't help but feel this pull to get to the Prenzlauer Berg, immediately. It's the hairs on the neck thing, the intuition prickling at her brain screaming, 'GO.'

"Carter, I have to tell you, I was pretty impressed with your quick pick up when we first got to Tomas' desk this morning. Score one for Team Carter."

"Thanks," he deadpans, "Maybe you won't treat me like a useless tool from now on."

"Let's not get ahead of ourselves there, big guy. It's a long game, Carter. What's the plan now?"

The town car is pulling back into the hotel. Carter grabs all their bags from Olaf and opens the door to head out, "We wait for Director Reed. We should go upstairs and get some rest before he arrives." Not the answer she was looking for.

They wait for the elevator together. The doors open, and Cara looks around to see the lobby in front of the elevator is empty, as well as the elevator car. She walks in and immediately turns to face Carter. His head is down, and he has the Olaf bags in both hands. She gives him a swift kick to the groin, and as his body involuntarily bends forward, his head is met with her knee. He goes down for the count. Cara quickly makes sure the Olaf bags are fine, she has her priorities, and then pushes all the buttons on the elevator before running back out into the lobby. She hails the first cab outside and heads to the Prenzlauer Berg.

Agent William Carter found himself on the floor of the elevator with the bags from Olaf neatly stacked next to him. There are several sets of eyes staring at him. He slowly pushes himself to a sitting position with his back against the elevator car wall. A short, round older woman asks, "Sie einen Arzt?"

Carter's very bad German skills assume she's asking if he needs a doctor. He shakes his head and leans towards the elevator panel to hit the five button. No one will get on the elevator with him as the doors close. When they re-open on the fifth floor, Carter drags himself off, along with the bags. His head is pounding and he feels nauseous. But worst of all, his nuts are on fire. What the hell is he supposed to do now? How could a woman in her 40's take him down? Reed is going to fire his ass. Oh no, Reed. He has to call Reed and tell him.

Carter makes it to his room. He takes some deep cleansing breaths and dials Director Reed.

"Reed."

"Director, Sir."

"You lost her, didn't you, Carter?"

"Yes, Sir. Sorry, Sir."

"She kick you in the nuts?"

"Yes, Sir."

"My bad, I should've warned you. It's her go to maneuver."

"Sir, I understand if you want to re-assign me off the case or out of the department. Hell, Sir, I would understand if you terminated me right now."

Reed lets out a soft chuckle, "Carter, don't be so hard on yourself, she is very crafty. She has taken them down bigger and badder than you.

Besides, I assumed she would lose you. Those Olaf boots I gave her, is she still wearing them?"

"Yes, Sir."

"There was no way I was going to let Agent Bennett wander around Berlin. The trick is to always be a step ahead of her. I had one of my local agents retrieve the coat and boots from the Olaf retail store and had the boot heel modified with a tracer and audio device inside. I set it up as soon as you both left. Give me a second for the satellite to uplink from my plane and I'll send you the GPS coordinates of her location. Are you in any condition to go after her?"

"Yes, Sir," Carter lies.

"I'm arriving in less than hour. I will proceed directly to whatever coordinates I get from the trace unless I hear from you otherwise. And Carter?"

"Yes, Sir?"

"No more slip ups."

Cara arrives at the address and is surprised to see a very fun, diverse neighborhood. There are coffee shops and restaurants, funky boutiques and music stores. There are lots of young people loitering around. Probably unemployed. A door between a coffee shop and a record store, with actual vinyl albums in it, looks to be the entrance she wants.

Carter didn't notice she swiped the Glock back out of her purse while they were in the sample room at Olaf's. He really is sort of slow on the uptake. But the gun, her phone and some Euros are the only thing Cara has in her coat pockets.

She tries the door and it's open. According to the address Olaf has written, they were able to pin point to an actual apartment number on the second floor. She wonders if they can be that accurate. It seems unlikely in a multi-tenanted space to be able to do that. But, her grasp on the latest technology is sufficiently lacking.

She arrives onto the second floor looking for Apartment 24. She places her hand in her coat, and around the handle of her weapon, which she has at the ready. Walking slowly, with her back against the wall, she stealthily moves down the hall reading apartment numbers on the doors. When she gets to 23, she looks across the hall to see a door with 24 on it. Facing the door to Apartment 24, she pulls out her Glock. She suddenly hears the door to Apartment 23 open behind her. Before she can spin around, her world jolts. She feels her body project off the ground, and her brain completely scramble. She loses control of her bladder, and everything goes dark.

When Cara starts to see light beyond her closed eyelids, the overwhelming stench of urine invades her senses, first. Holy Shit! She peed herself. Quickly setting aside the humiliation of that, she realizes she's been Taser'ed. She, again, wishes she knew more about the latest technology. She has no clue how many volts of electricity she just received, or if it's normal to lose your bladder, and will she have any permanent damage? Cara's feeling very inadequate. She can describe the entrance and exit wounds of every possible cartridge or bullet and yet, she knows nothing about a Taser.

Wait. Her arms feel dead. Her arms aren't dead; they are tied behind her back. Cara tries to remain calm as she ascertains the situation. She's on the ground in her own urine with her arms bound. She listens for sounds, next. She can hear breathing and movement to her left. Very cautiously, she lifts her eyelids. Her vision is blurry, but Cara is certain she's looking down the barrel of a semi-automatic pistol. Not good. She can reach her puddle of urine with her hands bound. Maybe she should leave a message? OK, that only incites this Einstein looking man more.

Feeling chastised but suddenly more focused, she glares at him.

Einstein speaks, "Agent Chase Bennett, welcome, or should I call you Cara Bianco, or is it Cara Andre now? My, you do have many names. Maybe I will just call you Reflex."

The man is quite unattractive. He's mid-fifties, short, big bellied with a large nose. Wisps of hair protrude out from the sides of his head. He accent sounds Russian, could be Slavic. He knows Cara, but she's never seen this man. Time to ascertain again before mounting a full panic attack. "You know my name or names, what's yours?"

"My name is Vlad, Vlad Chekov." The short man offers freely.

"Chekov, like the Star Trek character?"

"Yes, yes, you may have heard of me?" He asks looking for validation.

"No, should I?" Cara is attempting to gradually get to a sitting position with her back to the wall she is laying next to.

"Well, maybe you know me as Vlad the Impaler?"

Vlad the Impaler? Seriously? She has never heard of this guy. What the fuck? "That's not ringing a bell. Sorry, have we met?"

"No, we have never met, but I thought you may have heard of my reputation." His shoulders go back and his spine stiffens with pride.

"Your reputation? Are you former KGB? I know a lot of those guys. I can call some of them friends, even."

He deflates. "I was KGB trained, but I haven't been part of that organization for a long time."

Always keep them talking. Time for chatty Cara. "So, forgive me for being forward but, if we've never met, and I don't know who you are, why am I bound as your hostage at gunpoint?"

"Oh, yes, this…you're my shining star." He blurts with great pride, again.

"Care to elaborate, please?"

He shrugs out, "I'm a contract killer, now. But three months ago, I was asked to find the Reflex and kill her. Largest offer I ever had for a disposal. I've heard of you, of course, but I heard you were untraceable, as well. I started to think, maybe everyone was going about finding the you the wrong way."

"How did you go about finding me, then?"

He taps his temple. "I have a friend who's a wiz with computers. He owed me a favor. I wanted to see if it was possible to take a picture of the Reflex from the 90's, age progress it, and then search the Internet for any matches. I knew we were going to end up with lots of people."

So far, he's making sense. She asks, "How did you ferret out all the mismatched folks?"

"I didn't need to. I narrowed it down to about 50 people, 38 in the US. I focused only on the ones in the US. I eliminated age differences, background discrepancies, or any obvious inconsistences. That narrowed the list down to eight women."

"How did you get the backgrounds and pictures?"

"Social media, of course. I used professional sites like Linked In, as well." He's looking at her like she's a dumb ass.

Which, apparently, she is, and Reed is going to kill her if Chekov doesn't. "I still don't understand how you found me." Cara inquires, casually, trying to keep him talking.

"I didn't try for you, specifically. I used the music, the emails and the phone calls to get to all eight of you. I figured the only one that would actually react would be the real Reflex, right?"

"That was really smart!" She decides she should compliment him. "But, how did you find me here in Berlin?" He straightens to his full height, looking very smug. And it hits her. Olaf. Vlad must have known the story of Olaf and Lucien.

She trembles out, "Paris. You know what happened in Paris with Olaf."

With a wicked grin stretching his thin lips, he confirms, "Overheard an agent talking about it in a bar in Budapest one night. Confirmed it was true you shot Olaf in the foot, then shot Lucien's finger off."

It's all coming together in her mind. "You knew I would trace the call to here in Berlin." She wants to be devastated, but the only emotion she can feel at the moment is genuine praise for his plan. "You purposely hacked into Olaf's personal contacts three months ago from this address, but across the hall, knowing when I found out the blocked call came from Berlin, Olaf would be the first person I sought. Right?"

Cara is slowly rising from the sitting position to a standing position leaning against the wall. "So, essentially, eight women get the same messages I do, only one reacts, and that one learns the final call is made from Berlin. Olaf is set up to give the address, and abracadabra, you don't have to find me, I came to you! It's genius!" She exclaims, seriously underestimating the overweight, short man.

Using her peripheral vision, Cara takes in the apartment. She's looking for anything she can utilize as a weapon. It's empty. The apartment is completely bare. Could he have been sitting on the floor waiting for her for days? She catches a glimpse of the contents of her coat pockets lying on the counter in the grimy kitchenette area. Her Glock, her phone and the Euros are there. All she can surmise is Vlad must have known when she saw Olaf. Maybe he has a camera or some kind of surveillance on Olaf's building.

Cara stops her congratulations of him to ask, "Wait, how did you know when I would get to Berlin? You couldn't have been waiting in this apartment for days?"

"Easy, I paid someone to watch Olaf's building." They had the pictures of the eight women, and he knew she would only try to see Olaf when he was in town and at his office. "I received a call early this morning saying you had arrived with a tall, dark young man. I came to the apartment to wait."

"But what if I brought an army of people with me to this apartment?" She needs to buy more time.

"You underestimate me! My eyes at Olaf followed you back to your hotel. I was prepared to stake out the hotel, but I didn't have to, you were back out, by yourself, within minutes of arriving. I knew you were headed here."

Reed is really going to kill her if she doesn't die now. "Let's go back to my original question. Why are you trying to kill me?"

Cara notices her breathing is quick and shallow. Her heart rate is elevated. She's beginning to perspire. She's losing it. Focus! She can't. Pictures of her family are flashing in front of her eyes. Max, first, with all his beautiful out of control blonde hair and his constant smirking smile. The one he has because he's up to no good. The cocky walk and bold strides of her beautiful baby boy. And Mia, her Mia, all five foot ten of her is mouthing off some complaint. The raving beauty and confidence she doesn't even know she possesses. They act like they don't need their Mommy, but that's no consolation right now. Deep down, Cara knows they need her.

"I told you I will be paid very handsomely for your body. I'm getting on in years. I need this to retire. You understand." Vlad adds, almost apologetically. He's closer to Cara now. Gun still trained at her head.

He's getting ready to shoot. She can go for the head butt, but she needs him closer. He's angled prohibiting the old faithful kick in the nuts. It's like this guy knows all her tricks. Her arms are bound, so she has little leverage to work with. "But who hired you?"

Vlad shrugs his shoulders. "I don't know. It doesn't matter to me. As long as the second half of my cash arrives with your body, I'm good. They were very impressed with how I found you, though."

Her anxiety prevents all subtlety when she shouts, "This matters to me! I want you to tell me who hired you!"

"I don't know who. You are a dead woman in less than thirty seconds. Don't worry yourself about it." He takes his shooting stance.

● ● ●

Carter receives the GPS coordinates from Reed and it's brought him to the doorway between a coffee shop and music store. Based on the three-dimensional grid display on his phone, Bennett should be somewhere on the right hand side apartments on the second floor. He proceeds through the doorway. Once in the hallway, he withdraws his gun and takes a two handed search stance with it. He stays to the shadow side of the stairwell and climbs as quietly as he can to the second floor.

He waits on the top of the stairs to hear any movement. He hears water running, but no voices. He slowly precedes down the hall, passing the first two apartments, one on each side of the hallway. He releases one hand from his gun and searches in his pocket for his phone. He glances at the screen and the blinking spot is further down. Again, he moves cautiously towards the next set of apartment doors. He stops and listens, no abnormal sounds, no voices. Quick glance at his phone confirms coordinates are still further in. He approaches the doorways for Apartments 23 and 24. No sounds. He glances down quickly at his phone in his left hand. The target is on the right, Apartment 23.

Before Carter lifts his eyes from the screen, his right wrist is being jerked backwards by a hand from behind him with their fingers wrapped around the barrel of his handgun. To prevent his wrist from breaking, he releases his grip on the gun, but throws his head backwards to head-butt his assailant. The classic, surprise street-fight maneuver, except his head is met with nothing but air. Carter loses his balance and stumbles.

He regains his stability to find himself looking into the coldest, dead eyes he has ever seen. The tall, big man is just standing there, motionless, with both his gun and Carter's gun, one in each hand. No expression on his face. Just death. Carter goes for the lunge except the tall man is quicker. He steps forward and kicks Carter right in the nuts – again. Carter lurches over, and the last thing he remembers is being dealt a left upper cut to his jaw. Lights out.

Cara hasn't realized, but she's begun to tremble. She's shaking uncontrollably. And for only the second time in her life during a mission, she's crying. It's over. Her only clear thought is how unfair to meet death at this age rather than when she was young and felt invincible. She would've faced death with more honor, because she was irresponsible and imprudent. Now, like this, convulsing, crying, and coated in her own urine, she will die leaving a husband, two children and a beautiful life.

Her head is averted from the handgun. Cara is so hopeless; she can't look death in the eye. Her despairing thoughts are suddenly interrupted. Kabul. Kabul in 1998. It was the last field mission before she quit, the only other incident that left Cara in tears, and an emotional basket case. All of her emotions from Kabul are flooding back into her. She prayed for death in Kabul, and her prayers were answered in an unexpected way.

She finds the energy to pick her head up and look at Vlad with silent tears streaming down her face. She promised Reed she would be careful. She has broken her insincere assurances to her handler for the last time. Cara is crying so hard, her vision is blurring. She sees spots. No, it's just one clear spot.

She tries to focus, and there is a mark on Vlad's forehead. A red mark. Just about at the exact millisecond it takes for Cara to register what the spot is, Vlad makes the same connection. Both of their eyes travel the distance of the laser causing the red spot in slow motion. When their eyes finally find the source, Cara's jaw drops of its own volition. Standing completely still, with two hands wrapped around the handle of a Beretta M9, is the most frightening man with the steeliest, coldest dark gray eyes ever seen and…Cara's husband.

CHAPTER 12

NIC? NO, NOT NIC; SOMEONE that looks like Nic. This Nic is wearing leather pants, biker boots, and matching leather hooded fitted jacket. This Nic has the cruelest, coldest eyes Cara has ever seen. They're not blue. They're like gunmetal grey. This Nic is a thug, a badass. His hair is slicked back like a mobster. He hasn't blinked once yet. His eyes haven't left Vlad's face. He hasn't even glanced in her direction. He's like a doppelgänger or evil twin of her husband.

Cara peels her gaze from the Nic twin to focus on Vlad. Vlad's eyes are shifting at top speed between her and the Nic twin. A fine sheen of sweat has come to cover his face. The gun Vlad has aimed at her trembles.

Subtly shaking his head, Vlad hisses out of his mouth, "Nicolae? Nicolae Andrychenko?" Evil Nic twin doesn't blink. His face is still a total mask of any emotion. The Beretta's laser sight doesn't even flinch. Vlad takes a second to better compose himself. "They said you were dead. Died at the hands of Golov." He slowly inclines his head towards Cara and whispers in reverence, "Agent Bennett, have you met the Dark Angel of Death?"

Cara can only stare wild-eyed at Vlad. Tears are still falling from her eyes without any control. She feels nothing but fear.

Vlad lightens his mood. "Agent Bennett, you are a very popular woman. Seems you have incited the wrath of the Dark Angel." Vlad positions his arm so his weapon is against Cara's temple. He turns his head ever so slightly towards evil Nic. "Nicolae, do you remember, friend? It is me, Vlad Chekov."

For the first time, evil Nic speaks. His voice is lower, and there's a heavy Russian accent when he simply says, "No. I have no friends."

Her husband does not have an accent.

Vlad tries to shake him. "Yes, we worked some missions together, remember?"

There is uncomfortable silence before evil Nic states, "She's mine."

"It doesn't matter which one of us shoots her. Allow me the pleasure for old times' sake." Vlad tries.

Evil Nic says a little stronger and firmer than before, "She's MINE."

Vlad is growing petulant. "I found her first."

And like a moment of inspiration, all of Cara's training is back. She refocuses her gaze onto evil Nic. She keeps her eyes trained on him, unblinking, despite her tears. When she feels he may understand, she shifts her eyes to Vlad's leg, and then slowly looks back to evil Nic. She blinks three times, purposely. To her astonishment, evil Nic blinks three times back.

She starts the count in her head. One…Cara leans her weight to her right leg. Two…she bends her right knee. Three…she throws her head forward, raises her left leg and lands a chop kick right into the side of Vlad's knee.

The next thing she hears is the sound of a gun being fired and feels her body being propelled to the right side by something forced against her back. Her hands are bound so Cara can't control the fall. She's hitting the ground hard on her right side. She's not sure she's breathing.

There's the sensation of a cold blade against her hands and she's jerked up from the floor. Her hands are free but she can't feel them. Evil Nic has his hands on her body, and his lips are moving but Cara can't make out what he's saying.

Nic strips the Olaf coat from Cara and tosses it to the side. He starts running his hands all over her. When he's done checking her body for any damage, he places his hands on each side of her face. "Cara, look at me, baby, I need you to look at me. You're going into shock. I need you to try to focus. You appear mostly unharmed. Are you hurt?" He asks gently.

Cara raises her eyes and looks passed him to slowly shake her head.

"Good girl. Was Vlad alone? Was there someone else here, Cara?"

Again, Cara shakes. She forces her head left, to the spot she last saw Vlad. He lays crumpled on the ground. There's a small red dot in the middle of forehead; the back of his head is completely gone. She follows the trail of blood, skull fragments and brain tissue leading to her boots and legs. Raising her arm, she moves her hand to touch her hair. She brings her hand back towards her face and looks at it. Without any expression, she croaks, "I have brains in my hair."

"Yes, you do, baby. It was unavoidable. I'm sorry."

For the first time, Cara turns her face up and looks right at him. Her hand touches his chest. He places his hand over hers. She whispers, "Nic?"

"Cara mia."

"Who are…how did…" She stutters.

"I have a lot of explaining to do, but we need to get out of here, now. I need to get you cleaned up and we'll talk. Please, Cara." Nic pleads softly.

Cara looks closely at him, almost as if she doesn't believe it's him. He leads her by the hand towards the door. She glances at the kitchenette, and Nic immediately leans towards the counter and grabs her Glock, phone and the Euros, putting them in his jacket pocket.

They step out into the hallway where Carter is sitting with his back to the wall against the apartment right by the door. He's conscious but not moving. He looks like hell.

Carter's whole body breathes out a huge sigh. She's not dead and looks unharmed. He heard the single gunshot, but had no idea who was going to come out of that apartment. His attacker is clutching her to his side, but she's not resisting. Carter finds his voice. "Are you okay?"

Cara doesn't answer, but does move her eyes to him on the ground. She stares blankly at him before shifting a concerned gaze to the man that has her in his arms. She whispers to Death, "Did you do that?" pointing at Carter.

"Yes." The mean man speaks, and it's unapologetic.

Cara looks back at Carter. "Sorry," still only in a whisper.

Carter tries to move, but Death makes a stop motion with his hand and warns, "It would not be prudent for you to try to stop me."

The man gets down on his knees while watching Carter. He unzips Cara's boots and gently pulls her leg out of each one. When she's standing barefoot, he picks the boots up and tosses them to Carter. "Give your boss a message from me. Let him know I have her. He has clean up duty." He's gesturing towards the interior of the apartment. He unzips his jacket, pulling open the right side. Death pulls Cara to his chest and wraps the jacket around her, concealing most of her upper body and head. He turns her towards the stairwell, and walks away with his arm around her waist.

Carter barely caught the boots when the Devil threw them. He can't believe he couldn't save her. He keeps trying to get up, but nausea overcomes him, and he falls back down to his butt. He doesn't know how much time goes by, but suddenly he hears footsteps on the stairs. Director Reed appears frantically looking all around him. He has a Glock in his hand, and several men are behind him.

Reed looks right passed Carter and yells, "Where is she? Where is she?!" His eyes are wild with panic. "I followed the trace here when I didn't hear from you!"

Carter tries to articulate his answer to the Director. "Sir, she was here, in Apartment 23. She was being held at gunpoint by the man in there. I was on my way to her when out of nowhere I was attacked from behind, Sir."

Reed opens the door to the apartment and surveys the scene quickly. He turns to Carter and demands, "How many men and what did they do to her?"

"It was only one guy. Mean son of a bitch, Sir. He put me down, like I was nothing. He took my weapons and my phone after I passed out. I am so sorry, Sir. He went in there and he shot the man holding Agent Bennett. He came back out with her and threw her boots at me about 15 minutes ago."

"Was she hurt or struggling?" It's apparent Reed is trying desperately to keep control of his complete alarm.

"She seemed in shock, but she didn't appear hurt, Sir. She was just letting him lead her. He spoke to me. He said to tell my boss that he had her, and that you had clean up duty." Carter points to the apartment.

Reed stops dead from his pacing in the hallway. He rigidly moves his head towards Carter, "What did this guy look like?"

"Like I said, mean son of a bitch. Cold, dead eyes. Maybe around your age, but blonde, Sir."

Reed moves in closer to him. "A little taller than me, and a little bigger? Very good looking?"

Carter can't stifle a snort. "Handsome like the Devil himself."

Reed leans against the wall as he exhales very loudly, and let's all the built-up tension leave his body. Bringing one hand towards his face, he stares at it. His hand is visibly trembling. His legs give out and his body sags down the wall, he's practically sitting on the floor. He places his hands over his face while he replies, "You did meet the Devil, Carter, the Dark Angel in the flesh." Reed drops his hands to his side and numbly continues, "Consider yourself initiated. You're only my second agent, in almost 30 years, to survive a close encounter with the Dark Angel of Death."

If possible, Carter is more alarmed. "Sir, who was the first?"

Reed lets a slight frown cross his features when he answers, "Agent Bennett, 17 years ago."

"The man is a monster. How did she survive, Sir?"

Reed mumbles, "He can walk straight through hell with a smile," before dispassionately looking Carter directly in the eyes and admitting, "She married him."

CHAPTER 13

NIC KEEPS MOST OF CARA'S head and body covered with his coat as he makes his way to the motorbike he left in an alley. She has no shoes on and he lifts her onto the back of the bike. He doesn't have a helmet with him, but they do not have far to go. He mounts the bike in front of her but needs to reach back for her arms to make sure she wraps them around him. She is shaky and quivery against him. The tears are gone, but she hasn't said a word.

The only thing he offers, "I'm taking you to my apartment. We can get cleaned up there. It's only several blocks away."

It was late 1989 when Nicolae Andrychenko first heard of the Reflex. Talk amongst the agents was the Americans had a new operative that was beautiful, but in a much understated way. She could creep up on you undetected. She was very cunning and lethal. His superiors at the KGB gave everyone a description, but no pictures. Nic didn't pay much attention. By then, he was already considered one of their best. He was placed on the highest profile and most dangerous missions. He didn't think he would ever run into an American woman anywhere he would be.

Nic continued to hear the stories from other agents the Reflex had confrontations with. They all spoke of her talent and beauty. Some of the agents truly admired her. They said she was a woman of honor, no cheap shots, and always open to negotiate. Again, he didn't pay the fables much mental effort. Agent Chase Bennett wasn't in his league. He had bigger bears to hunt. His handler, Alexander Golov, managed a picture of the Reflex in the early 90's. It was taken at a distance, but it gave the office a general idea of what she looked like. Nic studied the photo for posterity purposes only. She was attractive, but not beautiful. He didn't share the sentiment of the others.

It wasn't until Kabul in late 1998 that would all change. By then, the communist government backed Afghani officials had been all but wiped out. Russia was losing the last tentacles of control in the province. The Taliban, with Osama Bin Laden as their leader, was closing in to seize Kabul. The Saudis and the Pakistanis were assisting. His mission was to, covertly, arrange for possible final assistance to the remaining Massoud forces. Their best intel was the US had backed the wrong horse with the Saudis and Pakistan. Bin laden was playing for keeps, and there would never be peace in the region with him at the helm. He was to find the Americans working with the Taliban, and extinguish them, if the opportunity presented itself.

There was chatter the Reflex was in the region. Nic couldn't believe her handler would place her in such a position. Women do not perform effectively, covert, in that misogynistic culture. He assumed the intel was incorrect.

He had a meeting set up with his six contacts in Kabul. He was on his way to the meeting when he heard some commotion. Nic stopped and took protective cover. When he peered around the corner he saw his contacts dragging a woman in full burka through the dirt street. He knew what their intentions were. These men were his contacts but they were animals, filled with hate and rage, depravity at its worst. He watched as the woman continued to struggle but to no avail. They groped her, unarmed her, and finally pulled her headgear off.

He recognized her immediately, except she wasn't beautiful like his colleagues had described, and she wasn't attractive. She was breath taking. He felt his heart tighten and his body stiffen when he laid eyes on her. She was the most beautiful woman he had ever seen. Never in his life, did he have such a visceral reaction to a woman. Worst of all, he could feel her terror. He stopped thinking straight. He knew those men would gang rape her and kill her. He pulled out his weapon and shot all six of them without remorse.

His heart was pounding so hard in his chest; he swore there was movement from behind, so he turned to see that he was clear. When he turned back, she was gone. Nic was fairly certain the Reflex hadn't seen him. He was still using the corner of the building as cover. He assumed she ran off. He wanted to run after her, but he finally had a clear thought. He would only scare her more if he gave chase. He rushed towards the bodies and removed any identification, quickly. He brought his hat down low over his forehead as he spied faces in the windows and balconies of the apartments facing the dusty alley.

He left Kabul shortly after that. His mission blown. His first failure. His handler was very disappointed, but Golov understood the mentality of the region, and how tenuous any associations were there. Nic never told him the truth about what happened. He never told anyone.

Nic pulls into an alley that opens up into a courtyard. This is the former East German side of Berlin. It's known as the courtyard district or Mitte, now. Clutching her to him as he lifts her off the bike, he scans around them to check for any eyes. Looking up at the buildings, Nic finds it ironic they are standing in an alley, once again. Although, Berlin's side streets do not resembles Kabul's. Using a key, he opens the back door and pulls her in. They walk silently up two flights of stairs. The hallway is well decorated. The building is clean and modernized, but at least a century old. Nic puts his arm around her, again, and approaches an apartment door. He pulls another key and lets them in.

They enter the small but very quaint apartment. The colors are all muted, and there are lovely furnishings. The compact kitchen is entirely updated with granite counters and stainless steel appliances. There is one bedroom with a European double bed and a couple of dressers.

Nic releases Cara and turns to lock the front door. At the kitchen table he removes all of the weapons from his jacket pockets. He pulls knives from his pants. Removing his jacket, he hangs it around one of the two kitchen chairs. He gets his leather pants off and places them over the jacket, next.

Cara only watches. Her eyes are picking out the large number of weapons on the table.

In only his briefs and a T-shirt, Nic leaves his holster on, which is outfitted with another two guns, one under his shoulder and one on his back. Sitting down on the only other kitchen chair, he pulls off his boots, but not before removing a smaller .22 automatic from the inside of one boot and a knife from the other. He approaches Cara and takes her hand, pulling her gently into the bathroom located between the kitchen and only bedroom. Closing the door to the bathroom, he locks it. He hangs the shoulder holster over the hook on the door before leading her into the large walk in shower.

The shower is renovated. New porcelain tiles cover the walls and there's marble on the floor. A shower seat is built in to one side. He turns on the water and adjusts the temperature, after he shifts Cara so she's not in the path of the spray. Facing her, he pulls his T-shirt off and throws it in the corner of the shower. Carefully, he unbuttons Cara's silk shell. He extricates it from her arms and throws it over his shirt. He reaches around her to unzip her skirt, letting it fall to the shower floor. She is now standing naked except for her matching grey lace bra and thong.

Checking the water temperature, and satisfied it's warm enough, he pulls Cara under the showerhead. She shudders when the water hits her. He wraps one arm around her waist, pressing his body close to provide warmth. Removing the showerhead from its mount on the wall, he uses it as a handheld. He runs it over her hair until it's sufficiently wet. Placing his hands on her waist, Nic spins her to face the spray with her back against his chest. He pours some shampoo on her hair and starts to slowly massage it through.

When it's thoroughly lathered, Nic spins her facing him and uses the handheld to rinse out the shampoo. When he's done, he places the handheld back into the mount on the wall and twists a dial to activate a large rectangular rain head centered above them. Gentle, warm droplets leisurely fall all over the shower stall.

Bending his knees to be eye level with Cara, he wraps both his hands on the nape of her neck. He hesitantly brings his lips to hers, brushing across them ever so slightly. Gazing into her still dazed eyes, Nic knows all of his apprehension has led to this moment.

When he and Cara first met, she gave him, what he would come to find out later, her real name, not Chase Bennett. Cara said she was a recently unemployed banker. Her lack of initial disclosure, forced his need for discretion. He kept with his cover history, and only disclosed that. But as that first evening progressed, Nic began to suspect she truly didn't know his real identity.

She was never frightened or concerned that first night with him, even though he knew she was completely unarmed. Had she known he was the Dark Angel, she would have never willfully gone back to his hotel suite with him. Even Reed never reacted to him like he knew the truth. The man was her handler, a CIA Team Leader and eventually, the Director, yet he let his best friend marry the Dark Angel of Death. In the 17 years to follow, Nic could only assume neither Cara nor Reed was aware of his true identity.

He breaks their visual connection to whisper, "Please, just remember, I love you more than you can ever know." Nic sits on the shower seat, placing her between his legs with her back to his chest. He wraps both arms tightly around her and confesses what he did and how he felt in Kabul.

After the incident in Kabul, Nic went back to Moscow a mental mess. He spent the next few weeks trying to get the Reflex out of his mind. She became a compulsion, though. He was feeling all kinds of things he had never felt before. Strong emotions are dangerous in his line of work. Emotions will get you killed.

His next assignment was still pending when he found out about the European and American mini Summit in Geneva at the UN. He heard through the grapevine the CIA would have agents there. Nic managed to talk himself into the mission to attend the Summit. His only hope was she would be there.

And Agent Chase Bennett was there, with Agent Connor Reed wrapped around her like a glove. The famed and feared Duo of the Reflex and the White Night were schmoozing it up at the dinner. He knew Reed was her handler. There was chatter and speculation, not only were they an effective team, but they were a couple. She wore an amazing red gown, and he couldn't imagine she could look even more breath taking than Kabul, but the Reflex was a total knock out. Every man in that room was watching her, but it was Reed who was all over her.

Reed was acting like a man in love. He was admiring her, gazing at her, and leaving kisses on her lips, face, bare shoulders and hands. He found himself trembling with rage and jealousy watching the two of them. It was only when he stopped looking at Reed and just watched her that he could see…she was smiling, but the smile never made it to her eyes. She appeared distracted, her mind elsewhere. Occasionally, her eyes would dart around the room like she was looking for something.

Nic stayed in the shadows during most of the evening's dinner. He decided to finally get closer to them when the dancing commenced. He grabbed a fellow female agent when the Duo headed towards the dance floor. He tried to steer his dancing in their direction. He wanted to get a better feel, and possibly overhear any conversation. But that damn Oksana he was dancing with was talking his ear off. She was running her hands through his hair and disrupting his hearing. He kept trying to tell her, discreetly, to shut the hell up and stop touching him, but she was incorrigible. And that's when he noticed Reed yank Cara abruptly off the dance floor in his peripheral vision. Nic turned to watch as Reed was practically dragging her out of the ballroom.

He ditched Oksana and decided to follow them, but it was too late, they were both gone. He took a chance and went to the hotel he heard the CIA had taken a floor on. He worked his charm on the girl at the front desk and got their block of rooms. Nic came out of the elevator and immediately had to take cover because Reed was storming out of a room. He had his luggage with him and headed straight into the open elevator car.

Nic came around the corner and headed towards where Reed had left. He heard the sobbing. It was coming from the room Reed walked out of, and he knew for sure it was coming from her. Nic wanted to break down the door to get to her. What had Reed done to her? Did he hit her? Hurt her in anyway? He tried to get composure before he did anything rash and that's when he realized her sobbing didn't seem to be physical pain but more emotional.

Nic leans into Cara's ear as the droplets of water roll down his face. "I decided to just stand outside your door and listen. My heart was breaking for your pain. I must have been there about an hour when you finally stopped crying. I presumed you and Reed had some sort of blowout. He left. He left you."

With that final statement, Cara leans forward against his restraining arms as if in pain, a wince on her face. She tries to speak for the first time since the shooting, her voice more of a croak. "I can't believe you were there, outside my hotel room that whole time. So close…if you wanted to check on me, why didn't you just knock?"

"Cara, when one is known as the Dark Angel, one doesn't bring death to your door." Nic pauses before continuing, "Honestly, I thought you'd recognize me and shoot me." If he was Cara, he would have shot first and asked questions later. It was one thing to try to see her in public, but knock on her door in the middle of the night?

He picks her up in his arms and sits her down directly on the shower seat. He kneels in front of her to force her to look into his eyes.

He waited outside her hotel room all night in Geneva, dodging other agents and any activity in the hallway. She finally emerged around 7:00 am with her bag. He followed her out of the hotel and to the airport. Nic watched her board a flight to DC. He assumed she was headed back to Langley.

Running back to his hotel, he grabbed his bags and his American cover documents, and boarded the next direct flight to Washington. He had to know what this thing was between she and Reed. Really, he had to know what this compulsive feeling towards her was.

He arrived in DC and used his contacts there to find out where she was living. It was easier than he thought. By the time he made it to her apartment, she was packing her car. She looked lost.

Not too differently than she appears now.

Nic runs his hands down Cara's hair and around to her shoulders. "I knew you were leaving town. I didn't know at the time that you had quit. I would learn that later. But I followed you for the next six hours until you arrived outside of Cleveland to Jinx's apartment. During the next two days, I staked out the apartment and trailed you, not that you left much."

Problem was Nic couldn't stay in the States. He would be considered rogue if he didn't check back in. He only hoped Cara was at Jinx's for a while. He flew out of Cleveland that afternoon back to Moscow. As soon as Nic arrived, he found Golov and told him he needed some mental health time off. Nic always had a very close relationship with Alexander, and he wanted to be honest. Nic explained he met a woman, and needed to explore the relationship, because she was causing all kinds of havoc in his head. He wouldn't be able to perform his job until his head was on straight. It was the truth. He was surprised when Golov was sympathetic about it. He told him to take three weeks, and then report in.

"Of course, I didn't tell Alexander Golov who the girl was. He would've had you shot." Reaching for the shower gel, he starts soaping up Cara's feet and legs.

After his conversation with Golov, Nic spent the remaining day making arrangements for himself. He had a sense he needed to put some insurances in place before he left Moscow. He packed everything he thought vital to his mission. For him, it became the most important mission of his life. He flew back to Cleveland and was relieved Cara was still at the apartment. He waited for his opportunity, finally deciding he had spent too much time being the creepy stalker.

Following Cara to the Ritz Carlton downtown, she was meeting three men for a late lunch. Her outfit, body language and what Nic could hear of the conversation led him to conclude it was a job interview.

Nic pauses in his confession here to massage the soap onto Cara's hands while very gently making his way up her arms. His eyes on what he's doing and not on hers, he continues, "I watched you wrap up your lunch and extend your thanks."

Earlier, Nic decided the restaurant and bar at the Ritz was his chance to make first contact, so he booked a suite to ensure their privacy to talk, if he could get Cara that far. As luck would have it, he never had to intercept her. She finished her meeting and walked right towards where he was sitting at the bar.

Cara places her hands on his shoulders causing Nic to still for a moment. When he looks up into her face, Cara can see the steel in his eyes is gone and they're back to the most beautiful ocean blue she has always loved. She whispers, "I didn't see you at the bar. I only saw the five women around you. I needed a stiff drink after that interview."

Nic finally flashes her one of his signatures smiles. The one that makes his eyes twinkle. He pulls her right hand down from his shoulder and places it over his heart. With slight cockiness, he delivers, "Those women were fodder compared to you."

Cara smiles for the first time since she's seen him in Berlin. "That's exactly what you said to me at the bar."

She was about to pay for her drink, when suddenly, there was a hand on her wrist. She thought one of the women grabbed her, but it was a man's hand. When she looked over, Cara could see Nic literally pushing a couple of girls aside to reach her. He told the bartender to put the drink on his tab, pulled the twenty out of her hand, and placed it on the counter in front of her.

Nic has more shower gel in his right hand and rubs it across her rib cage brushing the bottom of her breasts. When she doesn't protest, he releases the front clasp on her bra as he asks, "Do you remember what you said to me?" He has both hands rubbing soap on her shoulders while he removes the bra straps from her arms.

Cara brings her hand back up and into Nic's hair while she smiles in memory.

She politely thanked him for the drink but told him he had more than enough women at the moment. That's when Nic gave her the first, of many, 'killer' smiles. He replied with the fodder comment, rather loudly, right in front his other admirers. The women all huffed and stalked off.

Nic winces slightly at the 'killer' adjective. "I knew the instant my hand touched your wrist that if I didn't get you out of my system, I was a dead man. I felt all my blood rush to my groin. I had to turn my body towards the bar to hide my raging hard on from you." With his hands, he begins to skim over Cara's breasts, lightly brushing her nipples. She shudders from the arousal and moves her hands into his hair. "What did you say next?" he pushes her.

"I asked you why was I different from the other women. You said because I was the most beautiful girl in the room."

Cara laughed at him in the bar after he gave her that line. She accused him of using a very unoriginal pick-up. Nic turned really serious, though, when he looked her straight in the eyes and admitted he had never said that to any woman, ever.

Pulling Cara closer to him so she's barely on the edge of shower seat, he picks up her legs to wrap them around his waist. Their bodies are now chest to chest. Nic moves one hand in Cara's hair, pulling gently to bring her head back. He places tender kisses along her jawline. "It was the truth.

But I didn't think you believed me." He continues his kissing along her neck, occasionally letting his teeth lightly scrape her skin.

Cara closes her eyes as her husband's lips sensuously incite her and the memories of long ago.

When her drink came at the Ritz, Nic picked up his glass and clinked it to hers. He toasted to good girls and bad girls. She didn't understand the toast and asked him to expand.

With his lips against her jaw, Nic whispers into her flesh, "What did I tell you, cara mia?"

Cara smiles to herself as the memories are now pouring into her brain. "You said something about good girls are sweet and kind, and can be rather boring. Bad girls are hot and sexy, but too high maintenance. Then you asked me which one I was, good or bad?"

Nic makes his way back to Cara's chin and brings his lips softly to hers, brushing them across. His breath is hot against her when he whispers, "You didn't answer me at first. You paused. Then you did something I didn't expect. You leaned forward very slowly, eventually bringing your mouth to my ear. You said…" Nic moves his head in the same manner she had 17 years ago, bringing his lips to her ear. Whispering the words she spoke on that unforgettable day. "I am neither good nor bad…I am dangerous." Nic gently bites Cara's ear as she had done to him at the bar. Pulling back to look at her face, Cara slams her mouth down on his.

The kiss turns immediately fast, hard and passionate. Nic starts to run his hands down her back getting to her bottom and pulling at her thong. He rips them right off before picking her up to stand. She is still wrapped around his waist. "Baby, take off my briefs, now."

Cara leans to one side and tugs at his waistband, jerking his erection free, and getting his briefs halfway down his leg. He wiggles them the rest of the way off while still carrying her.

He turns and places her back gently against the side wall of the shower. The water has turned colder but neither of them notices. Nic gazes into her eyes and admits, "I knew then, with those words, I was a goner. I had to have you. No getting to know each other. No courting you, no romance. I just needed to be inside you. That was the only clear thought in my head." And with reconciliation, Nic lowers Cara onto his waiting erection. He slides slowly inside her watching her eyes again. "This is where I belong, cara mia. It was then, and it will always be my place and mine only, in your body, in your heart and in your soul."

He begins a slow thrust into her. His eyes never leave hers until her head rolls back and a moan escapes her lips. He thrusts harder and Cara groans appreciatively.

Taking one of her nipples with his mouth, her breath hitches, "Nic, more."

He moves his mouth to her other breast before quickening his pace. Cara arches her back, her head hard against the tile. Her mouth is open, but nothing but quick breaths are coming in and out.

Nic coaxes, "I can feel you, baby, you're ready, come with me." And with that command, Cara cries out and Nic slams her hard into the tile as he releases everything he has for her.

CHAPTER 14

CARA IS CLINGING TO HER husband as he drops her legs and leans in for a passionate post coital kiss. She wants to smile, but is resisting. He just took her exactly like he did for the first time in his hotel suite at the Ritz. He shut the door, pushed her into it, and fucked her with such need; they still had some clothes on when they were done. But, he was only getting started. Nic had her on every surface in that suite at one point or another. She couldn't believe any man could have the stamina and the ability to recoup with such speed. He was a machine, physically, but emotionally, there was always sensuality to everything he did. He had a deep desire to please and love her from the very beginning.

Nic releases her and grabs the shampoo for his hair. Cara grabs the conditioner for her hair, before taking the shower gel and offering, "You know the water is freezing."

He smirks, "I don't feel a thing."

Cara rubs the gel across his chest while he rinses his hair. She takes her time, working it all over the front of his body, making sure to spend a little longer around his already firming manhood. His head goes back, and all he can do is groan. Moving to his back, she rubs gel everywhere, again spending more time on his gorgeous ass. He abruptly shuts the water off, opens the shower door and grabs a huge towel. He spins it around the both of them, and with arm around her waist, lifts her wrapped up, and out of the shower.

He towels the both of them off, spending some time to get moisture out of her hair. He then grabs her hand with his left and leads her out of the bathroom, making sure to grab his holster with his right hand and taking it with him.

Nic brings Cara into the bedroom. He places the holster with two guns on the floor by the bed, and then picks Cara up to toss her onto it. He growls as he crawls onto the bed on top of her. "First time I needed fast and hard. The second time, you are going to get slow and torturous."

Cara's eyes widen, "That's what you said 17 years ago!"

Nic smiles and brushes his lips gently across hers before pulling her lower lip and biting it. "I may not be able to go 12 for 12 like I did years ago, but I have a couple more in me for today." With that he takes her mouth.

Cara awakes with a smile on her face feeling very satisfied. But as the clarity of the day begins to dawn on her, she frowns. Turning to the clock, she realizes she must have taken a short catnap. She reaches in the bed to find Nic, but she's alone. She leans back and stares at the ceiling.

She has never really understood why she was sent, or actually went to Kabul. In the past, she had only been with Reed, and only when a detailed mission script was in place. She has always disliked the region. Besides the obvious reasons, her hair never cooperates while she's there, her shoes get ruined, and it smells badly. The Deputy Director at the time insisted she go. He made it an order. Despite her own aversion to Afghanistan, lack of proper intel, and knowing Reed would have argued with the Deputy about sending her, she felt compelled to comply.

Cara ended up in Kabul at the right place but the wrong time. She heard the chatter about the Dark Angel's meeting. She was going to position herself in one of the adjacent apartment buildings with a hallway window facing the alley for the meeting. She staked it out the previous day, and was all set. And, she was sort of excited to finally see the Dark Angel in action. She arrived early, except, her so-called contacts got the meeting time wrong. She ended up arriving with his boys; literally walking into the alley at the same time as the six men.

Suddenly, they're all yelling, 'Hey green eyes', in their dialect, and they grabbed her. Her natural self-preservation gene took over and she started to fight them, except there were too many. The more she fought, the angrier they got. That's when two of them secured her so the others could start groping. They grabbed her breasts and placed their hands between her legs. They pulled her burka off, and Cara knew, she was about to die a brutal, horrific death.

She's not a religious person. But right at that moment she prayed. She prayed for some miracle of mercy to die before the men could do what they'd intended. And then, her prayers were answered when she heard the wiz of a bullet blow by her ear. She thought, oh good, someone will shoot her, except within seconds the arms restraining her were gone. The hands all over her body disappeared. She looked down, and the men were in lifeless piles. She didn't think. Cara didn't even breathe. She just ran.

Cara shudders at the memory. She notices a robe at the foot of the bed. Getting up, she puts it on, tightening the sash as she approaches the bedroom door.

She opens the door to see Nic finishing in the bathroom. He has rubber gloves on and has bagged all of their clothes and bleached the shower walls and floors. He's only wearing jeans and his shoulder holster. Cara checks out her husband, bare-chested, with only the holster on. He looks smoking hot. She decides the next round should be with only the holster. No, she needs to focus. Stop thinking about sex and talk to him.

Glancing up, Nic grins when he sees her. "Hey, baby, you passed out on me after round three. Figured I would start clean up. Bathroom is done, and I've cleaned the Beretta and my leather. All stored away where they won't be found. Unfortunately, I have nothing for you to wear. But I imagine it's only a matter of time before Reed shows up."

Reed? "Oh my God! I totally forgot about Reed!" Cara exclaims. He's coming to surely kill her.

"I'm actually glad to hear you say that." Nic teases.

As if on cue, there's a knock on the door. Nic quickly removes the rubber gloves and throws them inside the trash bag with all their clothes. He pulls the gun from his holster while walking towards Cara. Gently pushing her back into the bedroom he mumbles, "Just in case it's not your boyfriend." He walks towards the front door and listens.

They hear Reed say, "It's me, Nic. I'm unarmed. Well, not really, but come on, let me in, please."

Cara snickers when Nic rolls his eyes at her. He unlocks the front door and opens it wide. He's standing there looking a little less menacing in only jeans and his holster. Gun, of course, still in hand. Cara rushes forward from the bedroom opening, deciding she may need to place herself between these two. Reed is standing in front of the doorway with Cara's carry-on bag in one hand and four large shopping bags with 'Olaf' on them in the other.

Reed walks in, and while Nic shuts the door, Cara squeals, "You brought my stuff!" She jumps up into Reed.

● ● ●

He drops all the bags and catches her firmly in his arms. Reed doesn't even realize he's squeezing Cara too tightly. He's not sure if it's from relief or rage. He decides it doesn't matter.

She's rubbing his back knowing he's experiencing some mixed emotions at the moment. He can still feel the adrenalin running through his bloodstream from the fear something happened to her. He whispers softly in her ear, "Sweetheart, are you okay?" Cara lets him put her down and she smiles at him and nods while she holds his hands.

She refocuses on the overstuffed shopping bags. "What's all this? Olaf only gave me two bags of stuff."

"I was hoping your husband could answer that question." Reed inquires while peering over to Nic.

Nic shoulders his gun back inside the holster and just shrugs. He has retrieved Carter's gun and phone and hands them to Reed stating, "Agent Carter misplaced these."

Reed pockets them with no comment and explains a courier delivered two bags of merchandise to Cara's hotel room with a note for the 'Dark Angel'. "And they weren't Carter's size, so…"

Nic puts on one of his killer smiles nodding in recollection. "Olaf… this morning. I was waiting for him in his office when he returned from the sample rooms with you." Pointing to Cara, Nic admits he had Olaf in his sights, ready to torture him for intel. Olaf was unfazed by the weapon trained on him. Instead, he jumped up, ran to Nic and grabbed him into a bear hug. Olaf started yapping on and on about how he couldn't believe Nic married the Reflex. Apparently, his wife showed Olaf pictures of her family. Olaf told him Cara never mentioned anything about the photos of Nic. She only said, "This is my very hot and wonderful husband."

Nic shudders at the memory before his features turn to revulsion. He was able to rush through a quick recap with his old comrade, but Olaf wouldn't let him leave. "Olaf insisted he had to 'measure my inseam.' No one ever told me that was code for violating you."

Reed and Cara burst out laughing at him. Reed is trying to articulate through his giggles, "Nic, can you show me on the doll where Olaf touched you?"

Cara is howling but grabs Reed by the arm and raises her hand to him in a stop motion. Informing him he shouldn't laugh too hard. "Olaf has been following your career. He clips photos and watches all the TV coverage you're on. I am sure Olaf has developed a crush. He wants me to relay a message to you, Connor. Olaf doesn't appreciate Tom Ford on you. He wants to 'measure your inseam' so the only thing all over you is Olaf! He expects a visit before you leave Berlin." Cara giggles out.

Now Nic and Cara are laughing at him. Before he can respond, Cara continues, "And he said seeing you never married, and have no known serious dating record, Olaf is fairly certain you're the man for him!"

Reed is horrified. Nic's still belly laughing but begins poking through the bags. He pulls out a beautiful chocolate colored leather jacket and puts it on.

"Reed!" Nic exclaims, "This coat is amazing. It feels amazing." As he strokes the leather, "Please sleep with Olaf so we can get more swag." Cara and Nic both dissolve into more laughter.

He doesn't see how this is humorous. "I am not amused, guys, and I AM NOT GAY!"

"Oh, the lady doth protest…" Nic gets out.

Before he can rip back into Nic, Reed considers he might get laid more often if he was gay. And Olaf would be an amazing boyfriend. Maybe he should consider being a switch hitter. His thoughts are interrupted by an unfamiliar sound. Looking at Nic, it dawns on him. "Are you giggling? All these years, and I've never heard you giggle."

Before anyone can retort, Nic raises both hands and stops laughing. The expression on his face changes; his mouth tightens and his eyes go back to that weird steel color Carter was talking about. "What did you say when you came in, Reed? Did you say Olaf sent the clothes to the 'Dark Angel'?" No one answers. Nic looks with great disdain at his wife as the slow realization spreads across his face. "You both knew who I was, didn't you?"

Reed looks imploringly to Cara, but she's just standing there biting her lower lip. She only bites her lip when she's emotionally stressed. He glances back at Nic and can feel his rage. Reed's at a momentary loss. Looking at the scene in front of him, he should stay and assist, but better he leave this to Cara.

He stutters out, "I purposely gave you guys a couple of hours to sort this out. I knew where you went immediately because of C's phone. I had the SIM card switched…I traced it here…I…I…am leaving." Heading to the front door with speed, he adds, "I'll be across the street at the café waiting."

The door shuts behind Reed, and Cara is left with Nic glaring that awful, menacing stare.

Shit. Evil Nic twin is back. Reed and his impeccable timing. Cara tries, "Nic, my love, I swear I was just about to tell you when I came out of the bedroom." After Nic's confessional, Cara realized he didn't believe she knew his background.

"When?!" Nic barks out, cutting her off.

"When what?"

"When did you know who I was?!" Nic yells.

She blurts out quickly, "Kabul, I knew in Kabul!" Nic's face alters to show genuine rage.

Confusion overtakes her. "Nic, how could you think I didn't know? I mean on the surface that's rather insulting. Do you think so little of the CIA, and me and Reed, to believe we wouldn't have intel on what you looked like…or heard all the stories?"

Nic doesn't answer her. He only glares with those cruel eyes.

Still nothing but hostility from him, so Cara rambles, "Reed was one of your biggest fans." The Agency had pictures of the Dark Angel of Death; one was a clear close up of him. They feared Nic, while having the highest respect for his skills. Reed made a pact to never send anyone from his team up against Andrychenko or his handler, Golov. It wasn't that Reed didn't have faith in his team, but faith wouldn't save their asses against either Russian.

"Reed thought the deadliest weapons the Soviet bloc ever produced were you and Golov. He told us why they call you the Dark Angel of Death. He said you received your moniker because you looked like an angel but had the heart of the devil, and no soul to speak of."

Cara pauses to control her slight hysteria before continuing, "It was actually a mistake that I was in Kabul. Jinx was my regular analyst, you know that, right?" Nic nods very subtly.

Jinx had just quit to take the job in Cleveland, which she has always suspected was a front for the NSA, but Jinx will never admit it. Back then, Cara was assigned a new researcher, and he wasn't very good. They were having some difficulties getting along. Reed was out on assignment when she got the order to go to Kabul, immediately.

She was not to engage. Only witness and report. She should have called Reed, and reported the assignment, but didn't. Cara felt foolish tracking him down, while he was possibly covert, and whine about it. If Jinx was there, she would've had better intel, or she would've stopped Cara if she didn't.

As usual, Cara didn't follow Reed's orders and took the next transport to Kabul. Suddenly, she stifles a sob at the memory. She stops rambling and hesitantly continues the story.

After she ran away from the blood bath in Kabul, she stopped when it hit her. What the hell just happened? Who in the hell could have taken those shots? And then the only possible scenario occurred to her. It was him, the Dark Angel; it had to be Andrychenko…but why?

Because she had to know, she started to run back. This time taking the route directly to the apartment building she staked out. She ran up the stairs to the second floor window and carefully looked out. The Dark Angel was there. He was bent over the bodies removing any weapons and ID. His movements spellbound her. She was also baffled. What was his motive? Wouldn't the vicious, killing Dark Angel have a motive for everything? But oddly, she wasn't feeling it. From the distance and the angle of his face, he looked more resigned than calculating. Then it happened, a gust of wind blew through the alley and his hat came off. He turned his face so she had a clear view.

The strength in her legs escaped while she stared at his face. Her knees buckled, and she dropped down as the breath left her lungs with a clear whoosh sound when she saw his face. He was the most spectacular creature she had ever seen. The pictures they had did not do him justice. She was totally captivated by his face. He really looked like a sweet, beautiful, built with a body for sin, angel. Her angel. Her guardian angel. She was hanging onto the windowsill for support, looking like a Peeping Tom, when he started to move his head towards the window. Almost like he knew she was there. Cara backed away quickly, ran down the hallway, out the building, and kept running until she was safely on the next transport.

When she got back to Langley she had to report what happened. Essentially the transaction she was sent to witness didn't go down, but Cara started to hesitate about how much she should document. Reed hadn't returned from his assignment, so she hedged and didn't report anything. She made excuses, took some time off, and within a week, Reed was back. It felt like the longest week of her life. She couldn't get Nic's beautiful, angelic face out of her mind. It was making her crazy. She told Reed everything. Listened to him yell at her for even going to Kabul in the first place, and then listened to him lecture her for turning back to see the Dark Angel after the shootings.

Reed tried to convince her Nicolae Andrychenko did have motive, and if he had caught her, her fate would've been worse. She never would have made it back from Kabul. But, for the first time since she'd known Reed, Cara wasn't buying his judgment. And that made him even more irritated, except he didn't yell. Instead, Reed decided she was experiencing some sort of PTSD over the attempted gang rape. He furloughed her, and sent her to five sessions with a shrink before she could come back to work.

Nic speaks, interrupting her confession, and barking out, "Geneva. Tell me what happened in Geneva."

Cara is exhausted. She hasn't slept in 36 hours, she almost died, and now this. She walks over to a plush chair and sits down bringing her legs beneath her. Nic is still standing in the same spot, having not moved a muscle since she started confessing. Throwing her head back, resting it on the top of the chair and concentrating on the ceiling, she whispers, "I needed to see you again. Counseling didn't help. It just reinforced that I needed to see you and find out why I somehow felt connected to you. That's how I felt, linked. Like some thread had been sewn between us."

She found out Reed had been invited to Geneva. She knew several of the higher profile Russian agents would be there with their diplomats. She realized there was only a chance one of them would be the Dark Angel, but for some reason she thought, if he's there, it will be because of the thread. It will mean something.

She begged Reed to let her come as his plus one. He finally agreed on the grounds she had to act like his date. The Americans were to only have a certain number of agents present. They arrived at the kick off dinner Gala in Geneva, and she immediately spotted Nic in the shadows. Unfortunately, so did Reed. She would swear he dispensed the whole 'date' thing more than usual. Nevertheless, she felt excited Nic was there. It meant something to her more importantly; it proved to her the thread existed. Kismet, karma, mathematical improbability of coincidence, chaos theory, whatever it's called, she was feeling all of it.

Cara kept track of Nic all night, but he was always a distance away. She finally saw her chance when he came out towards the dance floor. She grabbed Reed and started in the same direction. She just wanted to see him eye to eye. She can't explain why she felt that way. She thought if they could make eye contact…but the leggy blonde Russian agent he was dancing with kept putting her hands all over Nic. She was practically fondling him. Every time he appeared to be turning his face so he would be in full visual of Cara, the blonde would yank his face back to hers.

She was so focused on trying to get Nic to look at her; Cara hadn't noticed Reed catching on to her intentions. He pointedly asked her what the hell she thought she was doing? And what the hell was she trying to prove? Her concentration only on Nic, she wasn't paying Reed's inquisition much attention when it happened. Nic's dance partner must have said something to him because he let out the biggest, most amazing smile…his killer smile. That smile wasn't even meant for Cara, but she went down, hard.

"The thread pulled tight, right there and then, Nic." Cara shuts her eyes recalling the intense emotion she felt on that dance floor so many years ago. "After your confession this morning, I know you felt the connection between us, too."

"But what happened with you and Reed?" Nic asks.

Cara takes a deep breath, letting the painful memories flood back. Slowly, she articulates her side of what happened the night after Reed dragged her from the party. As the story continues, the memories become more and more painful. She begins to sob as Nic stares, listening intently to every word she utters about the horrible night that ended with her walking away from Reed, her career and her home. As she finishes, she looks up at him, hoping to see her loving husband's gentle face, but she only gets the mask of the Dark Angel of Death.

Making no comment about her Geneva admission, Nic jumps forward to their first night together at the Ritz, and asks with piercing eyes, "I'm not sure if I understand why you weren't afraid when you saw me. Before, I assumed you weren't because you didn't know who I was, but you did recognize me, and yet…"

Cara rises from her chair and approaches her husband. She chooses to stand directly in front of him despite his still steely glare. She looks into those cruel eyes and answers, "And yet I let you drag me back to your hotel suite within an hour of meeting you, unarmed, and without letting anyone know where I was. I would NEVER do that with a complete stranger, yet, I let a known killer have me. Is that what you're asking, Nic?"

Before he can answer, she continues, "Because of the thread, Nic, the thread. You found me. You found me because you pulled the thread, and all of it was wrapped around me! If you were there at the hotel to kill me, then so be it. I would rather have died than continued the insanity. That's what I was thinking that late afternoon at the Ritz."

She raises her hand to place it on his heart, but he catches her wrist with his hand firmly preventing her. Nic snaps at her, "Don't touch me."

Cara tries to yank her hand away, but he's using force around her wrist. Nic has her hand and arm immobilized. Instead of fighting him, she steps in closer so they're mere inches apart and stares into his eyes. She can feel the rage rolling off him but she doesn't understand. Calmly she inquires, "Why are you so angry? I'm sorry I didn't interrupt your heart-felt confession earlier to add mine. I was traumatized by the events with Vlad, and I always wondered what led you to me. I waited 17 years for that story, Nic."

"You really don't get it, do you?" He snaps at her, again.

"You're beginning to agitate me, Nic. I'm warning you." She has no idea where this is coming from. They are both to blame for making the decision to deny full disclosure for all these years. It's not judicious to pin this lie of omission on just her. Nic isn't budging, though. He's still holding her wrist and glaring down at her.

Cara's eyes start to narrow, her mouth tightens, her teeth clench and she loses it. With her free hand she grabs the nape of Nic's neck to yank him down nose to nose with her as she commands slowly, "You can stop this right now. Stop being a smug, sanctimonious, ice cold BASTARD!"

And with that, Nic releases her wrist, grabs his wife by the shoulders and spins her so she is pinned between the kitchen counter and his body. All of his weight is pressed up against her, causing Cara to wince with the force of the maneuver. He places his hands on the counter to each side of her, leans into her face and spits out, "That's it, Cara! That's just it. I AM an ice cold bastard."

He's watching her face to see a reaction, but she only stares wild-eyed back at him. "More importantly, I am YOUR bastard!" Nic is practically yelling in her face now, "Your own personal lethal weapon!" Again, he searches Cara's face for something, but she still has the same clueless expression. Nic shakes disdainfully at her density and knows he has to spell it out for her. "What's the first thing you do when you determine there's a viable threat to you and possibly your family?"

Watching her expression finally change to one of complete recognition and remorse, he nails it home. "You don't come to the man who sleeps with you every night. The man you have children with. The man who would lay down his life for you. The man who, you know, can protect you better than ANYONE! NO! YOU. CALL. REED!" He pushes off her with this pronouncement.

She is dumbfounded. She's shaking her head for some clarity while her mouth is mumbling, "I'm so sorry, I'm so sorry," over and over. Her head is down because she can't look at him. "You more than deserve an answer." Her knees give out and she drops to the floor on her butt, leaning against the cabinets.

He feels justified, being very angry and disappointed with her. How could she lie to him? How could she exclude him from all of this? Federal secrets and loyalties aside, he is her husband. She's still on the ground mumbling something about Pavlovian reactions to threats and not thinking straight. The tears are streaming down her face, again. He has rarely seen her cry. Between finding her in tears with Vlad, having her finally divulge what happened in Geneva, and now this, he's starting to wonder what's going on with her. She's been an emotional wreck for the last six hours.

Walking away from Cara towards the Olaf bags and her carry-on, Nic opens the luggage and pulls a matching set of bra and panties from the contents and a pair of jeans. He then empties the contents of the Olaf bags, separating the men's clothes from the ladies. He wants to give Cara some time to sort this out, but he needs answers. He spies a cashmere sweater with a cropped front. He sees Olaf left camel colored soft leather mid heel, mid-calf height boots.

He takes all of it and walks back to Cara, dropping the outfit in front of her. "Start getting dressed." He commands her. "We need to go."

Nic makes another pass back to Cara with her cosmetic bag. His rage and jealousy has subsided, only disappointment remains. Her running to Reed when she felt threatened he can rationalize away as being habit, but not telling him? When she knew who he was? And how delusional was he to believe his wife, a prominent ex-CIA agent, would not know about the Dark Angel?

She's correct, of course, about him being guilty of the omission, as well. He didn't want to believe she could love a man like him. He couldn't imagine his life would take such a left turn, landing him blissfully happy and content with the woman of his dreams. He didn't deserve her or this perfect life after the sins of his past. A past he never wanted to contaminate his relationship with her.

As he hands the bag to her, she grabs his arm, "Nic, I love YOU. Please, never question that. You are a wonderful husband and father who has earned being happy. I need to be questioning if I deserve someone as amazing as you. Not the other way around."

Nic walks away from her; always astounded she can so clearly read him. Then again, except for this miscommunication, he can always read her. He knew she was lying about the DC job in his office. He could tell she was upset and distressed the night before. Yesterday morning when she flew to DC, every alarm bell in his mind was going off. He and his wife have been strangely connected and entwined like thread to each other from the first moment he laid eyes on her.

Cara sheds her robe to her nakedness and starts getting dressed. She's mumbling, "When we first met, aside from the obvious spy versus spy omission, I felt we were being honest with each other. I wanted to get to know the true Nic, the man who wasn't a monster. The man whose heart didn't belong to Satan but was full of love and passion. The man who had a soul, the sensitive soul of a poet."

She heads into the bathroom to do something with her hair while still spewing random thoughts out to him. Recalling the first few weeks and months of their relationship, she admits "Even though the passion between us was off the charts, we also spent time talking about dreams and desires; planning what the perfect business venture would be for us. And somewhere along the way, for me, the Reflex and the Dark Angel ceased to exist. The memories faded. The legends became vague. Of course having twins can fully dominate anyone's mind. I stopped seeing anything but Nic and Cara, couple, parents, and business owners."

He's getting dressed while she's still in the bathroom rambling memories of their early relationship. She peeks out with a loose, messy ponytail and an attempt at some make-up. "When I started to hear the music everywhere and sensing something was wrong, my first thought wasn't to see what the Dark Angel of Death thought about my predicament. My first thought was to run to my handler. The man who trained me and protected me for a decade. The man I still consider to be my best friend. I am truly sorry, my love." She appears devastated.

Again, he can overlook Cara's habitual nature of running to her best friend. Reed has the means, as the current Director, to make things happen, but it doesn't excuse her most recent lie. He cannot forgive her for the fear and trepidation she caused him when Nic sensed she was heading into danger yesterday. She may have been a formidable agent in her day, but she was half-cocked and sloppy this morning. She walked into peril with no strategic plan.

Good God, had he been only seconds later, the life he has treasured would have been destroyed. The woman who gave him a reason to love, two amazing children and 17 years of bliss would be dead. He shudders with how close they came to that.

Cara is walking out of the bathroom with her cosmetic bag when she adds, "But, on the other hand, this morning with Vlad, I didn't think you were my Nic."

Nic urges her, "What about this morning?"

"You looked different, like a mean, violent version of yourself. The cruel evil twin of my husband."

He was wearing clothes she has never seen him in. His eye color does alter when he is enraged. Years of training kicked in forcing his entire persona into a void of all emotion.

"It's like you are wearing a mask." She points to his face, "I don't know this face. I have never seen it."

She zips her bag closed while Nic places his shoulder holster back on. She notices his collar is caught on the leather straps of the holster, and leans into him to adjust it. The gesture feels natural. Fondling the holster, Cara whispers, "I have never seen you in action. I didn't have a visual of you shooting the Afghani men in Kabul. Until this morning, I've never had any first hand witness to your reputation."

Forcing his chin down to look at her, she gently rubs her fingertips to his lips. "Most importantly, Nic, you will always be the Zen Master of our family. You are the patient and impartial parent, and the devoted and loving husband. A brilliant entrepreneur, a hardworking business owner, a passionate, avid and talented musician, and to me, you are the antitheses of a killer. This morning was a total surprise." The way she is gazing at him with complete devotion in her eyes, Nic has to release the rest of his disappointment. He is a sucker for that look of love.

Her eyes turn reflective before she admits, "I think I was in shock because of you rather than Vlad. You really scared the crap out of me this morning."

He relinquishes and pulls her into a firm hug. She grips him back harder, both of them needing the contact. They stand clinging to each other until he whispers, "I scared the piss out of you, not the crap."

Cara stiffens at the humiliation of that, and whines, "It happened when I was Taser'ed."

"I know. I'm just teasing. Trust me, nothing can be worse than watching them slice you in half to rip out our two children."

"You didn't have to watch them give me a C Section."

"I wasn't taking my eyes off you or our children during any of that." Nic says sternly.

She spends a moment rubbing her lips along his neck before pulling away. "I've always felt safe with you. I know you will protect us. I just... didn't respect the extent of your talent. You are amazing!" She says with great admiration. "The way you took down Carter. The way you got into the apartment silently. The head game you had going with Vlad, and that shot from the other side of the apartment. I am your newest, biggest fan, Dark Angel."

Before he can speak, she continues, "And I promise the following. A. full disclosure on everything. B. I will respect the skill," she bows before him with that, "And C. we start the next phase of our marriage including our past, and learning to incorporate it into our future."

Nic pulls her into a hard kiss. The kiss turns passionate, but he breaks it off, and holding on to her jaw he concedes, "I'm good with that promise, Cara mia. Now, let's go meet your boyfriend. He's across the street becoming surely apoplectic."

Cara winces at the thought, but then asks as they're walking out with their bags, "By the way, how did you find me, and how did you rent this adorable apartment?"

Nic says as he's locking up, "The first part is a story for later, and the apartment...I'm glad you like it...because we own it."

CHAPTER 15

AS THEY ENTER THE CAFÉ, Nic takes a more protective stance with Cara, grabbing her hand and pulling her closer behind him. The café is mostly full, and they spot Reed at a table in the back. They place their luggage against the wall and sit down, Cara next to Reed and Nic across from him.

Reed breaks the initial silence after visually inspecting both of them. "Are we good?"

Nic retorts, "No, we are not good if my wife and I don't get some coffee, immediately. And we're starving. Otherwise, we're good."

Reed motions to the waitress to come over. She's very young and approaches hesitantly. Nic flashes his killer smile at her and she visibly relaxes. He launches into perfect German as he asks for a carafe of coffee, cream, and orders food for both he and Cara. He even politely asks her to bring the coffee as soon as she can. Not only can he speak fluently, he can speak the language including the local dialect.

When he's finished ordering, he turns his attention back to Reed, "I count seven plain clothes agents in the café with us. Tell them to stand down. They're nervous and jumpy."

Reed rolls his eyes.

Cara leans past Reed to the customer sitting with his back to him and his head down, "Carter, darling, how are you feeling?" she asks politely.

Carter slowly turns his head, so he has both he and Cara in his view before he replies, "I may never father any children between the two of you, but otherwise I'm fine. Thank you for asking."

His wife turns sharply to him. "You kick him in the nuts, too?"

Nic grins, "I couldn't help myself. I saw the way Carter took the stairs when I was following him. I presumed you got his boys earlier." He apologizes to Carter, but there's not much sincerity in it.

Reed whispers something to Carter who makes a gesture with his hands. The other agents in the café noticeably unwind. Reed reports they finished at Apartment 23. Swept for prints, but only some of Cara's and many of Vlad's were found. Otherwise, there was nothing of interest. It was pretty bare. Chekov had ID on him, and they have his phone, but analysis is still pending on that.

Vlad has only been in Berlin for less than a week. They have gone over the audio device implanted in the Olaf boots with the tracer, replaying Cara's visit with Olaf, and her capture with Chekov. No one thinks Vlad was working with anyone besides the hacker, who they hope to identify from his phone records. Speculation is the phone records won't yield any answers as to who funded the hit. The watcher at Olaf's building was found, a paid homeless man. He could only identify Vlad. Reed's locals will continue to work on any leads.

Coffee has arrived and Nic pours both Cara and himself some. Cara guzzles hers down and refills her small cup a second time, while Nic offers, "The hacker will be of no assistance, and knowing Vlad, I'm not surprised your search of the apartment yielded nothing."

Cara asks confused, "You told Vlad you didn't recognize him?"

"Really, Cara?" Nic mocks, "You think I forget anyone?"

Vlad was a substandard agent at best, and an average analyst. Nic worked a couple of missions, with him as the researcher, but never in the field. Golov didn't send anyone in the field with Nic that wasn't exemplary. He knows he sounds cocky, but when it comes to his skills, he is, and makes no apology for it. "Chekov was out by the late 80's. His usefulness had expired. I'd heard he became a contract killer and vowed to kill him if he ever crossed my path."

"Well, you're a man of your word, then. Any ideas, guys?" Reed inquires. He doesn't believe there is anything left for them to do in Berlin. They need to get back to Langley and do some research. Reed has the Gulfstream ready at the airport to take them. No need to stay in Berlin any longer and draw suspicion.

"I agree. This lead is cold." Nic concurs.

Seemingly out of nowhere Cara asks, "Hey, what time is it?"

Reed answers, "3:30 here, why?"

Cara turns to Nic with a knowing glaze in her eyes, "Can you check in with Sasha and see how the kids are doing? Let *her* know we're together. Tell her we will text her before we get in the air."

Nic stares blankly at his wife. For the first time, he's at a complete loss. Her eyes are boring into his. Sasha and 'her'. Oh my God. Cara knows. He smiles as blandly as he can and agrees, "That's a good idea. I'll call her outside."

Nic gets up to leave, turns his back to Reed and Cara, but inclines his head just enough to see them in his peripheral vision. He spies Reed grab Cara by the arm and drag her to him with some force. Good boy, Reed. Nic was wondering when Reed was going to reprimand her for the disgraceful mission conduct this morning. Be her handler. Don't make her husband play the bad guy and lecture her. Nic leaves the café to make his, what should prove interesting, phone call. He keeps an eye on his wife and Reed through the front window, watching them talk as he calls Sasha.

Cara has a bite of food on her fork when she's pulled hard towards Reed. She watches as the food falls from her fork onto the table between her and Reed's place settings.

Reed tries to keep his voice low, just above a whisper, "What the hell did you think you were doing this morning? You're fired."

"I can't be fired, I don't work for you."

Gripping her forearm, Reed gets in her face, "Disobeying direct orders, assaulting an agent, contaminating a crime scene, breaking and entering, cavorting with the enemy AND THAT WAS IN THE FIRST 3 HOURS YOU WERE HERE!"

"My personal favorite was the cavorting." She winks.

"Not talking about Nic, you pain in my ass, Olaf. Olaf is not cleared."

Cara counters, "Olaf gave me swag. You know I'm easily bought. He's my new Facebook friend." She waits for the FB lecture but it doesn't come.

Instead, Reed hugs her, tightly. "You're being glib, C. You were scared this morning."

Acquiescing and exhaling a breath, she confesses, "I totally lost control, Connor. I failed to see the threat, and then I failed to neutralize it."

Pulling away from the embrace, Cara sets her eyes on Reed. If it weren't for Nic, Carter would not have been able to take down Vlad without her as collateral damage. Nic determined that in his weird mental assessment thing he does. He took out Carter so he could control the confrontation with Vlad. He was brilliant. She owes Nic her life for a second time now, except, she's feeling very inadequate. "I think it was wise I quit 17 years ago. I suck at this now. I'm so sorry I kicked Carter in the balls and disobeyed your orders. Mostly, I'm sorry I made you worry."

Wrapping his fist around her ponytail, he yanks her head to him. "Argh, how do you do that? Turn this around so I stop being angry?"

Cara gives him another quick hug before pulling away, "I PROMISE to be careful and follow your orders from now on."

Nic's voice startles both Cara and Reed up from their chairs, "YOU WILL NOT MAKE THAT PROMISE!" He's standing directly behind them with his arms folded across his chest.

"Jesus Nic, how do you do that? Appear out of nowhere!" Cara exclaims.

"Baby, no promises to Reed. I will handle your protection and this investigation from now on. I'll work with Reed. You will report to me. Capice?" Nic states with full confidence.

Cara is about to argue, but then remembers the deal she made earlier with Nic, her confession to Reed just now, and most importantly, her total failure with Vlad this morning. Surprising them both, she concurs, "Nic is the lead on this."

Reed's eyebrows spike right up. "Wow, C, appears you have a new handler."

Cara contemplates her response while she eyes both men. "Not a new handler. I'm not releasing you of that honor, Reed. Instead, I have a new partner."

CHAPTER 16

ON THE LIMO DRIVE BACK towards the airport, Reed shares the details on all the information they have accumulated so far. He passes Nic ballistics from the crime scene. The records from Vlad's cell phone and rental information on the apartment, amongst other intel. Nic reads through all of it, occasionally asking Reed a question. Nic and Reed then work on possible motives and suspects, discussing strategies, protocols and research items.

Cara sits away from them in her own thoughts during the whole ride. Looking at the two of them, now, this is the most in sync she has ever seen them. They both appear in their element. Each of them is respectful of the other's talent and intelligence. To think it only took an attempt on her life to bring them together. It's their shared concern for her that's binding them, but maybe this is a turning point for all of them.

What's odder than these two working together is, she has no interest in what they're talking about. They both have glanced over to her, repeatedly, during the discussion looking for input, but she has none. Instead, she's letting something weave its way through her mind. It's there, but Cara can't catch a good glimpse of it. Something about Vlad that's a clue of some sort. It was in the conversational text she had with him.

She's replaying that conversation when it occurs to her this is her fugue state. Her seizure. She isn't zoned out, but more in a hyper internal focus. Shutting out the outside world and concentrating in her mind. After all these years, it's intriguing she just made the association. Possibly the stress of her recent ordeal brought some clarity for her. Her eyes snap up to realize they have pulled up to a hangar.

Reed and Nic exit the limo, first. Reed starts walking in, but Nic hangs back, takes her hand, and helps her out of the car. One of the suited agents grabs their bags from the trunk and starts into the building. Nic holds her back from walking.

When the suited agent is far enough away, he brings her close enough to whisper, "You knew. How long have you known?"

Cara doesn't bother to whisper her answer back. She is well aware of his new concern. "From the first appearance I knew. It didn't take a brain trust to figure it out, Nic."

"I am so sorry it didn't come up earlier during our confessions. I forgot. I owe you a vast apology for that one. It's possibly…unforgivable." Nic lowers his head, shamefully.

Cara grabs his jaw to force him to look at her. "Don't ever defend what happened." She scolds, "Not with this. Not ever. More importantly, how can you even think I would be upset by it? Keep it forgotten. We're good. It was long ago."

His beautiful frown lines between his eyes are still furrowed. "And Reed?"

Raising her hands in supplication, Cara tells him, "Obviously, Reed doesn't know, and he's going to have a complete meltdown when he finds out. He has to be made aware of it with all that's going on."

"You were having a seizure in the car. I was worried *you* were having a meltdown over all of this." Nic asks while leading them back towards the hangar.

Cara stops abruptly. "No, I was in my mind palace," She smiles at the nod to one of their favorite shows, the BBC's <u>Sherlock</u> series. "Not seizures. I just figured out I go to the palace for insight." She stands proudly in front of him like she won the spelling bee.

"Find anything of interest swirling in there, Sherlock?" He jokes.

"Something Vlad said is bothering me. I can't put my finger on what it was. I'm letting it float around in the palace for a bit." She motions to her head.

"How about you let me be your Watson?" Nic inquires as they walk into the hangar, hand in hand, to find Reed on the phone. Carter is there, as well as the agent with the bags, and two more men in casual street clothes.

Reed motions to them to follow him into a long office within the hangar. They comply as Reed hangs up his call and asks, "Who's Watson?"

Nic and Cara smile at one another while Reed takes a seat behind the desk, gesturing to the two chairs in front.

Cara shakes her head, "Watson as in Sherlock Holmes. And I don't feel like sitting." She starts to pace the long length of the office. Nic drags his chair halfway down the office, until he is centered on her pacing path.

"Okay," Nic directs to her, "Go ahead and start throwing those thoughts from your 'mind palace'."

Cara begins this game they play often, which evidently now has a name. As business partners and marriage partners, she and Nic have developed ways to cope with their conflict. Sometimes they do this to weigh out tough business decisions, sometimes to work on parts of their marriage, and finally, they have played this game when they have issues with the twins. She always leads with the pacing. For some reason her mind works clearer if she's in motion. Nic always sits within close proximity of her. No one takes any notes. The sessions are more productive if they are free and fluid.

Reed opens the small refrigerator in the office and removes three bottles of water. He delivers one to each of them, and then goes back to seat himself on the front edge of the desk. He's watching them with rapt curiosity. She has never played this particular game with him. And oddly, now that she thinks about it, she doesn't have her seizures as often when she's with Reed, alone.

Letting her thoughts spew out, she starts. "We know from the beginning with Reed at Langley that we're missing motive. No known adversaries for me that we can identify, so keep that in mind…I feel I'm missing something with Vlad…there's a clue there…something he said…" She looks to Nic, "Was he always filled with self-importance?"

Nic considers the question before speaking. "Yes. More so, the approval of others was important to him. I wouldn't say he was delusional, just insecure."

"That was my feeling as well…he was very proud of how he found me…as if finding me was more the prize than killing me." She is still pacing back and forth keeping her steps rhythmic. "Vlad said whoever hired him was impressed with how he found me…So he/she or they knew how he did it."

Nic interrupts her, "Why do you say he/she or they? Are you getting any thoughts on which?"

"They. Definitely leaning on the 'they'…collective group, small…the inflection of Vlad's voice leads me to they. Could be to throw him or me off, but I don't think so."

Nic affirms, "I agree. Let's work with a 'they.' What is their objective?"

Cara continues her pace, except the rhythm has slowed and she shakes negative to Nic's question before asking, "Could there be others hired to find me, multiple contracts?" She directs the question to no one in particular.

Reed answers as he and Nic discussed that in the car, while she was zoning out. It's possible there are other contracts. Reed placed tracers on all of her social media accounts. Going forward, they will be able to see any access to those accounts outside of 'friends only', he says using air quotes, "I did that earlier when I heard how Vlad found you."

Cara turns to Nic, "What made Vlad leave your group in the late 80's? Specific event?"

Vlad was a good analyst, sharp mind, pretty focused. He was always trying to be Nic's analyst. Golov told Vlad he needed to work harder to earn the right to work for Nic, but Vlad would whine he wanted to work for him because it made him feel good. Golov thought that was creepy, so he kept them mostly apart. Vlad finally left because he wasn't happy with his assignments, and they had no use for him as anything but an analyst. The odd thing was Vlad wasn't a good field agent. Nic thought it strange Vlad would find work as a contract killer after he left. "He really didn't seem the type to…"

"That's it!" Cara interrupts. "He doesn't seem the type, and I would venture to guess his forte was finding people, not killing them." No one speaks, so she continues to throw thoughts. "So let us go with this coincidence; the one person in this world to locate the Reflex in almost two decades happens to also have some strange obsession with you, Nic."

Nic tilts his head. "I did have quite a few fans. As feared as I was, I could draw people to me like a moth to the flame. Hence, the moniker's real origin, like the Dark Angel of Death, attractive, tempting, and alluring but ultimately fatal. Judge and jury damning someone to hell for an eternity." Nic utters with disgust in his voice. "Nice, huh?"

Her eyes roam up and down over Nic's body. If getting to fondle that is hell, she means to live there indefinitely. Refocusing her thoughts back to the issue at hand, she inquires, "But do the math thing in your head, Nic. You know where you calculate probability? What are the odds of the actual connection? Me, you, and Vlad. Furthermore, what are the odds that we would end up together in that apartment here in Berlin?"

Nic's face changes slightly as he thinks, and then his face grows blank. "Less than 1 percent on the first, fractional from that for the second scenario."

"Now calculate the odds that it wasn't a coincidence that Vlad was chosen to find me, but chosen because of my known connection to you."

Nic is ready with an answer, having already predicted Cara's direction. "46.54%"

Reed lets out a slow whistle. "I will take those odds in Vegas any day."

"So, this isn't necessarily about you, but about me or us, which was my initial reaction for coming here, to be honest." Nic states matter-of-factly.

This admission gives both Cara and Reed pause. She eyes her husband carefully before speaking, "Your gut thought I was being led away from you, wasn't it?"

"Yes, and then I discounted it. I thought I was being super paranoid and possessive. Making it all about me instead of the threat to you." Nic confirms.

"That's very sweet of you, babe, but I'm thinking your intuition was accurate." Cara smiles at her husband. She wants to continue with this train of thought, however likely or unlikely. She was led to Berlin as a diversion, whether she's killed here isn't important, what's important is Nic follows her or loses her in the process.

"Well, Vlad was definitely surprised to see me. Shocked would be a better word, so he was unaware, despite being privy to your fairly active social media posts." Nic adds.

Nodding, Cara adds, "Yes, agreed. But if Vlad wasn't aware of your existence in my life…and he was an average analyst…would he have picked up on any possible connection?"

As usual, Nic is quick on the uptake. "Conceivably no, but would he have shared what he found in detail with the folks that hired him?" If they we were profiling Vlad through a software program, the program would say he would want to share all the details to garner more accolades and improve his self-worth based on what they know of his personality. "But…"

Cara chimes in, "But you think he wouldn't have showed them all those cards in his hand-at least not initially."

"Yes, but he may have shown them when he had you in Berlin this morning, when the timing was to his advantage. Garner the praise when the risk was minimized by playing his hand."

"Would you say you are a habitual hunter? One that uses patterns that can be mimicked or followed." Cara inquires.

"No." Nic states vehemently.

"That's what I thought, whether you follow me here or not, it doesn't change the odds of you being here with Vlad and me. Is it still less than 1%?"

"Yes, but if you included the pre-knowledge of our association with each other, the odds go to 5%." They both nod to one another as if only the two of them are following this discourse.

Cara has her back to both men as she paces North away from them. "Stick with the diversion scenario, first. I am led away from you…" She turns 180 degrees to return her pacing South when she notices Reed shaking his head and smiling, absentmindedly. She stops pacing to take a sip from the water bottle before pointing inquiringly of Reed, "What so humorous?"

Reed smiles broader and raises both his hands in a protective gesture. "I am enthralled by the both of you." He points, waving his finger between them. This process they have mastered with each other, "It's fucking remarkable." Nic and Cara are getting more analysis in the last five minutes than Reed's whole team has in the last six hours. He let his mind wander, and Reed couldn't think of a time that Cara was this good. Partnering with Nic suits her, intellectually. "I was smiling because I determined here in front of me is my perfect dream team of operatives. Together, you make a perfect pair. I was shaking my head thinking how I wish I had you *both* 25 years ago."

Cara's face suddenly changes, and a broad look of horror forms across it. She walks stiffly towards Nic, grabbing his shirt and bunching it in her hand as she stares at Reed asking him to elaborate.

He rises from the desk, knowing she's upset, and apologizes for the 25 years ago comment. He didn't mean to make a jab about their ages.

"No!" Cara barks out, "Before that!"

Reed tries to think, and then it dawns on him, "You mean the dream team thing?" he offers. "I couldn't help myself. Just pointing out the combined talent and genetics with the two of you."

Cara's water bottle slips from her hand, and crashes to the ground. Nic rises so quickly from his chair, he knocks it over. Cara still has his shirt bunched in her hand, but she tightens it while Nic grabs her shoulders and roars, "It's 78%. It's fucking 78%!" He releases Cara's shoulders, brushes her hand off his shirt, rifles through his pocket for his phone, and runs out of the office.

Reed is left feeling more horrified than Cara looks. "What the Hell did I just miss?" he shouts. Cara turns to him, and immediately tears spring from her eyes while she slowly approaches.

"Sweetheart, tell me!" He demands, stalking towards her.

Cara is shivering and stuttering, "Missing motive…always about finding…diversion…Dream team…genetics."

It hits him with full force. This is most likely the rationale for hiring Vlad. Reed grabs Cara as her knees buckle and she drops. The overwhelming need to protect seizes him. Lifting her up, he has her cradled against his chest. He walks to the end of the desk and sits down, placing Cara on his lap. He's wiping the tears from her face, gently, murmuring, "It's going to be okay. They're going to be fine."

Cara stares at him with a look of loss he has never seen on her face, "My babies, Connor, someone wants my babies."

Bursting back into the room, Nic is frantic, totally uncontrolled, with panic written across his face. Reed has never seen Nic look like this. He informs them "Sasha with Jake are on their way to the school to get all three kids out of class and bring them home. Jinx will meet them there. Sasha will phone when they're safely home. Carter is having the crew refile their flight plan to go directly to Cleveland Hopkins airport. We should be on board in 15 minutes."

Nic adds, "Carter may need your influence with the tower in Cleveland, and he would like permission to send some local boys to the house to await our arrival."

Standing up, Reed delivers Cara to her husband. He drops her legs, placing her in front of Nic, and without a word, he darts quickly out.

CHAPTER 17

CARA CAN HEAR REED'S VOICE barking out commands on the phone just outside the office. She's standing entirely wrapped around her husband. He is clinging to her so fiercely; she's having difficulty breathing. Nic is murmuring words, but Cara can't make them out. Maybe he's humming. Either way, she isn't sure who is comforting whom. They stand like this for what seems like hours but must only be minutes when Nic's phone rings.

He breaks the embrace and grabs his phone. Reed hears it and walks back into the office, still attached to his cell phone. Nic answers but doesn't say a word. Nodding his head, he covers the phone and tells her, "They have the kids in the car. Jinx has secured the house. They have an ETA of two minutes to the gate of our neighborhood."

Cara exhales loudly, her tears drying out.

Reed touches Nic's arm. "Tell them 5 men, local FBI, will be there within 20 minutes in two cars. Let your gate guard know. Code for the men is 'Sold the Renoir'." Reed walks away again to continue his conversation.

Nic relays the info to Sasha and tells him to text when they arrive, and are completely secure in the house, and text, again, when the FBI arrives. He lets Sasha know they will call when onboard, and the pilot issues their ETA at Hopkins Field.

Ending the call, Nic forces her chin up to meet his eyes. "Sold the Renoir? That's funny, actually." He presses his lips on hers with the only the slightest pressure, easing her tension.

Reed reenters the room and starts apologizing he can't get the FBI to the house sooner. "I need to go across agency lines. FBI has jurisdiction and should be involved. Besides, I don't have any agents in the vicinity."

Nic raises his hand at Reed, stopping him. "Sasha and Jake are armed to the hilt. I have full faith in them until the FBI arrives." Nic relays this without any thought of the consequences.

Questioningly peering at both Cara and Nic, Reed inquires, "Why is your babysitter 'armed to the hilt' and who is Jake? Isn't he Jinx's husband?"

Nic's head tilts in submission. "How much time do we have before the plane is ready?"

"They needed more fuel for the flight, but the flight plan is in, and the tower in Cleveland is alerted. About 15 minutes to board. Enough time for you to answer the question." Reed barks with authority.

Nodding her approval to Nic, she sits in one of the chairs, while he takes a seat and turns his attention to Reed. Nic advises he may want to shut the door and sit down.

"Why am I suddenly feeling like things are going to go from bad to worse?" Reed replies as he shuts the door and heads back to the chair behind the desk. "Hit it, Nic."

Taking a big breath, Nic's feeling some apprehension. He offers how seventeen years ago, when he found out where Cara was in Cleveland, he went back to Moscow and made arrangements with Golov to take a three-week leave because he met a woman. "As our relationship developed, I realized I needed to deal with Golov and my desertion."

Reed interrupts him, "Word on the street was Alexander Golov killed you, and then he died in Britain."

He continues without answering Reed. He kept buying more time with Golov, using the truth as his excuse, but again, not divulging who the girl was. He got about four months out of it. He did do some work here in the States for Golov on the side. Not that he wanted to, but it bought him a deep cover story with their superiors.

Golov did that for Nic. He made it happen because they had always been like family. When he and Cara got engaged, Nic had to decide to either tell Golov he wanted out, or risk another option. Because he and

Alexander were so close, and he had been very understanding so far, Nic decided on telling him. He knew it had to be done in person. Golov deserved the truth, all of it.

Using his American cover, Alexander made his way to New York. Nic met him there. "To say the meeting went well…he basically went bat shit crazy on me." Nic looks to Reed, and then to Cara before continuing, "I suspect Cara got the same reaction from you, except I'm hoping you didn't take multiple swings at her like Alexander Golov did."

Reed gazes over at Cara as if recalling their reveal, but otherwise he lets Nic go on.

Nic and Alexander went nine rounds with each other, trashing a hotel room, but when they were done, Golov just stared at him. They were both bruised and bleeding and he said, "Do you love her enough to risk everything?"

Nic told him, "1000 times over."

And that's when Golov said, "So be it," and left. He and Cara married, and she was immediately pregnant with the twins. He sent a message to Golov about the babies. Nic didn't hear from him until a few weeks before the twins were due.

Cara interrupts him at this point and looks to Reed directly. "Sweetheart, I want you to try and stay calm, because this was over 15 years ago. Just keep that in mind." Motioning to him to continue, Nic can't. Cara has caused him to pause where he can't find the right way to start again. She proceeds for him. "Connor, you know the Russians have nicknames like we do, Dick for Richard, Bob for Robert? What's a common nickname in Russia for Alexander?"

The silence in the room is epic. He can actually hear Reed's brain working.

The light bulb goes on in Reed's mind only a split second before he stands up and shouts, "GOLOV IS YOUR NANNY!" Reed shoves everything off the desk causing a huge crash.

The door swings open and Carter, with the suited agent who took their bags, appear with their guns drawn. Reed pays the weapons no attention as he continues to trash everything breakable within arm's reach. Carter motions to the one agent to stand down, but he keeps his gun out. Cara is calmly sitting with her legs crossed as shit is flying all around her.

While Reed is gesticulating wildly with his arms, trying to form words with his mouth, Carter whispers to Cara, "You seem to have this effect on men." He leaves and shuts the door behind him.

When Reed is finally able to speak, all that comes out is, "Someone better start talking, NOW!"

Nic decides he does need to man up here, so he continues. Sasha, or Golov, showed up at their door two weeks before the kids were born. He basically offered to work something out so Nic could be permanently released from any issues with their group. That's when Sasha met Cara for the first time. Nic introduced him to her as his brother, Sasha. He thought, until today, that's who Cara thought he was.

Looking to Cara, he apologizes. "Sorry, baby, for selling you out." Cara waves him off like no problem, but takes over the conversation.

She doesn't know, nor does she care, what Nic and Sasha worked out, but by the time they did, Sasha was at the hospital with them while she gave birth to the twins. To say the man fell in love that day would be an understatement. Alexander Golov cradled her babies like a man possessed to guard and protect until death. Cara knew that day, just like she knew when she met Nic, Sasha was going to stay with them and be welcomed.

Ignoring Reed's scathing sneer at her, she calmly says to him, "You recall what you and I went through when you found out about Nic and I. To be honest, I had just undergone an emergency C-section with not one, but two babies. The last thing I wanted to deal with was telling you about Sasha."

Reed finally injects, "So, you're telling me the original Widow Maker of Russia, the notorious Alexander Golov, has raised your children since birth." He says this as a statement for effect, wanting to hurt her.

Cara takes a deep, cleansing breath, trying everything in her power to maintain control. When she feels she's ready, she simply stands, leans over the desk into Reed's face, and with conviction recites, "Yes, the great Widow Maker, the handler for the Dark Angel of Death, and unarguably one of the most lethal men in the world, helped raise our children. He has been the grandfather who dotes on them. The uncle who plays with them. The father who loves them, without disciplining them. My right hand after

Nic, and most importantly, our children ADORE him. He has taught them everything that is good and kind and wonderful in this world. And as I told my husband earlier, when he realized I knew about Sasha, no one, and I mean NO ONE, will EVER need to defend Sasha to me." And with that, she leans back to her seat, and sits down.

Reed is rendered momentarily speechless. Nic gets more of his story out with, "Sasha had contacts in the UK. He arranged to have the story spread of Golov killing the Dark Angel for desertion. He then had one of the Britain's MI6 agents set up to kill Golov as far as stories go. A few people were paid off, and we have both been left alone from mother Russia ever since."

Now Reed has his words back glaring at her, "But when you told me about Sasha, I ran a full background check without your knowledge."

She explains how she enlisted Jinx's assistance. They made up a different last name than Andre for Sasha, and created a cover for her fictional nanny. She knew Reed would run a check. She was counting it.

Jinx, also, hacked the profile and cover Sasha had created for himself, just in case the name Sasha Andre was ever let loose. Jinx put in some additions and changed it from a him to a her.

"I don't think Sasha knows this." Cara smiles at Nic because Sasha as a girl is too funny. She's never discussed it with Nic, so it's been like that for 15 years, she assumes. She, also, told the twins they weren't to talk about their Uncle Sasha when they saw their Uncle Reed because he would get jealous. "I feel badly for placing them in the scam, but it had to be done."

Now Nic is staring at her with disbelief right along with Reed. Neither man gets a chance to speak when Carter opens the door and announces the plane is ready to board.

Nic rises from his chair and heads towards the office door, but tells them as he's walking away, "Sasha has texted to say they're in the house, and the FBI agents are outside waiting for Reed for further instructions." Nic can only shake his head as he grabs Cara's stuff and his own, while making his way onto the plane.

It's written all over her husband's face. His memories are rushing back to him. He was in complete denial about her knowledge of Sasha. Just like Cara knew Reed would run a background check on her new babysitter, she knew Nic would never put two and two together when he spent time with Reed. He would not be able to look past his own jealousy to realize she and the kids never talked about Sasha in front of Reed.

She never invited Reed to visit the house when Sasha was around, and there are no pictures of Sasha up around the house. She mostly took trips with Reed and the kids without Nic, using the excuse he and Sasha could be left to have boy time together. She maintained her relationship with Reed over the years with only her children or alone. Not only was her husband in complete denial about Cara knowing his true identity, he was in denial about her acceptance of Sasha.

Of course, Nic wouldn't want Reed to meet Sasha, so he would collaborate her antics without even realizing it. That's the beauty of manipulation. If done well, the minds you're controlling truly believe they are acting of their own accord.

CHAPTER 18

REED IS IMMOBILE. SHOCKED, ANGRY and disappointed as he glares at Cara from across the desk. For the first time in decades, he really wants to choke her. The last 24 hours have given him the fear that her life may be threatened, to sending her on her own to Berlin so she could assault Carter and almost get herself killed, to this.

She gets up and walks over to him. Leaning in, she wraps her arms around for a hug, ignoring his fury. "I feel like we have all leapt a great distance today. Nic confessed his secrets to me this morning, then I confessed mine to him in the afternoon, and now, we both gave you the Sasha story. Please understand, as with all secrets, sometimes we do what we think is the right thing to do at the time. I never meant to hurt you, or jeopardize your position. I simply did what I needed to do to keep my family together. And Sasha is family to me-just like you are." Cara pulls away to leave a kiss on his lips.

He grabs her sweater, two fisted, and draws her close. They are practically nose-to-nose as he stares into her eyes. He knows Cara all too well. She has another motive for keeping Sasha a secret from him. He wants to shake it out of her, but she has enough to concern herself with at the moment. He can wait for the truth. He traces her lips with one finger before shaking his head slowly at her. He would like to blame himself for this. He created this woman. He trained her, coached her, and taught her everything he knew. But there are aspects of Cara no one will ever comprehend. Some truly gifted, wicked impulses only she can navigate with such ease.

Cara just dealt him a serious sucker punch. The kind of blow that could damage any relationship, even theirs. He can't imagine anything could reassure him and make everything 'all better' until she kneels between his legs with her hands on his knees and admits, "Back at the apartment, Nic wasn't infuriated because he thought we didn't know who he was. Nic was enraged that I did know. I knew, and yet…the moment I felt threatened…I went running to *you*." Cara raises her eyebrows at him, tilts her head, leaves a small kiss over his heart, then gets up and walks out of the office.

Well played, Cara, well played.

Leaving Reed to digest that, Cara boards the jet. The plane is parked and running in front of the hangar on a stretch of connecting runway. It's a Gulfstream GV. The jet is a smaller twin engine commonly used in the US for corporate and military VIP travel. She hasn't seen this jet since he was assigned it a couple of years ago when he was confirmed Director. Reed is very adept at playing around the rules, but he's shrewd when it comes to his budget and avoiding red flags. He strictly utilizes the plane for business. She wonders what Reed has spun about this unscheduled trip to Berlin, and now, a flight to Cleveland.

There is only one plush chair, resembling a first class seat, on each side of the plane. The first three sets of seats swivel, allowing for a conference set up. The next two rows of seats appear to slide and lock on a track so they can be relocated next to each other for conversation purposes. The back part of the plane is more of a conference table set up. The only bathroom is in the front of the plane behind the cockpit across from a small galley. The interior is not overly decorative, but much better than the military transport, and certainly plusher than a commercial flight.

Nic is seated in one of only two sets of side by side placed seats when she boards the plane. He's typing on his IPad and his leather duffle is on the seat next to him. She notices her carry-on bag is in the overhead compartment above.

Signaling her bag, Nic inquires if there's anything she needs in there for the flight. Cara lets him know not at this point. "I'm just emailing

Sasha a heads up, and sending him some things I want him to investigate while we're in the air. So...that went well," as he gets up to move his duffle off the seat for Cara to sit. "I'm afraid to move onto round two with this game of Secrets and Lies we're playing."

Cara sits and turns her body to face him. She's afraid of what round two is as well. She would like to admit she has no idea, but that wouldn't be true. She has suspicions. If those fears are valid, it's going to be a knock out for Reed. "Please, wait until Reed has calmed down from this revelation before you hit him with the next."

Nic looks at her with utter amazement on his face. "You're telling me you have the next blow mapped out, too? Who are you?"

A small smirk crosses her lips. It's wonderful to always be underestimated. "I knew who you were, and I knew you knew who I was." Wow, that's a mouthful. "Figuring out Sasha is Golov was cake. This next blow is a lesson in observation and ignorance. Observation, because you made mistakes. And ignorance, because I really didn't want to know the truth."

"Tis folly to be wise." Nic smirks at her.

"Absolutely. By the way, did you catch that I said I knew who you 'were' and who I 'was' just now? Again, I think in past tenses. You ARE the Dark Angel, and I AM the Reflex, but I'm still having trouble reconciling that in my head. I'm sorry."

"If you're referring to my complete disappointment of your running to Reed instead of me, I'm so over that." Nic waves his hand in a mocking gesture. "No, seriously, I get it. Sometimes, that pretty head it's absolutely brilliant, and sometimes it sticks itself in the sand, and goes off to the Land of Denial. Apparently, I spend some time there, too." Nic places his tablet to the side and leans over to grab Cara in an embrace. "You're compartmentalizing right now. You're very worried about the kids, and I know your mind palace is still searching for some answers."

"I am terrified for the kids right now." She does feel better knowing Sasha, Jake and Jinx are protecting her children. And she is still doing a mental Google search in her mind. She's concerned with how long they can keep them safe. "You know we have to tell *them* the truth."

"Sasha asked me if we were going to come clean with the kids. The twins are asking questions. Not many, mind you, these are our mostly absent teenagers, but they did ask some." Nic pulls Cara to him by tugging her hair and placing one of his signature soft lip-to-lip caresses. "I love you. I…no WE…will make this right."

Just then Reed walks by them. "Are you two always making out?"

Cara retorts, "No *Mia*, we are not always making out," and makes a face at him.

Reed takes one of the doublewide seats behind them and throws his stuff down in a bin at the back of the plane. He brings his laptop and phone out, and places them on the seat back tray table. Apparently, he doesn't need to adhere to FAA rules governing the use of seatback tray tables during take off and landing. He gets comfortable, and she can hear him typing away on his laptop.

Leaning out into the aisle, she sees Carter is sitting in the first seat on the left, and across from him is the agent who came in with Carter and had his gun drawn when Reed flipped out. He hasn't been introduced to her at any point. He must be Reed's far guard. She believes that's what they call themselves these days.

Political VIP's get a near guard and a far guard. The near guard acts as a personal bodyguard and the far guard has his back, or six, from a distance; checking for any incoming threats. Reed would have opted out of a near guard, considering it unnecessary with his training, but he may still respect a far guard.

The flight attendant comes on and makes the usual announcements, then the pilot announces they are getting into cue for take off.

Before the plane is off the ground, Cara has fallen asleep and Nic is working on his tablet. He can hear Reed still typing furiously on his laptop behind him. He listens to Reed type while watching his wife sleep. He needs to figure out how he's going to break Part II to Reed, and when. Hopefully, Cara will sleep for the flight. She's exhausted, and it's only going to get worse for her with the kids when they land.

Once airborne, the pilot makes another announcement about their flight time, wind speed and altitude. He turns off the seatbelt sign, and the flight attendant starts to make her pass through the cabin. Carter and the suited agent are asleep. She walks by them and heads towards he and Cara.

He flashes the attendant one of his killer smiles and asks for a couple of pillows and blankets. When she returns, he asks her for two glasses of bourbon, straight up, to be served to Reed's seat. Nic releases his seat belt and gently leans Cara down across his seat, placing the two pillows on it for her head. He maneuvers out into the aisle and spreads the blankets on her.

He steps back and leans into the area where Reed is working. Pointing to the empty seat next to Reed with his briefcase on it, Nic asks, "May I?"

Reed hesitantly points to the briefcase, and then motions to the table behind them. Relocating the case, Nic sits and brings his seatback tray down. The attendant immediately arrives with the two glasses. She hands them to Nic, who takes one and hands Reed the other.

Reed takes the drink with a narrow look. "What's this for?"

"In Russia, it's customary to start an important exchange with a drink."

"Do you know what the percentage of alcoholism is in men over age 45 in Russia, Nic?"

"I'm well aware, Reed." Nic toasts his glass. "To new beginnings, I hope."

Reed eyes him warily, but takes a sip of the bourbon. Swishing it around his mouth, he grins devilishly at Nic. "Angel's Envy bourbon. How serendipitous of you."

More relevant the he can know, and Nic forgot Reed's a bourbon connoisseur. He matches him, sipping plentiful, but doesn't say anything more, or try to speak. Nic only sits looking forward waiting Reed out. They finish their drinks in silence, and Nic catches the eye of the attendant, waving the empty glass in the universal gesture for a refill.

Before she can return, Nic decides he should start small. "I want to sincerely thank you for keeping my presence in the States all these years a secret." Nic comprehends what Reed did for him, now. By being aware of his true identity, Reed essentially harbored a criminal, as did Cara. If Reed wanted to separate Cara from the relationship, all he needed to do was make a phone call to the SVR. But he didn't. Reed never got in his way. He could have made Nic's life difficult or impossible, but he looked the other way. "I know you and Cara must have gone to blows over it, figuratively I hope, when she told you about me. I can't thank you enough."

Reed seems hesitant to respond, staring straight ahead. "I would do anything for her. She loved you and I knew it. What could I do?" Reed winces before offering, "You're a parent now. If Mia comes home with a boy you dislike, but she loves him, what would you do?"

Without hesitation Nic states, "I'll kill him."

This gets a small chuckle from Reed. "Very funny, but you would break your daughter's heart? I think even the Dark Angel would avoid that."

"It's true."

"Don't get me wrong, I never gave my blessing to C, either. I simply let her go."

Reed shakes his head after he says this. There is nothing simple about his relationship with Cara. Their relationship was or is different. It started out odd, and progressed to incredibly abnormal, but through it all, she has been his closest friend and confidante. For some strange reason, she's the only person to truly understand him on an entirely different level. He realized that, quickly, when they first met. "It was hard for me not to take advantage of our friendship if this is a confession."

Nic assures him he's not asking for a confession.

Sighing, Reed admits, "Well, maybe I do need a priest."

Cara's a total pain in his ass, but at the same time, she's easy to be with. She can second-guess Reed's thoughts and feelings, and ultimately she always made him a better man. He has valued her wisdom and support over the years. They were so close; he ran his every move by her, first, like best friends do. He wasn't sure if that was normal, because he never had a best friend before. He was never sure what was acceptable, so he didn't worry about it, and their relationship just was or is.

"My wife pesters you on a day-to-day basis more often than she bothers me." Nic admits he peeks at the texts they send each other all day long. "The two of you act like an old married couple. The couple that stays together, but bicker and nitpick with one another." Reed laughs at the apt description. Nic requests, "But why do you call her C?"

"That's an easy one." When he first met her she was Cara Bianco at University of Connecticut. After he recruited her to the Agency, the deal they made was no one was to know about her employment there. Her parents would have freaked out, her mother going ape shit with worry if she knew what her daughter was really doing.

Consequently, he created a paper trail for Cara Bianco to be employed by the World Bank as an assistant in the International Banking department. She even had a little desk in a corner of their building in DC with a phone and voicemail where her friends and family would leave messages. Cara received a check every other week directly deposited to a bank account in her name. She was even promoted a couple of times in her tenure at the World Bank.

Reed created an alias for Cara to work under at the Agency. She became Chase Bennett. She had a manufactured past, education and a new social security number. No one at the Agency knew her as anyone else, only he knew. In the beginning, though, he was having some issues remembering to call her Chase. He kept catching himself calling out 'Car', so, he called her 'C', instead. Little by little, Chase became easier to recall, but he still called her C. "Which thankfully I did, because when it was time for Chase to go back to being Cara, I would've been fucked."

Nic smiles at this. "I was thinking it was far more sentimental."

"I was thinking you were, too."

"May I ask another question?"

"Shoot, hopefully, they're all this easy."

"My understanding from your published bio is you went to Harvard undergrad, and then did a year at Law school there. You eventually finished at Georgetown with your J.D. If that's true, how did you and Cara meet at UConn?"

Inhaling a deep breath, Reed has to think about how he wants to respond. Those first few months after meeting Cara changed his life, in every way. How does someone explain to the husband what a profound impact his wife had on another man's life? If ever there was a time for diplomacy… "I left Harvard and joined the FBI, in the Hartford office. My first field assignment, when I was only an analyst, was to assist in the investigation of a series of rapes at UConn."

Nic's eyebrows furrow but Reed cuts his concern off quickly. "I was interviewing anyone associated with the victims. Witnesses and such." Cara was his third interview on his first day. To say he left that interview shaken and stirred would be a serious understatement. "She marched in, yanked the file out of my hands, and was examining all of the evidence before I could stop her." Of course, the fact she is disarmingly beautiful may have contributed. "Before I could protest, she had processed the info and was spewing out conjecture and possible leads, all of them viable."

Cara already knew the MO the rapist was using since she had found his fourth victim. The vic was a housemate of hers. She was very invested in nailing the perp. "She blackmailed me. She promised she would not tell anyone I let her see the file if she could assist in the investigation. My first chance to prove my worth in the office and I get Cara Bianco stuck up my ass."

Nic is stifling a laugh. Reed decides pulling the comedic value of this story will not only benefit him but help Nic. Glossing over all of the details will be necessary. "While I was investigating some of C's ideas, a fifth rape occurred. The Special Agent in charge decided I needed to go undercover as a collegiate."

From that point on, every move he made on the investigation was orchestrated by Cara. "I went undercover as her boyfriend so I could get into the frat parties. We had determined the perp was mostly likely a frat boy based on the evidence." He became Cara's boyfriend from Harvard as far as the sorority house she was living in knew. He was only 24 at the time so it wasn't a stretch.

"She had the lineup for the weekend's frat parties we're attending, and a list of appropriate wardrobe choices for me. Not only did she have my schedule, she's going to tell me what to wear! And what did I do? Exactly what she told me to do!" They both dissolve into silent hysterics at this, the two bourbons and 35,000-foot altitude surely contributing.

He motions for Nic to relocate towards the table at the back of the plane. He doesn't want to wake Cara, but he does wave to the flight attendant for another round as he follows Nic. "So we spent the next 6 weeks as a couple with me on campus every weekend to attend the frat parties."

Nic stutters, "Wwwait, you spend the night with her?"

Reed turns serious, knowing where Nic's mind went. "As a senior she had a single. It was this tiny room with a double bed in it. The first night together I panicked because what's supposed to happen? Before I could overthink it, she said…"

From directly behind them Cara yells, "Don't panic, Connor, clothes on and nothing is going to happen!" He and Nic are so startled, Nic spills the remaining bourbon across the table and Reed bangs his knee on the table leg.

CHAPTER 19

NIC SHOUTS AT HER, "HOW the hell did you…" pointing ahead of him, and then behind him.

"I guess sleeping with you has its benefits. Ghost by injection." Cara teases, raising her eyebrows at Nic.

"Seriously, what the fuck, C, you were sleeping two rows up. You made me bang me knee and wasted a perfectly good drink." Reed whines.

"The drink? That might explain how I got behind you both without you noticing. How dare you drink without me?" She catches the flight attendant eyes and raises three fingers on her hand. Might as well join the boys.

Having let the shock of her appearance pass, Nic inquires, "What did you say when you startled us?"

Reed jumps in to respond, "She repeated what she told me all those years ago when we got to her bedroom in the sorority house."

Nic questions purposely, "And that would be…" using his hand to make a roll on motion with it.

She hesitates to respond. She heard most of what Reed has already told Nic. He left the details out to minimize the intimacy of the story. That's what a best friend does. Protect your back. But their beginnings happened ten years before she ever met Nic. As far as she is concerned, her relationship with Reed supersedes her marriage to Nic. At the very least Nic should finally understand why Reed is so important to her. It's overdue.

Setting her stare on her husband, Cara responds, "I called him Connor when we got to my bedroom for the first time." Reed places his hands across his face and growls. She giggles out, "Reed doesn't like to be called Connor."

Reed yells, "Connor is my father's name! I like going by Reed."

Cara interrupts his whiny explanation. "That's what starts our first evening alone together in bed; Reed confessing to his Daddy issues and me listening." Reed flicks her head at the dig before grasping her hand.

Looking back, it had been an intimate evening. She told Reed all about her family and what they were like. They ended up sitting up in bed for hours, just talking. It laid the basis for what would be their relationship.

Reed confesses, "I told her shit that night I had never told anyone. I still don't know why I did, but it was oddly cathartic." He releases the deathgrip he has on her hand and subconsciously strokes his thumb over her palm.

Narrowing his eyes on their clenched hands, Nic inquires calmly, "You mean to tell me you had my wife in bed with you for a dozen nights and you don't try to fuck her?"

Cara winces at his choice of words, and then glares at her husband. "You really are stuck on this sex thing, aren't you?" Wait, of course he wouldn't understand. Nic always wants to have sex with her. It's at the core of their relationship. The more she thinks about it, the more she comprehends. If they are mad at each other, they have sex. If they're happy, they have sex. If they are feeling vulnerable, they have sex. It's their cure all. No emotion can get in the way of having sex. It's non negotiable in their relationship. And honestly, it's pretty fucking awesome.

Reed is evidently alarmed, but quickly responds to Nic before thinking. "I was a 24 year old with a strong sex drive; of course I wanted to fuck her. But, that would've been pretty inappropriate on so many levels. I went to bed stiff, and woke up the same way, but between feeling guilty for having her involved in the cover, possibly ruining the cover over a failed attempt at it, and knowing I wasn't hanging around after the assignment; it was just not possible."

Nic murmurs, "How gallant of you."

"Precisely!" Cara shouts, but then points to Reed. "White. Knight." She cocks her head at her husband. "Get it?" White Knight became Reed's moniker at the Agency, because Cara called him her white knight as a joke to pester him all the time.

Nic's only response is to blink several times at her. She's going to let this go. Sasha is his best friend, and he was a girl, she'd have serious issue with that.

"Anyway, we went to all the frat parties for six weeks but nothing happened." On the seventh weekend, though, they decided to change things up. They arrived at the party together but separated once inside.

She partied and danced with the girls while Reed acted like a typical frat boy and flirted with another group of girls. A very unassuming boy she didn't know asked her to dance. "There was something about him." She muses.

Reed scowls at her before adding, "C decided it was fine to go out to the backyard with this boy and retrieve more beer from a cooler back there. I was not happy she was out of my sight."

Sighing, Cara recalls the evening that altered the direction of her life. That boy, Ed Grotto, had her follow him to the darkest corner of the yard before pulling a knife on her. He was suddenly crazed. Telling her he had been looking specifically for her all this time, and the other girls were mistakes.

She knew Reed probably followed her outside, but she couldn't see him in the dark. She didn't try to call out to him because she didn't want Ed to know he was there.

"When I got to the yard, I could hear Ed saying, 'You are mine. We can be together forever now.' And I knew C had found our serial rapist." Reed says before shaking his head at her. "I removed my gun from my boot and cautiously approached them. I could see the knife in his hand but he was too close to C for me to take a shot."

Reed studies her for a moment before turning his gaze back to Nic. Poor thing. He looks as grim as he did that night so long ago. "I knew Ed intended to make his move so I bolted forward, but before I reached him, C stepped into Ed. She threw her arm at his forearm, pushing the knife away from her, while simultaneously landing her elbow directly into Ed's throat. She spun back, landed a full on kick into his nuts, and as he was going down, she grabbed his head and forced him face first into her knee. I reached them with Ed writhing on the ground, blood pouring from his nose, and C with the knife in her hand. Ed was groaning and Cara was screaming, 'I'm going to cut off your nuts for what you did!' waving the knife at his crotch." Reed concludes.

"I will never forgive you for stopping me from slicing his balls off. That was the least he deserved." Cara intones.

"SPD moment?" Nic questions his wife.

Reed responds, "Her Sicilian Personality Disorder aside, there is a process in this country, and I certainly wasn't going to have her jeopardize that process, or find herself compromised. I wanted Ed Grotto put away for a long time. I cuffed him, gave him his Miranda rights, and called it all in."

Nic is doing that blinking thing, again. Like if he moistens his eyes, the story will have better clarity. He's not going to get it. "While Reed and I were waiting for the police, the adrenalin had worn off and I began to freak out."

Nic looks like he's about to offer some consolation for her trauma but Reed cuts him off, "She wasn't losing it about Ed. She was a mess because she didn't want her mother to find out."

Comprehension dawns on Nic's face. He has had 17 years of dealing with her nutty family. Her father's boisterous personality and her mother's strict, overbearing, and protective treatment of her children. Nina, her mother, would have shit a brick if she found out her daughter put herself in harm's way. Cara learned early on the less her parents knew about her life, the better. She ingrained the same standards to her younger sister as well. It was never about disrespect as much as survival.

"I started begging Reed to shield me from this. It couldn't get out about the cover, or my assistance in the case. I didn't want my friends or family, anyone on campus, or the press, to ever know. I was simply Ed's next victim and Reed figured it all out."

Despite his initial guess, more clarity is dawning on her husband's face. It's turned contemptuous as he glares at Reed. "You took all the credit for the capture. You based your entire career trajectory on Cara's ordeal."

Cara jumps in, needing to diffuse the obvious tension, "Nic, it's what I wanted. The ramifications to both of us were too damning. If Reed was going to be the only recipient of the capture success as a side effect, so be it. It made no difference to me."

"Where is this Ed now?" Nic demands.

"He got life in the State pen with no parole. I make sure of that and keep tabs on him. Unlike C, I'm convinced she was his intended target all along." Reed advises as he glances at her. She and Reed used to argue about this often. She believes Ed was simply nuts, but Reed insists she was always his target. Ed didn't use the same MO with her, but Cara thinks because he didn't get the chance.

Her husband is processing all of this. She can practically hear his scrambled thoughts. Before he can come to any more judgment on the matter she adds calmly, "Nic, my love, you are the first person to know this story. Reed and I have never shared it."

Taking a big breath, Nic exhales, "What happened to you, Reed, after the ordeal?"

Reed slumps forward over the table and hisses out, "Give me a moment before I divulge federal secrets to a former high level KGB agent, whose live-in nanny was considered the most notoriously cunning handler and politico in Russia's Foreign Intelligence history."

CHAPTER 20

BEFORE THE TRIAL WAS EVEN over, Reed received a call from his contact at the CIA. The man wanted him to come to Langley to talk about opportunities. Of course he had heard of the UConn case, and believed Reed would be a good fit for a new program they were starting with a younger, more 'hip' group of operatives to address some of the newer concerns with the predicted fall of the Soviet Union. The new team would be autonomous within the Agency with only a few guidelines to follow. The program was going to be given two years to see results, and then evaluated.

During the interview, Reed was asked a series of questions with scenarios. Before he could answer the first one, he thought about Cara. How she manipulated him, taking advantage of the mind of a 24 year old. He tried to forget his Quantico training, and anything he had learned, and answered like the young man who just broke basic rules to find a serial rapist.

Then Reed was asked if he was team leader, how would he choose his team? He was floored by the question; thinking he was interviewing to be on the team, not head it up. Again, he thought of Cara before he answered. She would be fair and ask to interview all current employees interested, but would be cautious about bringing aboard anyone with too much old school baggage to shake off. They would have to be willing to think outside of the box, use technology as it becomes available, consider training at a different level, and always be fluid to opportunities.

After more discussion, Reed signed a non-disclosure and was headed back to Connecticut when it hit him like a freight train. He interviewed for a job he really wanted based on his last four months with Cara. Did he answer as Cara, or as the man he had become because of her?

"It was then I realized what a profound difference she made in my life in such a short time. I was different. I had changed because of her. I didn't feel guilty for what happened at UConn, or how I handled it, because in the end, I got the job done. Some rules are meant to be broken. Others can be bent if your gut and intuition lead you there."

Reed is getting some hostility from Nic but he doesn't care. Besides, he is not the one referred to as the Dark Angel of Death.

"You got the team leader job." Nic says as a statement. Reed nods in acknowledgement. "You then hired Cara." Again, a statement. Before he can correct Nic, Reed feels Cara placing her foot against his under the table. She simultaneously scratches her hand and itches her nose.

During the course of training and running missions with one another, Reed and Cara developed intricate hand signals to communicate, very reminiscent of a Major League Baseball coach. This is the signal to omit from the script and quickly summarize.

He's not entirely sure why Cara doesn't want to divulge the pivotal evening when Reed decided to hire her. But then, he catches her putting two fingers into her mouth in his peripheral vision. That's their signal for spoon feed. She wants to spoon feed Nic this info. Reed touches his ear in confirmation.

Cara sighs out louder than she intended, relieved Reed has understood. With all of the confessions today, she is going to neglect this one. Reed did not hire her after he took his position. He didn't hire her until 6 weeks later. She went to DC and stayed with Reed the summer after she graduated to attend an interview at the World Bank. The interview was a bust, but what occurred after led to her employment with Reed and the CIA.

It's better if Nic learns those details when there isn't as much tension. She does want him to finally know the truth about Jinx, though. "I surmise you know Jinx worked for Reed, too?"

"Eleanor Evans, aka The Jinx, yes, I know she was your analyst. Did you hire her?" Nic inquires.

Reed takes on the answer for her. "No, Jinx already worked there when I was hired. I wanted her on my team but no one would work with her. Hence the nickname. She was and is a brilliant analyst and black hat. Nothing the woman can't hack into. But for some reason, everything she touched at the Agency would turn to stone in the field." Reed smiles at her to continue.

"So, Reed had Jinx escort me from the lobby on my interview day." Cara finds herself grinning at the memory. Jinx was wearing a dowdy navy blue suit with a white shirt. She was a blonde bombshell trapped in plain Jane clothes. Her body wanting desperately to be free. Cara, of course, was wearing ripped jeans and a halter-top. She thought she was having lunch with Reed. No idea she was on an interview.

By the time Jinx walked her to Reed's office, Cara was in love. Jinx chatted her up the entire way and asked her if Reed was available. Jinx thought he was, by far, the hottest guy at the Agency and warned Cara she was determined to get into his pants. Jinx did not succeed with that quest, but she did become Cara's right hand, her roommate and her dearest friend.

"Jinx left me at Reed's office, which was shittiest office I have ever seen." He had a gray metal desk and one metal folding chair. The walls were painted a dull gray like the rest of the facility. The whole place elicited anxiety and degradation. "It was like fifty shades of gray, but not in the great BDSM way."

"And from that day forward, you became my best employee, my best friend, and the biggest pain in my ass to ever live." Reed declares.

"Wait!" Nic stops them, "That's it? You just said, yes, I will be an agent?"

Cara looks at her husband with total disbelief. "Nic, besides sex, how many times have I said 'just yes' to you in almost 17 years of marriage?"

Nic ponders the question before answering, "I can count on one hand."

"Exactly. I said yes to Reed, with a short list of conditions."

"Short list!" Reed snorts. "Try like twenty conditions. Besides the whole Cara Bianco needs to be employed somewhere else, and you need an alias to work there, she said she was not wearing the uniform."

Those hideous blue and black suits with the white, gray or light blue shirts are a travesty. "It inhibited creativity, and if you sought an inventive team, you needed to let them wear what they wanted." Cara argues.

Reed concedes, "This, I agreed, was a good point." She said the team needed to be able to paint their area any color they wanted. She listed all her conditions, which of course were entirely calculated to maximize Reed's efforts for his team. "As usual, C had revamped an entire project after stepping into the building for twenty fucking minutes."

"Jinx was also looking for a roommate to share rent, so I had a job, a place to sleep, and a new name all before lunch. How awesome was that?" Cara takes a gulp of the bourbon.

Nic is looking at her like she has three heads. "Just like that? No formal background. No training. No military exercises. Nothing."

"Jesus, Nic, are you starting the Russian Angst on me?" She turns to Reed, "Have I told you I call Nic and Sasha, Moody and Broody? Nic is dark and moody, and Sasha is dark and broody. I attribute it to all the dark, torturous Russian training they put these guys through. They can produce unmitigated killing machines, but at the slightest provocation of emotion, they fall apart. Total angst."

Cara turns back to her husband, "And to answer your question, yes I took the job without over thinking it. I was unemployed, and living with my parents! I was in purgatory. I would have worked for you Russians to get the hell out of there!"

Nic lowers his head and says very quietly, "I'm not Russian."

Both she and Reed jerk at him, "What?!"

CHAPTER 21

NIC'S HAD THE WIND KICKED out of him. "Did I tell you I was Russian when we met?"

He told Cara he was a freelance interpreter. He traveled all over the world working for various clients. He inferred his schooling was in Europe, and his career took off from there. Of course, she never pressed him for details, just as he never pressed for her banking resume. Because both of their perceived jobs required international travel, he suspected neither of them ever lied about where they had been, only the circumstances of why they were there. They even thoroughly discussed destinations they had been to and enjoyed when they planned their honeymoon and subsequent vacations.

"Um, no. You only said you were born in Germany, but I assumed that was a cover." Cara finally responds after much thought.

"No cover. I'm German."

Nic waits for someone to interrupt, but neither does. They only stare at him in shocked puzzlement. He watches his wife, carefully. Nic has only omitted the cause for his travel and circumstances. He always shared his true emotions about his childhood and his work. He told her he had no family except for a brother he was once close with, but they had lost touch. He always led her to believe his childhood was painful, and he spent a good portion of his life alone. Had she inquired about the details, he was prepared to share them, but she never did.

Letting his eyes shift from each of their faces, Nic decides it's finally time to share those specifics.

Nic was born in Berlin, coincidentally, but on the wrong side. His parents were teachers at the University. He's pretty sure they both taught sciences, but they were also gifted musicians. He is an only child.

They adored him. He was very loved and very protected. His parents entertained all the time. Sometimes, they would play music and dance and sing. Sometimes, they would argue over books and propaganda, but it was always lively and enjoyable at their apartment.

One night, when he was eight years old, Nic was sleeping in his parents' bedroom. He woke up to the sounds of loud arguing. He thought his parents were having one of their lively debates with friends, but the arguing turned to pleading, and he can't recall why, but he crawled under the bed, afraid. And that's when he heard the two gunshots. Nic froze. He didn't move or try to do anything. He just froze.

Cara rises from her chair and makes her way around the table to him to sit on his lap. Reed is immobile, staring doe-eyed. He feels her hand rest against this heart.

Nic was so frightened, he couldn't move from under the bed until he heard the neighbors calling his name. He crawled out and they ran to him to try to cover his eyes. But he saw them, his parents. They were shot execution style in the head. The police questioned him, but he didn't speak to them. He couldn't speak at all.

He was placed in an orphanage, after that. The boys there were very cruel. They told him he would die in that place because he was too old to ever be adopted, and no one would want him. But still, he didn't speak.

Only two weeks went by when a Russian couple arrived at the orphanage. They came to see him. They spoke very quietly to him in Russian, but he couldn't communicate.

They said he was coming home with them, and everything was going to be fine. He knew enough Russian to make out what they were trying to communicate. At the time, Nic wasn't sure what was scarier, going with two complete strangers, or staying at that wretched place. But still, he did not speak. They brought him to St. Petersburg, Leningrad back then. They had a nice apartment for Russians. They told him his name was going to change to Nicolae, and his new last name would be Andrychenko. He had his own room. They bought him books and were very nice, but he couldn't say thank you.

"I was sent to a school for children who are…special." Nic admits.

The teachers tried diligently to get him to converse. His new adoptive parents would come in every afternoon and check on his progress. About six months in, he was at school when the fire alarm went off and they could smell smoke. Nic knew they were supposed to use the fire exits to vacate the building, but the teachers were running out without taking the children with them.

He retrieved all of the kids who were very special and made sure they exited safely. His parents heard of the fire, and arrived to find him escorting the other children out, and talking to them in perfect Russian trying to keep them calm. His adoptive parents hugged him and cried. When they stopped crying they said, "You can talk. But how do you speak Russian so fluently?"

Nic just told them, "I listen."

That's when they changed schools. They sent Nic to a new school, a private school, which is quite elite in Russia. This school was for children who are the other kind of special. He really liked this school. He was able to study whatever he wanted, languages, mathematics, any of the sciences. There were even books to read that were normally banned in the Soviet Union. At the time, he didn't understand the ramifications of where he was, or what was expected of him; he only flourished and thrived.

He had difficulty making friends. Nic would have acquaintances, but he didn't interact much with the other children. He was happy, by himself, learning. He lived with the Andrychenko's for seven years until they were killed in a car crash when he was fifteen.

Nic stops his story to look up at Cara. Bringing his fingertips to her lips, he says, "Same age as Max and Mia." A lone tear rolls down her cheek. He wipes at the tear, subconsciously, while Cara wraps her arms around his neck, burying her head into his chest.

There is silence for a few minutes until Reed, using a calming voice, asks, "Nic, what happened when they died?"

"I didn't have time to process their deaths." He was yanked out of his school, his home, and the life he had finally come to enjoy. He was told his school wasn't affordable anymore, but they had recommended Nic for a private military school, as his grades and attitude were exemplary. He was told to pack one bag, with anything he valued, and was shipped off outside of Moscow to an all-boys military academy.

It was not an academy. It was a training facility. Nic was highly intelligent for his age. He already spoke seven languages fluently, was doing math at a graduate level, and studying chemistry, physics and biology at the college level. His IQ tested over 180, but he had never been in a fistfight. He was a pacifist, a student.

Nic looks at his wife and again digresses to the present, "It would be like throwing Max in prison, now, and asking him to try and survive." Cara shudders and even Reed reacts with a frown over his otherwise impassive face.

Placed in a large open dorm room with 13 other boys in his age group, Nic was tormented. The boys were terribly cruel, taking their shots at him. He was pretty beat up by the end of his first week there.

He was able to hold his own, one on one, without getting killed because he was bigger than most of the boys in size. By the end of his first week, they would come at him in groups of two to four. Nic was at his breaking point. He would rather die than continue to endure the beatings.

He was ready for death when four boys approached him in a quiet hallway. They were taunting him, calling him pretty boy, mama's pet, and geek. They manhandled him before holding him down and beating him, hard. Just when he believed it was finally his day to die, the boys suddenly stopped.

They all stared at a lone older boy who had entered the hallway. He was bigger than all of them, his face cold and hard. He didn't say a word, but started to approach them. When he was within a few feet, one of the younger boys holding Nic down asked the boy what he wanted. The older boy responded, "I want you to leave and give me the pretty boy."

Another of the boys, who had been hitting Nic, and was the biggest, challenged the older boy saying, "You will need to fight us if you want him." Before that boy could register, the older boy punched him in the throat while kicking out his leg at the second boy. The third boy went for him from behind, but the older boy seemed to anticipate it and spun, connecting an upper cut to the boy's jaw. The smallest one holding Nic down ran away.

He was left on his knees, cut up, bleeding, and alone in the hallway with the frightening older boy. The older boy dragged him up by his shirt and pulled him outside the building to a dark corner. Everything in his mind was trying to process his next move, but he was badly hurt, scared and couldn't muster the energy to fight him. The older boy placed Nic on the ground leaning against the building.

Then he did the most unexpected thing. The boy offered, "I've heard stories about you; that you're extremely intelligent. Is that true?" Nic wasn't sure how to respond, so he just shrugged. He got down on his knees so he was eye level and asked, "You've never been taught how to fight?" Nic admitted he had never been taught anything but academics. He didn't know why he told the menacing young man the truth. He thought right after he said it; he had made a huge error in judgment.

The older boy began to examine his injuries. Nic flinched at his touch, but the boy didn't notice. He was rough, but somehow gentle at the same time. Then he stood back up and just said, "I will teach you to fight, Nicolae. The other boys won't bother you for a while as you are under my protection now. But that will only last so long. You must work hard and train with me every chance you get. Do you understand?" Nic was shocked by the offer, but somehow felt the boy could be trusted. Really, what choice did he have? He responded he understood, and then he said thank-you.

The boy put out his hand to help Nic stand, and that's when he said, "My name is Alexander, but only my friends get to call me Sasha. You will need to earn that right."

Silent tears are rolling down Cara's face over the tale of his childhood. Her hands are both clutched around bunches of his shirt.

Alexander found time to work with Nic every day the next week. They started with the basics of physical combat. Nic began to understand the patterns and psychology of hand-to-hand strategy. It was all he needed, to let his brain process the mechanics. He was catching on very quickly. Alexander told him he was impressed with the progress. He recommended some books to read that would assist Nic in understanding the art and science of combat.

Nic read all of them over the weekend between other schoolwork and training. By Monday, he was feeling better, like he was getting it. He was in the commissary, eating alone at a table, when Alexander came over with another boy his age. Alexander was pointing at Nic to the other boy. He said to the other boy, "This pretty face has angered me. Please, teach him a lesson."

Nic was stunned. Alexander was asking the other boy to fight him. Why would he do that? Before he knew it, the other boy, who was much bigger than Nic, was throwing a punch at his head while he was still seated on the bench. Then, the most amazing thing happened inside Nic's mind. He started to map out everything around him, instantaneously, calculating their use as weapons, and the distance between him and the punch. He was computing mass, speed, and volume, all at a lightning pace.

Everything he had learned from Alexander and the books was there in his mind. He grabbed the food tray and blocked the punched to his head. Then he flung the tray hard into the boy's nose, giving himself time to get up from the bench. Nic was at the boy's side, throwing punches into his torso, when he heard Alexander say, "Stop." Alexander looked at the boy with a broken nose and said, "Sorry, this isn't the right pretty boy. My mistake." He leaned into Nic's ear and whispered, "Now, you can call me Sasha."

"Sasha left me standing there while he walked away with a smile on his face." Nic concludes with a little smirk.

"HOLY SHIT!" Reed lets loose.

This exclamation breaks Nic from his memory trance. "I know, right? There were many boys in the commissary that day, and they had all witnessed the fight. So, needless to say, I was left alone for a few more weeks."

During that time, he trained with Sasha one on one. They became friends. Nic never had a friend before. Despite Nic's social issues, Sasha and he grew to be very close friends over the next year at school. Sasha was easy to be around. He understood him in a way the others didn't. Sasha was also very intelligent, and could follow any train of thought without much effort.

"Interesting." Reed muses again. "So what happened with you at school after the first year there with Sasha?"

"I learned everything I could from him. I trained hard. Hand to hand, guns, knives, anything. We worked all aspects of weaponry, first. Then we went on to more of the psychological aspects for covert operations, concealment, blending in, and role playing."

Sasha gave Nic everything he could handle for a 15 or 16 year old. Sasha assured him he was headed for a more covert type position with the KGB, rather than the military positions many of the other boys would get. Sasha advised to work towards that, because it would give him better latitude and freedom. "He really explained the whole 'game' to me. Making sure I understood what my limited options were, and which would ultimately suit me best."

When Sasha turned 18, he was sent away to a special training. It was given to boys turning to men who the school felt could benefit from the additional instruction. Nic didn't understand at the time what it entailed, but he did notice only the better looking boys were sent there. When Sasha returned four months later, he was colder and harder than before.

When Nic pressed him, he admitted the training was sexual in nature. Sasha described it as the worst experience of his life. Of course Nic would later find out what this training was, a cruel, violating assault on the men to teach them sexual stamina, control and seduction. They had come to call it Whore School.

He got another year in at the training facility before Sasha was assigned a position with the KGB. By then, Nic was 17 years old. He was targeted for Whore School in six months. Right before Nic left for that training, he received an order to report to KGB headquarters in Moscow. Upon arrival, Sasha greeted him, explaining due to Nic's expertise, extreme intelligence and willingness to advance, he had been chosen to the KGB for early assignment. He would later find out Sasha had pulled a multitude of strings to get him out of Whore School and get him placed on Sasha's team. They shared an apartment together, and have been together since.

Sasha was an expert with deep covert missions. He could alter his appearance completely and become anyone. Nic had that talent as well, but with his size, blonde hair and blue eyes, it was harder to send him to certain areas with success. He was, also, too noticeable. "Remember the moth to the flame?" he stops to ask Cara, "You and Jinx tease that I'm too beautiful, but that's fairly true, unfortunately. I'm too easy to recall. That can be very detrimental in a deep cover as you know."

Sasha would be assigned the longer covert missions; sometimes he would be gone for months. It was after one assignment in England Sasha came back damaged, not physically or mentally, but emotionally. "He's never talked about it, but after that, he was reassigned as a handler. I was assigned to him. The rest you know." Nic concludes.

Reed commences the questioning first, "Golov protected you, always."

"Always, since I was a scared 15-year-old boy. He really has been the big brother I never had. He even always made sure to get me the best back up and the best missions during his tenure as my handler. I owe him my life. You understand, now, when I had opportunity to give him something in return, a family, a life and love, I didn't hesitate to repay him."

Cara asks the next question from her position on his leg, "The apartment in Berlin we were in this morning? It was the one you shared with your parents, isn't it? Where they were murdered?"

An overwhelming sadness seizes him. "Yes. I've always suspected the motive behind my parents' homicide."

When Nic had opportunity, he investigated as much as he could, but the case was cold. He never gave up, but the longer time went by, the harder it became. When the apartment became available for rental, he took it. Nic thought somewhere in that apartment was a clue. He found many secret hiding places, but nothing interesting inside of them. Eventually, the apartment building went to condos and he bought it.

Reed's turn, "Do you suspect the Andrychenko's death wasn't an accident?"

"How do you put it, there's no such thing as a coincidence? The question becomes are they related, and was I being manipulated? The math leans to that."

"Last question from me." Cara states. "If Nicolae Andrychenko was your adopted name, what is your given name?"

The emotional choking he felt telling them his story is back. He slowly inhales and hesitates, "Herrmann. Maximillian Herrmann. My father was also Maximillian. My mother was Maria Herrmann."

CHAPTER 22

CARA IS RENDERED SPEECHLESS. SHE'S staring in awe at her husband before whispering, "Max and Mia."

"Yes," is all Nic can respond before losing it.

Reed rises immediately, excusing himself, but not before placing one hand on each of their shoulders and squeezing as he passes behind them. It's the simplest, sweetest gesture she has ever seen Reed do with Nic. As soon as Reed is towards the front of the plane, Cara runs her hands into Nic's hair, pulling his head towards her chest and cradling it. She is still sitting on his lap, where she's been since his whole admission of his childhood. Neither of them speaks.

It's all so dreadful, and yet, Cara always knew Nic's angst came from somewhere. She just didn't know the details. Do the details make it better? It makes it real. She feels his pain right now, his pain and his shame. Why shame? He never did anything to deserve or cause this life. Shame because somewhere in there is an eight year old boy who thinks he could have saved his parents. Somewhere, there's a man who thinks he should have been able to solve their murder. Somewhere in there is a man who feels responsible for the position they are in now.

She gently cups Nic's face with her hands and brings her lips to his. She gives him their soft lip-to-lip caress before placing her cheek against his. "I love you. Thank-you for sharing all of that with us. I didn't think it possible, but I may love you more for it."

Nic moves her so she's straddling him over both his legs instead of sitting on just one. He pulls her close, chest to chest. He looks into her eyes and gives her slow kisses that grow longer and deeper. They stop, not wanting to lose control, but Nic gazes into her eyes. "Cara mia, I will never have any regrets knowing my life has led me to you and our children. For that, I am eternally grateful."

It's surreal to think she and Reed's story borders on the sublime, but Nic's background is tragic. "We're on different ends of the color spectrum." Yet, despite the disparity, it always feels very comprehensive between them.

Nic cups her cheeks, and the sadness is back in his eyes. "After hearing you and Reed talk about your past, I realized how much you two are alike. He's your synonym and I'm your antonym."

She shakes her head at him. "That's a bit extreme, but I won't deny Reed and I are like alter egos of each other." Cara's not entirely sure when that occurred, but somewhere along the way it happened. She and Nic are different but complementary to each other. "We fill in all the empty spaces with each other. I mean what's an alter ego anyway? It's just an imitation."

This makes Nic give out one of his killer smiles. "I like your analogy better."

Reed is approaching with more drinks, but nonalcoholic ones, and some snacks. Nic pulls her from his legs so she's standing, and directs her back to her chair across the table. Placing the tray on the table, Reed pushes past Cara to take his original seat in the corner. He informs them the flight attendant will serve trays of dinner, shortly. She is serving the pilots, first.

Everyone is looking and feeling haggard at this point. Cara's messy ponytail is hanging in strands around her face. Nic's hair is partly standing straight up and he looks wiped out. Reed has only his suit pants and dress shirt on; the shirt is wrinkled and the sleeves are rolled up. Serious shadows are evident across all of their faces.

The sky outside is growing darker as they approach the East coast time zone. Lights in the cabin appear to be dimming, casting a supernatural radiance across the table. They are preoccupied inside their own thoughts as they help themselves to the drinks. Cara pours some coffee for all of them as her eyes stay on her husband. She's willing him to comprehend it's time to get his last confession out.

With a subtle nod to her, Nic voices, "So…there's one more thing…"

"Wait, wait!" Cara exclaims after she hears it. "It's…Something's Always Wrong by Toad the Wet Sprocket." She sings the first verse of the song he's humming, completely off key.

Nic leans over the table to cover her mouth. "You know you're not allowed to sing." He continues the song's next verse with perfect pitch, sounding like a professional.

It's after the chorus that Nic and Cara notice the look of complete confusion on Reed's face. Nic stops singing and Cara starts laughing. "Sorry Reed, Nic was doing that 'Soundtracks of His Life' thing, again. You heard him humming, right?"

"You told Reed about my little tic?" Nic asks, affronted.

"Yes, long time ago, though. You remember, don't you Reed?" Reed is sitting there looking bewildered. Cara realizes he still has no clue. She offers, "The weird coping mechanism Nic has where he sings songs in his head, and then starts humming the tune when he gets really emotional." Reed still looks befuddled.

"I'm feeling humiliated right now, Cara. Must you tell everyone?" Nic snaps.

"Reed isn't EVERYONE, he's, you know, just Reed." Cara counters.

Reed feels his stomach drop, his blood pressure spike and his heart race. He's trying desperately to keep his emotions contained. Everything is wrong. His eyes darting between Cara and Nic as they continue to argue, he can sense his body perspiring. A cold sweat is covering his forehead. In an involuntary move, his hands come up and rest over his face. He's swallowing hard trying to keep down the bile rising in his throat.

Reed closes his eyes and tunes out their bickering. His mind is racing over the last 25 years. From the moment he met Cara in that campus police interview room to now. His brain is systematically picking through events and processing. It was all there. He's beginning to tremble, but he hasn't noticed. He's falling apart. Everything is wrong. Cara is still trying to get him to recall the coping mechanism. He drops his hands to stare blankly at her.

Grabbing his wrist, Cara says soothingly, "Sweetheart, it's fine if you don't remember. Please, don't get so upset."

He can't articulate. His stunned face shifts from Cara's eyes to Nic's, and then back to hers. She knows he's distraught. But, she doesn't understand why. It's a moment of illumination for him filled with knowledge, insight, reconciliation, regret and guilt. His heart is hammering in his chest. He can't take his eyes off Cara…because Nic was not humming just now. Everything is right but for the wrong reasons.

Trying desperately to gain composure, he places a small smile on his face and addresses Nic. "By the way, I've forgotten what an amazing singer you are. Is there anything you can't do?"

Nic quips, "Control my wife."

Before he can retort to Nic, or consider the huge epiphany he just experienced, the entire plane plummets forward. Instinctually grabbing the stationary table, he reaches for Cara, just before she flies out of her seat. Nic seizes the edge of the table and somersaults over it. The flight attendant is screaming while Cara is trembling against his chest. Still holding on to support himself with one hand, Reed places Cara back down in her chair with the other arm. "Buckle up, sweetheart." Once she has the belt around her waist, he raises his eyes to Nic. "Turbulence?"

Nic is easing off the table with care as everything is tilting downwards. "I don't think so, Reed. We're rapidly descending." He gives him the head jerk to make their way to the front. Cautiously gripping seats along their way, both men find Carter and the other agent strapped in. Carter has the flight attendant gripped on his lap; the contents of a dinner tray all over them.

He can't remember the name of the flight attendant. This screaming one isn't his regular. Bonnie? Connie? Lonnie? "Are you hurt?" he finally asks without a name. She stops screaming long enough to shake her head. He grips her around the waist and shifts her off Carter and into the seat next to him. "Buckle up, and please try to stay calm."

"Reed!"

Reed's head whips back to see Nic standing in the now open cockpit doorway. Beyond him, both pilots are passed out over the controls. Holy shit. He turns back to look down the cabin. Cara is leaning over, her eyes locked on the sight. That's his girl. She's not a screamer. He trained that shit right out of her, but she most definitely isn't breathing, either. Her eyes are wide and her lips are turning blue. He turns back to see Nic pulling the pilots away from the controls.

"Reed, stop gawking and help me!" Nic demands.

The sound of Nic's shout startles him forward. He reaches the doorframe as Nic is yanking a comatose pilot out of his seat. He quickly motions to the empty dinner trays on the jump seat as he crawls into the now vacated pilot's chair.

It takes a moment for Reed to comprehend Nic's direction. And then it clicks. Calmly, he turns back to Carter and crew and inquires, "Have any of you eaten dinner yet?" Carter motions to the food all over him before shaking his head as a response. "Good. I wouldn't recommend the selection this evening." Turning to Nic, who is flipping switches on the control panel, he asks, "Poison?"

"Probably, but they're still breathing. Get this other pilot out of here and see if Carter can rouse them and make them vomit. Do you have any medical supplies on board?"

Reed is staring blanking at Nic because he has no clue. Thank God, the flight attendant finally decides to do her job. She tells them there are a defibrillator and IV for fluids on board.

Nic looks back at Carter as the plane is leveling off. "Carter, we're stable. Get to work on these two." He's giving Carter detail instructions on the medical care for the pilots and the only thing Reed can do is stand stock still with one hand on the captains' chair. "Reed! Look alive, please, and get into the other chair."

He doesn't hesitate at Nic's command, climbing in and buckling up.

"Cara! Get over here!" Nic continues barking.

Her eyes are still wide while she steps over the two pilots in the aisle to get to the cockpit.

Calming his voice, Nic changes tactics. "Baby, clean the trays from the jump seat, dump the contents, wash your hands, come back, sit and buckle up."

Following her husband's instructions, Cara makes it back inside the cockpit and into the small seat. She doesn't look at Nic, though, her eyes are locked on him. Reed reaches one hand back to her and she entwines her fingers into his.

With her warmth starting to reach him, Reed finally focuses. He takes a big breath and asks, "So, Nic, you have a plan?"

Giving him a double take, Nic let's the killer smile loose. "I'm going to fly us to Cleveland."

Reed stops himself just as the words, you can fly a jet, are about to rip from his mouth. Of course Nic can fly a jet. He kills, he sings, he can leap tall buildings in a single bound. Fucking Superman in a golden god's facade. He decides to take an alternate approach. "Now we know there isn't anything you can't do besides control your wife. But, can you get us on the ground?"

Nic glares at him before asking, "Do you have Wi-Fi on here?"

"Of course."

Leaning his head back to his wife, Nic commands, "Get Sasha on the phone for me." Cara's lips are returning to their natural color as she digs out her phone from the pocket of her jeans. While she's dialing, Nic's attention turns back to him. "Reed, do you think you and my wife can do something productive, like start an investigation as to who had access to the food service?"

Cara starts giggling as she hands her phone to Nic. Jerking her finger towards her husband, she blandly asks Reed, "Did you think it was always easy for me living with Mr. Cockypants and the Brilliant Bastard he's on the phone with?"

Finally being able to relinquish a smile in this otherwise disaster, Reed responds, "You must have held your own, sweetheart. You should be very proud." He squeezes her hand with affection before letting go and getting to work.

Nic has placed the plane back on course and turned on the autopilot while he waits for Sasha to research the schematics on the model jet. Cara and Reed have their heads over his tablet as they Facetime with his office. Apparently, the dinners were placed on the jet before take off from the government hangar at Dulles, where Reed keeps the jet. It was never restocked in Berlin. His staff is scrambling to identify how the meals were tainted, when and by whom.

Meanwhile, Sasha's voice brings him back, "Have you told Cara and Reed about Jake yet?"

"No, I was just about to when the pilots keeled over. You, have come out of the closet, though." He tells Sasha how Reed trashed an office after the news.

"How pleasant." Sasha deadpans.

Snickering, he asks, "Has Jake offered anything?"

"No, but he and Jinx are sequestered in your bedroom. I can hear yelling from here."

Averting his head from Cara and Reed, he offers, "So our guess Jake never knew who Jinx and Cara are and who they worked for stands? And Jinx never knew exactly what Jake does is an accurate assumption?"

"Based on the contention coming from your room, that's my supposition." There is silence from the other end of the phone before Sasha adds, "Nic, land the plane safely before you tell Reed. Sounds like he might put a bullet in you when he finds out."

"I will take that under serious advisement. Now, feed me the details on the jet."

Getting up from the jump seat, Cara shuts the door to the cockpit. Both pilots have not been revived. Their vitals are stable but they appear to be heavily sedated. The suspicion is the dinner may have been laced with Rohypnol, the date rape drug. Carter assures her he has it under control. Nic is still on the phone with Sasha and Reed looks like he's just finishing a call with the FAA.

In the military this is called a Charlie Foxtrot. A cluster fuck. For the second time today, her life has almost been wiped out. This time they were willing to take down a whole plane to do it. But was she the only target? If the food trays were the culprits, how could they know Reed and crew wouldn't have consume them on the way to Berlin? It was an overnight flight taken late in the evening, so they ate the breakfast aboard on the way over, but the dinner could have been eaten. And how could they know she would be on board on the way back? And Nic?

Carter is trying to extrapolate what the pilots did and consumed while they were waiting in Berlin. It's very possible the dinner trays are not tainted. They will be tested after they land. Tracking the pilots' movements on the ground is proving difficult without their participation.

Her eyes lock on her husband. The man of the hour. She isn't surprised he can fly a jet. She's learned to take in all of his and Sasha's natural and learned talents over the years. Their faculties have seeped into her life in subtle but piercing ways. She's had to work hard to keep up with them. She isn't joking when she says living with Moody and Broody hasn't always been easy. They are demanding and controlling.

Her eyes shift to Reed. He is demanding and controlling as well. What's wrong with her that she has wrapped her life around all these alpha men? More importantly, she has persevered and thrived with them. Nic and Sasha tease her relentlessly, but Reed has admitted she can give as good as she gets. Which is quite true. They may push her around, but they certainly don't get past her.

Speaking of attempting to get one past her, Nic was just about to admit to the Jake connection when the plane plummeted. Jake Bishop is a man of mystery and Jinx's husband. He came on the scene a few months after she met Nic, and just after they started living together. Jinx suddenly had a boyfriend, or at least a guy she was fucking on a regular basis. Which for Jinx, constitutes a boyfriend.

She has told Nic all about the porn terrors of living with Jinx and how she cohabitated with Reed, instead. She never omitted the details of their interpersonal relationships. She only lied about where they worked. She told him Reed was a government employee while Jinx worked for the Defense Department. She and Jinx were friends through a roommate ad, and she and Reed were friends in college. Years ago, when Reed's position as Deputy Director of the CIA became public, she only said he was promoted to the position from outside the agency.

She feels a tug on her ponytail and snaps out of her thoughts. "C, Please come back from wherever you are. You're zoning out, again." Reed is in her face. Her hair wrapped around his hand. He's looking at her with concern.

Nic pipes up from the left side chief pilot position, where he's looking forward and off the phone. "Baby, how come you let your boyfriend snap you out of your petit mal seizures but not me?"

"They are not seizures! In my mind palace! And…I was thinking about Jake." She waits to see Nic cringe before offering, "In specific about how I used to live with Reed to get away from Jinx and her sexual escapades." This gets a chuckle from Reed before Cara adds, "Well, mostly I lived with Reed unless he was getting laid, too. Then, I was homeless."

"Hey, I always tried to get laid elsewhere when I could. I thought it was the best I could do, leave you in peace at my apartment. Don't I get credit for that?" Reed offers.

Cara pats his hand "Yes, you get points for that, but you also had to make sure I had rest. I was your best agent, so the sentiment is deluded."

"Wait, you had dates and got laid?" Nic stops to ask.

Reed's body jerks in the co pilot chair. "What the hell…you think I'm some sort of eunuch? C. WAS. NOT. MY. GIRLFRIEND! I'm not sure when you will finally get that straight inside your thick, GERMAN, skull. She makes a hell of a wingman, though."

"You helped him get laid?!" Nic announces a little too loudly for the tight quarters they're in.

Very indignantly Cara puts her chin up towards her husband, "I'm an awesome wingman. Pity, you will never find that out."

Just when he thought they were going to get the Jake story they are digressing again. Reed takes a big breath, amazed by the emotional roller coaster he's on. He lowers his voice explaining how Cara is amazing in a bar full of beautiful women. He would pick one out, and she would lay it on thick. Whether it's a break up scene with him, leaving Reed broken hearted and looking for a sympathetic heart, or the jealous past lover pining for the great lay he was. She had a million tricks up her sleeve. Cara always knew exactly what was going to get the girl practically undressing for him. When he thinks back, it's another illumination for him.

Before Nic can make some snide comment about needing assistance to get laid, Reed adds the circumstances around this. He refused to date anyone at work. No one, any way, shape, or form related to the government. Shit like that comes back and bites everyone in the ass, especially as he climbed within the Agency. So, he and Cara would get out of Dodge and go trolling where no one knew them. He was looking for a simple one nighter, quick, safe and fulfilling.

Nic ponders Reed's admission, and then his light bulb comes on. "Cara, was Reed your wingman? Did you go trolling too?"

Reed can't contain his mocking laughter. Cara sneers at him before responding to her husband. "First of all, I never needed a wingman to get laid. Second…I'm not comfortable with the direction of this conversation. Let's get back to the Jake story, please."

"Answer the question, baby." Nic commands.

Cara looks to Reed before answering, wondering if he's going to sell her out or not. "No, mostly, no."

Reed decides to out her. "C doesn't need sexual activity in her life. She could've been a nun."

"Really?! YOU don't need sex?! That's breaking news to me." Nic says way to loudly, again.

"This is why I don't like the direction of this conversation. Jake. Please, tell us about Jake." Cara tries.

Reed has to drag this out. If he wasn't in a state of desperation already, he needs to make matters worse for himself. "Wait, are you saying you two have an active sex life?"

"ACTIVE?! My wife is insatiable!" Nic is practically screaming by this point, his voice reverberating around the cockpit.

Cara is banging her head on the fuselage. "Nic, please, TMI, TMI!" She raises her head to look at him. Reed's jaw is hanging open. Nic is obviously fuming, arms folded across his chest, hands off the controls. She snaps Reed's jaw up, while giving the hairy eyeball to her husband. "Nic, this is not relevant, and we need to hear about Jake. You can have an intimate discussion about our sex life with Jinx. She is the one who hears the details. Not Reed."

Letting the news sink in before he nods, Nic seems appealed until he adds, "But ah contraire, our sex life is what started this whole Jake story."

Reed has to interrupt. He's going to ride this coaster even if it kills him, because this is not how he has ever envisioned Cara, or understood about her relationship with Nic. "What did you mean when you said 'mostly no' to getting laid?" He's staring down Cara as he asks.

Cara stares back at him, blankly. "Um, I didn't really share your 'no sleeping with anyone that works for the government' mantra. When Jinx and I would go out without you, I might have taken a boy, here and there, home with me." Cara raises her brows at him. He's speechless, so she adds as she narrows her eyes at him, "I'm no nun, Connor."

Nic shouts, "Amen to that!"

"Wait, what do you mean our sex life started this?" Cara pokes at her husband.

CHAPTER 23

HE WAS SERIOUSLY HOPING TO push off this Jake discussion until he either landed the plane, or one of the pilots could take over. They have left him in a precarious position. If he admits what's really going on, there is a very good chance Reed will kill him in a fit of rage, and they will all die when he can't land the aircraft. Giving Reed a sidelong glance, Nic inquires nicely, "If I tell you two this story, you have to promise to not hurt me until we land. Then, you can kick my ass. Deal?"

The scowl on Reed's face is not helping to make him feel better. "I promise to wait to hurt you. I happen to value my life and the lives of everyone on this plane. But, on the ground, no promises."

Taking that as affirmation of an agreement, Nic considers his words. It's a long sordid story when it comes to Jake. The details will either exonerate him or indict him depending on how his wife and Reed construe them. Deciding the details are better for another time, Nic blurts out, "Jake blackmailed Sasha and I to run missions for him."

His wife's mouth drops open but it's Reed face that seals the deal. The man has turned so red, even his ears are inflamed. Turning to his wife his adds, "It happened right after the twins were born. Jake figured out who Sasha and I are. He told us if we didn't run missions for him, he would have us immediately deported and given to Interpol for criminal charges."

Now Cara's eyes are bugging out. Reed has dropped his head. Before either them says anything, Nic adds, "We thought about killing him. But...I couldn't do that to Jinx. They weren't married yet, but I couldn't leave Elijah without a father."

Reed is glaring at him, but Cara's mind is whirling. He can almost hear her connecting all the dots in her head. She leans into him and barely whispers, "All those boys weekends the three of you would take. All missions."

Nodding to her, Nic admits it started with Jake questioning him about his relationship with Cara after the sex they had on a weekend away with Jinx and Jake. "Those two heard us having loud sex from their room adjacent to us. Jake knew who I was, and he interrogated me about my intentions with you. He wanted to know why the Dark Angel of Death was carrying on with Cara Bianco." Jake made it sound like Nic was taking advantage of a poor, unsuspecting civilian. "I don't think he knew who you are. And he doesn't know about Reed from me."

To this day, neither Sasha nor Nic know who Jake really is. They have run over 30 missions for Jake in the last 15 years. Most missions were kidnap and rescues, but some were more political in nature.

"And Jinx?" Cara whispers, again.

"Based on the dissention between them right now at our house, my guess is Jake had no clue until today that you and Jinx worked CIA." Looking at Reed, he's ready to burst, but Nic must get this last part out. "After the initial six missions, Jake decided to stop blackmailing us." He inhales deeply and let's out, "He offered missions to us, instead."

"And you took them." Cara says as a statement of fact.

Exhaling for the first time since his confession, Nic admits, "Not all. We picked and chose the ones we were confident of, and the ones we thought we could make a difference." He and Sasha really wanted to contribute and help.

Eventually, they became close with Jake, and Jake wanted to be the husband and father Jinx and Elijah deserved. Without revealing too much about himself, Jake asked Nic and Sasha if they could always watch over Jinx and Elijah when he wasn't around. He wanted to propose to Jinx, and make them a family, but he would only do it if Nic and Sasha would ensure their safety.

"He married Jinx when he trusted you and Sasha to keep them protected." Cara says as a statement, again, before her head drops and she pulls the tie from her hair. It cascades around her head in beautiful waves he would give anything to run his fingers through.

●●●

Shaking her crazy hair out to bring some circulation to her brain, Cara asks, "Is it the Q&A, now?"

"WAIT, both of you. Before you go at each other, I NEED to have some questions answered, NOW!" Reed barks out actually causing her to jump. His finger is in Nic's face and she can feel his rage.

Nic backs away. "Shoot, but not literally, please."

Reed's fists clench. "You really don't know who Jake works for?"

Raising his hands like at gunpoint, Nic volunteers, "No. And trust me, Sasha and I have really tried. I can tell you we've had back up from various military units as well as black ops type personnel. There's no patterns we can find." Reed is speechless, so Nic adds, "Jake's job disappearances are teased about so much amongst our little group, Cara started to refer to him as Jack Reacher."

Reed snaps his head so hard towards her; it actually makes a clicking sound. "Why do you call him that?" He barks.

"Um, I don't know. Sasha has nicknames for everyone, and Jake didn't have one, but we always teased him about his 'walkabouts' away from home, and he's really big and mean looking. He just reminded me of the Jack Reacher character. You know, roaming around the country as a vigilante looking all disheveled and scary." She spills out as quickly as she can.

Reed shakes his head at her, scowling. "Yes, I know the fictional character, but doesn't he resemble Nic? Isn't he handsome, big and blonde?"

"Well, yeah, but he's supposed to be even bigger than Nic, the size of Jake, and the wandering thing is what jumped out at me. He hates it."

"Who hates it?" Reed demands.

She and Nic respond simultaneously, "Jake!"

Nic goes on, "He hates that we all started calling him Jack instead of Jake or just 'Reacher'. He gets all riled up about it. So, we do it more, of course."

Reed starts snapping his fingers, "Pictures, do you have a picture of him?"

Nic looks down at her phone in his hand. Flipping through her photos,

Nic finds the file from the Twins' last birthday party. He hands the device to Reed. "If you flip through, you may see some more."

Reed's swiping through the photos and stops at a couple of them. His eyes illuminate. She is watching Reed's face closely, and at one point she swears a very small smirk develops on his lips.

Suddenly, there's tension filling the area around them. Cara senses that Nic feels it too because he quietly asks, "Are there any more questions?"

When Reed looks up, his face is hard, and he appears foreboding. This is the Reed most people see, the serious, no mercy Director of the CIA with his piercing, ice blue eyes. "No more questions."

Nic hesitates, "Do you want to hit me?"

Reed gives Nic his iciest glare and speaks very slowly, enunciating each word. "No. I will say this once and once only, and you WILL concede. You or Sasha will no longer do anything for Jake EVER again. You want to work? I will put you to work. Any questions?"

"No," Nic responds immediately.

Knowing their lives depend on this, Cara grabs Reed's arm and suggests they check on Carter and the pilots. She needs to separate these two.

Reed is still glowering at Nic, but he unfastens the harness and follows her. They speak with Carter, but both pilots are passed out and belted into two seats. Carter offers how two town cars and an ambulance will be waiting for them when they arrive.

Reed pulls her to the back of the plane and the table they were seated at. He sits down with a humph sound and places her on his lap. Wrapping the seatbelt around both of them, he sits quietly.

She leans back and wraps her hand on the nape of his neck. Slowly, pulling his face down to hers, they let their foreheads touch. This is their thing. When one of them has been upset or emotional, they have always done this. It's weirdly intimate, yet perfectly innocent, and it centers them.

He breaks their connection but only to roam his eyes all over her face. He looks battered and beaten while studying her. As if all of life's answers are written on her face and in her eyes. She feels horribly guilty for the day he's had. The resignation on his face is foreign to her. Has she finally managed to fry his last nerve? Lifting her fingers to his temples, she rubs slow circles. While he still watches her closely, she whispers, "How are you feeling?"

His eyes close but he doesn't answer her. Just a sigh escapes his lips. Moving into his hairline, she works his scalp. His head tilts back but otherwise he doesn't react. After what feels like 5 minutes, he finally responds with a question. "Can you play co-pilot for a little while? I need to get some things done before we land."

She gives him a serious nod before rising from his lap. Quiet Reed is a bit scary. "I understand you need some alone time to process all of this. For what it's worth, I am sorry. And…I need to go deal with my Angel."

CHAPTER 24

NIC IS ON THE PHONE with Sasha when he hears Cara make her way back into the cockpit. She takes the copilot's seat and fastens the harness.

"Look, I'm flying." She tells him while he's listening to Sasha talk.

Interrupting his conversation, he states, "You will do nothing of the sort. Only touch what I tell you to touch."

She grabs the phone from him, but before she can say anything to Sasha, he can hear Sasha ask her if she knows anything about aviation. She cocks her head in thought before telling him, "Sash, I know the appropriate size luggage I'm supposed to bring to fit in the overhead cabins of various planes. Does that count?"

Nic rips the phone away from her and bids a farewell to Sasha. "We have about 30 minutes before I need to turn off autopilot, contact the tower, and cue into our descent and landing pattern. Are we going to 'talk' now?" He questions.

She shakes her head, unfastens the harness, locks the cockpit door and straddles his lap.

"Baby, I don't think this…" She covers his mouth with her own.

She breaks the breathless kiss to nip at his jaw, then down his throat. Unbuttoning his shirt, she kisses her way down to his abs, and his happy trail leading into his jeans.

"You don't seem as angry and disappointed as I expected once again today, or is this the third time you're surprising me with your composure?" He asks in an effort to keep his cool as his wife devours him.

"Third time's a charm." She unbuttons jeans.

"What are you doing?"

Her perfect pout disables him. "I need some skin. It's been a very draining day, and it's only going to get worse."

She wins. He unzips his jeans, before bunching his fists with her hair. A small moan escapes Cara's mouth.

She wedges herself in front of him in the tight compartment, and releases just the head of his cock from his boxers. Placing her tongue along the waistband and pulling gently at his pants, she tugs them down just enough to expose a little more skin. His erection is straining against the effort of being constricted. She takes pity, and pulls his jeans down further, just enough for his cock to be freed. Running her tongue from the base to the tip, he inhales sharply.

She delivers those long licks paying special attention to the underside of the head, wrapping her tongue and mouth slowly around and sucking only there. She teases him, licking and sucking in small sections wanting him to squirm. His wife is so very talented at this.

His hands give her a push, but she resists. "Are you going to lie to me anymore, Nic?" She whispers as she continues her deliberate assault of his manhood.

"Is that what this is? My punishment?" He softly moans. He needs to misbehave more often. Cara's teeth nip at his sensitive nerve endings. He shudders from the pain. Damn, she always knows what he's thinking.

"This is your penance, my love. Beg me for more." Cara eyes shift up to his face with a wicked gleam.

"Cara mia, please, give me more." He pleads in a whisper.

Cara gives him just a bit more, grasping the base with her hand and slowly bringing it up and down with firm then light touches, all while keeping her mouth teasing his head.

The tension is excruciating. "Oh God, please more."

"God has nothing to do with this, Nic," but she complies and lowers her mouth leisurely down, keeping her tongue flat to let it run the ridge. She sucks a little harder until she hears his familiar soft moan. She starts to run her hands into his thighs, gradually towards his balls, massaging behind them while her mouth goes deeper. She's moving painfully slow. His legs are beginning to tremble from the pleasure and pain she's inducing.

She knows his breaking point, and he's so close. She moves her mouth with marginally more speed to give him more pleasure while making sure she still teases his head with every pass. This is torture for him, the teasing bringing all his muscles taut throughout his body. His legs are stiff to prevent her from hitting any of the controls on the plane. She only needs to speed up, suck slightly harder, and he will lose it. But she waits a little longer. It's cruel, but his pleasure will be stronger. Just when he can't take it anymore, she draws him all in and sucks hard, hitting the back of her throat.

It only takes seconds and…he can't breathe. He's sucking in air, but his body isn't processing it anymore. It's taken every ounce of energy to refrain from screaming. His body goes limp. "You're such a fucking bitch," he tells her through panting breaths as she licks her lips. "And I LOVE it." He tries to pant out again.

"I know."

Cara straddles him, again, taking his mouth passionately, and preventing him the air he so desperately needs. He finally uses one hand to pull her hair in an effort to break the kiss for oxygen. With his hand still in her hair he places small bites on her jawline. His other hand reaches under her sweater to rest on her ribcage, brushing beneath her breasts. He releases her hair and moves both hands under her sweater. He shifts deliberately over her nipples, letting the lacy bra rub against them, and watches as Cara drops her head back in pleasure.

"I know how turned on you get when you tease me. Torture is a two way street, baby." He breathes out to her while unclasping her bra and letting her breasts drop into his hands.

His fingertips continue to rub lightly, teasing her nipples until they are hard pebbles. He knows she loves this. The anticipation of a firmer pinch, and then a lighter brush will send her anywhere he needs her to go.

Cara's breathing catches but he continues by raising her sweater to place his lips on her breast. He gets the desired effect when he sees Cara cover her mouth to prevent any sounds from coming out. He lets one hand drop to her jeans and places it between her legs, rubbing lightly at first, but then firmer. Her hand goes for the button to undo them, but Nic bats her hand away. "No, baby, I'm not ready for that. Beg for it."

Cara doesn't hesitate, "Please, Nic."

He unbuttons her jeans, pulling down the zipper and letting his fingertips brush across her sensitive spot. Cara shudders just from the light touch. He pulls her jeans down further before dipping one finger into her tight sheath. She bucks from the penetration but he holds her hips firmly, preventing her from any movement.

He continues to taunt her with his fingers, bringing her so close, then backing away. Trying to move her hips closer, he pushes her back. "Say that you trust me, baby."

"Always, my love."

He pulls her closer; just enough to get two fingers in while his thumb strokes her clit. She gasps with eagerness. "Look at me, baby." Her eyes meet his instantly, and he gives her the killer smile. "I need you to watch me enjoy this as much as you are." He whispers to her right before she let's loose.

Watching Nic's pleasure distinctly written across his face, she can't contain hers anymore and grabs his head to hold him tight against her. Her hands are shaking and her mouth is open. She reaches her limit and the sounds of life around her cease to exist. Nic takes one final, long, slow swipe to send a post-climatic shudder through her.

Before Cara can process the pleasurable aftershocks, Nic is yanking one pant leg from her. He takes her wrists and moves her hands to the chair arms. He's not finished with her just yet. He grabs her ass with both hands and lifts her over his new arousal.

He gathers her hair to one side so he can place his lips by her ear. "Perfect...so perfect...it will never be anything but perfect."

Cara can't think, he feels wonderful. She lets the arms go with one hand to cradle his head to hers with it.

Nic thrusts up harder, bringing them both to a fever of pleasure. Moving his hand back under her sweater to stroke those light touches across her nipples. He knows just when she's about to shatter and lets himself go.

She giggles in his ear. "We have done that while you drove a car, but never while you flew a plane. It's a first for us." He grabs a napkin and cleans between them before carefully pulling up her panties and pants.

"You are a very wicked woman, cara mia. Proving to me once again how you love danger." It's then they both hear the buzz indicating the need to release the autopilot.

"Timing is everything." She smiles. "Do you need me now, because I have to pee."

"You always have to pee afterwards. It's your rule."

"It's a universal rule, babe."

Getting around him, she makes her way to the door. She winks at Nic before she unlocks and swings the door open.

Standing with his arms crossed in front of her is Reed, glaring. She pats her hair down, knowing it must be all over the place. The look of outrage on Reed's face is mortifying.

She pushes past him to head to the bathroom, but he grabs her arm. She whispers, "We needed some privacy to work things out."

"I'm sure you did." He leans in and actually sniffs her.

Lowering her head, she doesn't bother to answer him. He steps into the cockpit and closes the door. As she passes Carter, he puts his hand out, palm out and mouths, 'mile high'.

Cara giggles. It's become more rare for she and her husband to achieve any firsts concerning their sex life. Besides, she feels a whole lot better now.

CHAPTER 25

CARA AWAKES WITH A JOLT when the plane hits the ground with a thud. It takes her a second to recall where she is and what is happening. As it slowly fades back into her mind, she realizes both her husband and Reed have headsets on and are high fiving each other.

"We're on the ground." The sounds of clapping from the cabin can be heard as Cara states the obvious.

"C, you fell asleep. You could not have been too concerned." Reed notes while he directs Nic to the NASA Glenn Terminal at the airport. You can't miss it. There are fire trucks and ambulances in front of it.

"I was tired." She hasn't slept in days. "Sorry, I wasn't much assistance."

"It's fine, baby. We didn't need any info on overhead baggage compartment sizes." Nic leans back to smirk at her.

She takes the opportunity to squeeze his shoulder in appreciation. She never doubted he would get them safely home. Nic is a superhero that casts a long shadow.

She is still so tired, Cara doesn't even take an active role in assisting to get the two pilots off the plane and into the medics' hands. Reed and Carter do most of that while Nic confers with some other agents. This is one of the moments where hanging out with alpha men pays off. She only finds her luggage and exits the plane. Reed, of course, managed to avoid the concourse and customs for all of them. The man can truly make miracles happen.

Two town cars are empty and parked by the emergency crews. Seeing the one suited agent, 'far guard', that was on the plane with them jump into one of the cars, Cara enters the backseat of the other.

After all the macho men conferences, Carter and Reed get into the first town car. Nic approaches the driver's door on the town car she is sitting in. Once seated, he peers over to her. She makes no acknowledge but to open her door, walk out and approach Reed's car.

"Get out, Carter. I need to talk with Reed on the ride there." She's tugging on his arm, pulling him out of the front seat.

Carter is horrified. "You want me to ride alone with Mean Man?"

"Yes, and I promise he won't bite." She assures as he rises from the seat and exits the vehicle with Cara still dragging him.

She approaches the other town car and pushes Carter in. "Hop in, big boy." After he's seated next to Nic she adds, "Oh…I promised Mean Man wouldn't bite, but I didn't say anything about kicking and scratching," She slams his door shut to Carter's protests. She can hear Nic's laughter through the windows while she opens the back door of Reed's car and climbs in.

When they're on their way, Cara decides to commence. "Um, there are some things you need to know before we get to my house."

"About?" Reed asks without looking at her.

"Mostly about Sasha."

Reed nods slowly, turning his head towards her. "Oh, I thought we were going to have the 'what the hell you were doing in the cockpit earlier' discussion." Cara immediately turns a bright shade of red. "And judging by your new skin tone, I was correct in my assumption."

"I thought we were quiet." Cara whispers, embarrassed.

"You were quiet, way too quiet for a couple looking to have a fight in private, C. Nic wasn't exaggerating about your sex life. Why would you never talk about that with me? Maybe not the details, but you kept your level of intimacy with Nic totally off the table."

Cara, feeling a little less embarrassed and a little more defiant, retorts, "After what happened in Geneva, you expected me to freely discuss my raging sex life with Nic? You and I went almost four months without speaking to each other after Geneva."

She is fairly certain the topic of sex, who's getting it, and with whom, and how often, is not open game since they have never discussed what happened in Geneva. She is well aware he's getting laid, but no offers of frequency and detail. He's never shared any of that. Why in the hell does he believe she should divulge? "If you want the sordid, sensual and erotic details of my sex life, you need to man up and discuss Geneva." She composes herself and states, "Is that what you want to do?" This shuts Reed down completely. He stares out his window ignoring her. There, she threw it out for discussion. When he's ready, she WILL go there with him.

Reed sits in his thoughts. Geneva. Fucking Geneva. Switzerland was the biggest disaster of his life, and another fucking Illumination. He makes yet an additional attempt to get his emotions under control as the roller coaster they are on careens and banks hard to the left.

A few moments pass before he turns back to Cara calmly, "Tell me about Sasha."

Cara releases the tension she's been holding in her shoulders and starts, "Sasha is…different. Do you remember any photos of him?"

"No, he was always an enigma." They had photos, but one never looked like the other. Golov could transform himself very easily. The Agency always feared him the most, because they wouldn't see him coming.

"Well, in a way, he's still a mystery." Cara confirms.

She struggles to describe her brother in law. "He is many things and none at all. There's Uncle Sasha, who spends hours with my children on a daily basis. He was always able to gauge what the kids wanted to do, and how they wanted to play. He was their more physical clown and running around partner when they were toddlers, to the patient man who introduced art projects and the alphabet, to the man who developed his own, individual, bond to each child."

Her eyes go soft as she reflects, "Whereas Nic and I would group our children as the 'twins', Uncle Sasha entertained each child, specifically. With Mia, he cultivated her love of hands on projects. Finger-painting, tie-dyes, macaroni necklaces, anything Mia wanted to make. Sasha, of course, would wear whatever she made him. That escalated to elaborate artwork she would draw on all his clothes with fabric paint, even bejeweling jackets of his. They would work on the craft together as part of their bonding.

"Uncle Sasha, with Max, was the roughhouser. He had him shooting baskets by three. Sasha was the one who investigated all of the sports options in town, made sure to sign Max up, and took him to all of his games. If the team needed a coach or assistant coach, it was Uncle Sasha that volunteered, first. I would spy him researching all of the rules and strategies for each sport. As Max grew older, the two of them became more partners in crime. Sasha allowing Max more freedom to act like a typical boy."

Reed always prided himself on having a great relationship with her children. He wasn't local, but Reed did see them at least 5 times a year and for two weeks in the summer when they would vacation together. He loves those kids, but envy for Sasha is adding to the multitude of emotions he's feeling. The Widow Maker, of all people, was privileged to see all their firsts.

Rationally, he now understands the close relationship Sasha really had with Nic, but still, it chafes his ass he was left out. Especially, more recently, in the last couple of years, when he's been busier, and the kids have been busier with activities. Come to think of it, it's been at least 6 months since he's seen them.

He's shaken from his jealousy and regret as Cara continues, "Although it was both Sasha and Nic that introduced music to the twins, it was Uncle Sasha spending endless hours with the instruments. He always made learning to play something fun, and they excelled under his tutelage.

"In a lot of ways, Max and Mia have a real relationship with Sasha separate from us. They have TV shows they only watch together, interests they only explore together, favorite places to dine together, the list is endless."

She is not even intimating Uncle Reed could have done more, and yet, that's how he's feeling. Reed won't project his feelings on her, but he can't prevent the words slipping from his mouth. "Sounds to me like Uncle Sasha has spoiled your children."

"Incredibly spoiled them!" Not the reaction he was expecting. "Nic and I, well, we're their parents. It's a role we sometimes feel slighted in, but a role we know we have to perform. We're the ones that play hardball with them, the disciplinarians." Cara points out.

Reaching over to entwine her fingers with his, she whispers, "Then… there's *my* Sasha."

Cara's Sasha? He inhales sharply without consideration for her. Wasn't it painful enough to share her with her husband all these years? To think he lost her to even another man is devastating.

Sensing his distress, she squeezes his hand, "For me...Sasha is the man who always knew when I was at my wit's end. When I was overwhelmed with work, it was Sasha that saved the day by going grocery shopping or cooking dinner. He would help me around the house with anything I needed done. He would even take the kids to run errands. A task I would avoid like the plague! Sasha never complained, though. Everything he did always came with a small smile and with love."

Reed is very uncomfortable with the direction this is going in. "Just how close are you and Sasha?"

"I love and adore him. Honestly, I don't know what I would have done all these years without him." Cara admits.

"So, you two have a relationship more like you and me?" He inquires with hesitation, not convinced he truly wants the answer. He turns his head to stare back out the car window because he can't look at her.

Her fingertips make contact with his chin and gently turn him to face her. Shaking her head slowly, she makes direct eye contact when she replies, "Sasha is like a brother to me. You and I...not the same."

Why is he relieved by that? Not an emotion he wants to explore with everything else going on. Instead, he lowers his voice and asks, "What does he look like?"

Reaching into her tote bag, Cara pulls out her phone and finds her favorite photo of Sasha with her children. "They were five years old on the morning of their first day of kindergarten." She turns the photo towards him. He can see each child under Sasha's arms and a broad, proud smile on his face. "It's his eyes that have endeared me to this picture. His eyes tell the real story. They are filled with fear, trepidation and loss."

She expands the photo, so the picture is a close up of Sasha's face. "We dropped the kids off at school for their first day, together, and sat on the couch when we got back. We didn't even communicate. I silently cried while Sasha held my hand." She takes a sharp breath before adding with a chuckle, "Nic danced all day long, thrilled the kids wouldn't be underfoot for 6 hours, five days a week."

Studying the photo while Cara seems lost in mixed memories, Reed can see what she means by his eyes. They are sad, but filled with love. It isn't the only thing he notices, though. "He's handsome."

"Very."

"Like Nic, he doesn't look Russian." Reed observes.

Cara takes the photo back and studies it. "All these years and I've never really considered neither man looks Russian. Sasha is more Mediterranean in his coloring, except for his eyes. He has the most captivating indigo blue eyes." She goes back into thought before she adds, "I don't know his history, but you can see how he can pass himself off as Spanish, Italian, Lebanese, even Iraqi. He can be anyone from anywhere."

He has so many questions; he doesn't know where to start. "Does he live with you?"

"Most of the time, but he keeps an apartment just outside our neighborhood. I think he needs alone time, occasionally. When the kids were young, Sasha would entertain them at the house while Nic and I would utilize his apartment to fool around," she giggles, "Sometimes, we still do. We tell the kids we need to go out of town for work, and then spend the night alone at Sasha's. The privacy is VERY rewarding."

Trying to shake the image of any of that from his mind, he redirects with, "Does Sasha date?"

She releases his hand and shrugs. "You and he have more in common there. I believe he trolls outside our general area. Nic and I have run into him on dates, but he never gets serious with anyone. I think he just gets laid. He's a fuck boy like you."

"Does he work at all, or just raise your children?" Reed jabs after the last comment.

Cara gives him her hairy eyeball before softening. "Sasha is both mother and father to my children most times. After they started school though, Nic recruited him into the business. Sasha is Nic's right hand man, now. He runs the crews and does a lot of the daily fieldwork required. The crews love him. They see Nic as the 'boss man' and Sasha, one of their own. It works out well. We don't normally have him interact with the clients. Nic and I maintain those relationships."

He is staring at Cara. His mind is racing with questions, some of which he doesn't want to ask.

Sensing his hesitation, Cara offers, "Sasha is many, many things to me, but the one thing he is not, is the Notorious Alexander Golov. As soon as I met Sasha, I assumed he was Golov. I answered our front door looking like a whale at nine months pregnant. He didn't even look at my face. He just stared at my belly and his whole body softened. Nic wasn't home so I invited him in. This Golov was no monster."

"I can't believe you didn't grab a sidearm!" Reed blurts.

Cara waves him off, "Golov didn't have an evil thread in his body with me. His body language was gracious and accommodating."

"Still! It's not like you to be so vulnerable." Reed has to stop himself and remember this was years ago. And he's grappling with Cara's so called "intuition" at the moment, as well.

Before Reed can calm himself, she gets more hostile and states, "Connor! Sasha has had the patience and fortitude of a saint with ME and my children. He has given all of his love to us, unconditionally."

In other words, Sasha deals with her, and loves her anyway. Cara is not your average homemaker and soccer mom. He, of all people, knows this. The woman is a demon. His thoughts turn quickly, though, as a slow realization creeps into Reed's mind. It was easy for them to forget the past and live with the secrets, because they weren't secrets. Their collective past was the anomaly. Their lives, all these years together as a family, is their truth.

For Reed, it's a tough pill of truth to swallow, but it finally makes sense. Her motive. Again, as if she can read his distress, Cara places her hands gently to each side of his face, and whispers, "Can you ever forgive me, Connor, for keeping Sasha from you?"

Reed studies her and decides it's time to call her out. "C, I know you better than you know yourself. You didn't tell me about Sasha because you *were* keeping him from me. You were hoarding him for yourself."

She bows her head to him. "You always figure out my motives." If Cara told him, he would taken Sasha from her. And eventually, Nic would follow. She knew they missed being in the field. And she knew how much Reed respected their skills. With Sasha concealed, the past could stay in the past, and they could continue to live their ideal, happy, never talk about missions lives.

Cara inhales hard, trying to control a sob. "Everything has changed today, Connor. My life won't be the same going forward. A large part of me will miss that. I'm afraid my happily ever after will end."

Pulling her in for a firm hug, Reed holds her against his chest. "You looked the other way with Jake on purpose, too. If you anted up, and admitted the truth to yourself, they would have ran more missions for him. You never wanted them working and risking their lives for Jake… or for me."

Reed can feel her nod against his chest. He runs one hand down her hair. He wants desperately to give her courage. She is going to need it, because he's prepared to send her world spiraling out of her Land of Denial fairy tale. Everything hasn't changed completely, yet. There's one more monumental reveal.

Still holding her to comfort, Reed picks her phone back up to study the photo. Finally, he questions, "I can't tell from this picture, because it's a head shot, but is Sasha big and buff like Nic?"

"Sasha and Nic work out all the time. He's slightly shorter than Nic but," Cara gives Reed the once over before finishing, "He's more your height and weight. About six foot two and built like you."

Running her hands up his chest, she moves one down his arm feeling his shoulders and biceps. She knows he's wondering if he could take Sasha in a fight. She's accessing him. She lets her hand skim back down his chest while she considers if he could win. She pinches his nipple and adds quietly, "My money is on you."

"Ouch, but thanks. Glad to know you still have some faith in me."

She grabs him by the nape and yanks his face to hers. "Always, sweetheart, my faith in you never wanes. Feel free to question my motives, but never question my faith." Looking all over his face for a few moments, she admits, "I take full responsibility for being a selfish bitch and keeping Sasha hidden, but the decision had nothing to do with a lack of trust in you."

"That's why you called me, first." Reed watches her shrug. Honestly, he hadn't even thought to ask Cara if she discussed it with Nic when she came to Langley. His natural inclination was to go into protection mode with her. He's done it so often, and for so long, it is second nature. He understands why Cara's kneejerk reaction to feeling threatened was to reach out to him on instinct. But Nic knew to question her. He knew enough to go after her, despite her silence. Illumination.

For the second time after Cara directly disobeyed one of Reed's orders, it was Nic that saved her. Reed still can't believe he never connected the clues until now. She's always been teased about her seizures, but damn, the fucking truth is going to break her.

Cara pulls Reed from his deep thoughts. "We're almost home. We need to talk about one more thing before we arrive. Jake. You know who he is." His lips twitch and it's all she needs for a confirmation. "Don't tell me. I leave this in your hands. But, I do need to explain Jake's position in my family."

He cocks his head for her to continue. "Jake has become part of our little Cleveland clique. His son, Elijah, is always at my home. He's Mia's best friend, and very close to both Max and Sasha. Sasha has sort of the same role in Elijah's life as he does with my kids to a certain extent.

"Jake is married to Jinx, and you know we are each other's support system here. We are closer now than when we worked for you. And although Jake is gone a lot, when he is home, he's very present in our lives. He's also developed a real friendship with Nic and Sasha. I suspect the fact they did run missions together fueled their trust in one another. Just like soldiers do within their platoons. Nothing is going to change that, Reed. Nic promised you he wouldn't work for Jake anymore, but he will be Jake's friend."

Ah, Jake. Antagonizing Jake is going to be more fun than Reed has had in awhile. It's the only confrontation he's looking forward to. "I understand that, C. I could see the respect Nic holds for him."

She lets a big smile take over her face before winking at him. "In conclusion…you're about to walk into enemy territory. I think you know that already. But like always, and I mean ALWAYS, I have your back, sweetheart." Cara waits for him to respond, but instead he pulls her in for a tighter hug. Just then the vehicle enters the driveway.

Reed releases her and looks towards the garage where one door is wide open. Standing with an umbrella is a man wearing a T-shirt saying, 'Fuck, Fuck, Fuckity, Fuck' and jeans decorated with painted skulls, demons, and pentagrams. His long peppered gray hair is loose, hanging halfway down his neck, and partially covering a face with 5-day beard growth on it. His arms are covered in dark hair. Same hair is pushing its way out of his collar. He looks like a vagrant. He doesn't resemble the photo, at all.

"Ahh…Sasha's sporting a halfway decent look this evening." Cara muses.

"This is decent?" Reed is horrified.

"For Sasha, absolutely."

CHAPTER 26

NIC BOLTS OUT OF HIS town car with their luggage in hand. He greets Sasha quickly, speaking a few words. Sasha grabs Nic's shoulder in a display of affection before Nic walks into the house. Making his way to Cara's side of the car with the umbrella, Sasha opens the door for her.

"Vizzini, so nice to have you home." He greets. She gets out, staying under the cover of Sasha's umbrella, but manages to punch him in the chest for the jab. Sasha grabs her with his free hand and pulls her into a hug. "You gave me a scare there, Ms. Reflex. You will not do that again, capice?"

"Sash, please, don't add to my list of overprotective men. I'm fine, and we have a lot of work ahead of us."

Sasha releases her from the hug but pulls her arm towards him so he can whisper in her ear. "I heard you knew, all along. I can never thank you enough."

Cara leans closer to him and places her cheek against his. "I should be thanking you for everything you've done for me and the kids. Please, never forget that, and let's not speak of it again."

She runs his hair away from his face and behind his ears. They stay looking at each other in understanding for a moment. With Sasha and his emotions, less is more. Cara has learned to refrain from any demonstrative displays of affection with him. He carries an underlying anguish. She can feel his love for them, always, but there is a deep pain beneath it. She suspects it has something to do with the assignment in England Nic spoke of when Sasha was young. Any answers she would like to acquire on the subject will need to be drawn out of Broodyland, carefully.

She leans back into the car where Reed is picking up his belongings, and eavesdropping on their conversation. "You need any help there, sweetheart?"

Reed gives her a dirty look before opening his door and walking out of the car. Cara places her arm in Sasha's, and he strolls them towards the cover of the garage. The steady gentle rain a welcomed constant of Ohio's spring. When Reed reaches them, she decides introductions are in order.

While Sasha is folding the umbrella, Cara announces, "Director Connor Reed, I would like to introduce you to Sasha Andre." There's no sound and no movement; the two men only stare at one another. Cara lets it go about ten seconds. "For God's sake just shake hands and stop being assholes. You can swing your dicks later."

"Nice mouth, Vizzini!" Sasha calls out.

"Says the man wearing that T–shirt!" Cara calls back, pointing at his chest.

Reed can't control himself and starts chuckling. "Did he just call you Vizzini? Like from the <u>Princess Bride</u>, the little Sicilian guy that kidnaps Buttercup?"

She nods unhappily while Sasha breaks out into laughter. A rare display.

"Now, that's very funny." Reed continues, still smiling, "And something else you haven't shared with me."

"Shut up, Reed. I guarantee you Broody will have a biting nickname for you by the end of the night. Now shake or I'm kicking some ass." She announces.

Reed reaches out with his hand and Sasha doesn't hesitate. They shake, but it's quick, borderline cordial.

The door leading to the house opens and Nic leans his head out. "Have they started fighting yet? We've commenced the betting in here on when and who wins."

Reed answers him, "Is there a line on 'Vizzini' kicking both of our butts, because she just threatened it?"

Nic's face falls. "I hadn't considered that scenario. Shit, this is going to mess up the wagers," He closes the door, going back inside behind it.

All three of them are smiling when Cara turns very serious and addresses Sasha, "I rode separately here from Nic, so I didn't get any updates. Tell me what the kids know so far."

Sasha turns serious as well as he offers, "It was difficult to keep everything from them. They're smart kids. They know they were pulled from school. They know the FBI has the house surrounded and they can't leave. Max has a great fantasy going that you and Nic made your money drug running and have been caught. Max thought that was 'awesome'. Mia, on the other hand, is convinced your Sicilian ties finally caught up to us, and the FBI is in take down mode for your organized crime connections."

"Sasha, I'm seeing a pattern here." Cara says with disgust.

"They're your children, what can I say? They think the worst of you." He smirks at her before admitting he was just teasing. "Remember, they are teenagers, and the idea of their parents going all gangsta is far more exciting to them than the truth will be." Sasha assures, "The only thing I told them was their parents were not being arrested for any crimes. They were sorely disappointed."

Reed snickers at this admission. Cara feigns a glare at him for laughing about her children. "Okay, let's get in there and get this over with." She starts for the door.

Reed stops her for a moment, "Are you expecting either Sasha or I to be a part of this discussion?"

She assumed only she and Nic would. "No. Why?"

Addressing Sasha, Reed inquires very formally, "This would be a good time for you and me to have a little conversation. Get to know each other?"

Sasha replies in his usual deadpan, "I expected it. We can go to the Music room downstairs. It's soundproof."

With this, Cara rushes to the front door. Jogging into the kitchen, she finds Nic at the table with Max and Mia running numbers on some paper. "Are you guys odds making?" They all look up and nod affirmative. She offers how the two men are going to talk in the Music room as she enters the kitchen.

"That changes everything," Nic states with disgust while he rips the paper he's working on with the kids into shreds. Max and Mia get up to greet Reed.

Reed envelops Mia in a big hug, "It's been too long, sweetheart. You're growing more beautiful all the time," he says really meaning it.

"Thank-you, Uncle Reed." Mia responds graciously.

"Does that get me your bet in the fight?" Reed pokes her.

Mia leans over to her Uncle Sasha and embraces him with one arm, "I have to give Uncle Sasha my money, Uncle Reed, you understand, don't you?" All while she winks at Reed and motions she really has her money on him.

Sasha leans into Reed and whispers, "Master manipulator like her mother."

"Yes, I see that." Reed confirms.

Mia pulls her Uncle Sasha's hair reminding him, "You promised to let me braid your hair later." Then she winks again at Reed and whispers, "That should help emasculate him enough so I get the assist."

Sasha leans back into Reed, "Did I mention manipulator? How about cruel?"

Max approaches Reed while Mia is still in Sasha's embrace. He places his hand out to shake, but Reed grabs it and yanks Max in for a firm hug. Cara's heart swells. It's such a thrill for him to see and spend time with her children. He has always loved them. He didn't get to see them as often, but knows he cherished the time he did have. They have called him Uncle Reed since they could talk, and as she glances at Sasha, she can appreciate how easy it is to really see them as uncles.

As he pulls Max away, Reed looks closely at the young man, "Max, has anyone told you…you're looking more like your mother, but with your father's coloring?" Looking over at Cara, he adds, "I see much more of you in him now that Max is maturing."

"Uncle Reed, are you saying I look like a girl? Dad, my money is definitely on Sasha," Max calls out.

Reed pulls him back for another hug, whispering loudly in his ear so everyone can hear, "No, I'm saying your mother looks like a boy."

This comment gets all four of them laughing and a giggle from Nic. Cara can only scowl at her boyfriend, which makes them laugh even harder.

Pulling both of her children away from the two men, Cara points them back to the kitchen table to be seated. She turns to Sasha and Reed and motions them towards the kitchen island. "Kids, pay attention, this is tonight's admission number one." Turning back to the two men, she demands they surrender every weapon they are carrying onto the counter. She wants a clean and fair fight. "Do it!"

Both men look at each other and shrug, deciding that's only fair. Reed removes his suit jacket to reveal a black snakeskin holster.

She jumps at him. "OH MY GOD, you did go see Olaf, you dog, and he gave you this!" Cara exclaims touching the snakeskin leather on the holster. Even Sasha reaches to admire the holster.

Now Nic is hysterically laughing. "Oh goody, Reed has a new boyfriend! And we're going to get a lot of swag!"

Reed growls at him, "Of course I went to see Olaf. You didn't think I was going to miss the opportunity to make that connection, PROFESSIONALLY, Nic."

Sasha is still admiring the holster. Nic decides to tease some more. "Sash, don't sweat it, Olaf gave me two, one's for you. Um, he wanted you to have it. Something about how he *owes* you? Care to elaborate?"

Sasha stops fondling the holster and flips Nic the bird behind Cara's back so the kids don't see.

"You boys don't fight over Olaf, too." Nic continues tormenting. Now they both flip Nic off so the kids do see.

"That's enough," Cara injects. "Back to work, guys, lay it out, come on."

Reed takes the holster off and Sasha reaches behind him to pull a semi-automatic from the back of his T-shirt. They both stand there like they're done.

"Really, have you both forgotten who I am? Reed, pants, left leg, now. Sasha, right leg and in your waist band." Both of them look slightly defeated as they locate and surrender the additional weapons. The counter is beginning to clutter. "Boots off. Sasha you have a knife in one and a small revolver in the other. Reed, the .22 and a poison dart." Cara looks to her children as the men remove their boots; their eyes have grown wider. Turning back to the guys, she can see them standing, shoeless, looking emotionally naked. "Nic, did I miss anything?"

Nic glances over quickly, as if he wasn't paying attention earlier, and narrows his eyes for a moment, "Sasha, switchblade left pocket. Reed has a garrote inside his waistband, otherwise, they're clean."

"Gentlemen?" Cara cautions them.

While they remove the final accouterments, Nic adds "If either one of you damages anything in the Music room or the house in the process, I will personally kick both your asses. And you know I'm capable of doing it. I've already calculated the odds in my favor." At this statement, Max and Mia grow more solemn. "Now, go have fun, gentlemen."

"Oh, and Sasha, can you please give Reed a tour of the lower level before you hurt each other? I can conclude the tour later. Thanks." Cara adds and walks to the table to take a seat.

Both men look at each other for a moment before Sasha gives Reed the head motion to go. They start down the long hallway and Sasha says very politely, but loudly, "Director Reed, on your right is the Great room, commonly known as a living room. To your left is the butler's pantry and entrance to the formal dining room. We will be utilizing the front stairwell system to gain access to the lower level." Both men can hear the four of them in the kitchen giggling.

Sasha stops talking when they hit the stairs. He walks down them, quietly, heading towards the large recreation room with kitchen, bar and billiards table. He gets behind the bar and pulls a chilled bottle of Chopin Vodka from the cooler and two shots glasses. He then leads Reed to another room and opens the door to reveal a small theater set up.

After he feels Reed has had ample viewing time, he closes the door and continues silently to another door to reveal a large bedroom with attached bathroom. Again, when he feels Reed has seen enough, he shuts the door and moves around to another section of the lower level. He brings Reed into Nic's office with the tables and boards. He walks him through it, and then back out.

Sasha stops at an open door leading to the beautiful room with all kinds of musical instruments laid out. There's a drum set, electric guitars, acoustic guitars, a cello, electric basses, a violin, an electric keyboard with a small upright piano. Several brass instruments sit on a shelf. One wall has all kinds of mixing equipment on it.

Reed enters the room with total amazement on his face. Walking around the perimeter, he begins investigating everything. Sasha, meanwhile, pulls two chairs to the center of the room. He grabs a small table and positions it next to them. He places the vodka and glasses on the table before heading over to the door and shutting it.

Reed breaks the silence. "You guys can play all of these?"

"What can I say? It's a hobby, yes." Sasha replies with no inflection.

"I'm impressed. Cara said Nic and the kids are musicians. But I had no idea." He says while waving his arms around the room.

"Music was very important to Nic. I found myself getting caught up in it with him and…I guess I had some natural talent. The twins are very gifted. They both can play several instruments and have great singing voices." He says again with no inflection, until he speaks of the children.

"They didn't get it from their mother." Reed cracks.

"No, Vizzini isn't allowed in here, and she can never sing. Her voice hurts us."

This gets a small chuckle from Reed who heads to the chairs. He starts to roll up the sleeves of his shirt while Sasha opens the bottle and pours two shots. Then Reed does something unexpected; he sits down and crosses his legs. It's a completely inoffensive position.

Sasha picks up the two shots glasses, handing one to Reed. "We are not going to fight, are we?"

Reed toasts his glass to Sasha's and downs the shot. Sasha does the same, placing his glass back on the table. He's still standing in front of Reed. "If we are not fighting, please, let me introduce myself more appropriately." He puts his hand out. "Alexander Golov, it's such an honor to finally meet you, Director Reed."

Reed smiles warmly and shakes his hand. "The honor is all mine, and please, just 'Reed', though. There's no need to fight, but you and I have much to discuss."

Sasha sits down and pours two more shots. "Nic's told me you know of Jake and what we've been doing for him."

"Yes, and we'll talk more of him later. I'm not prepared to play my hand with him...yet. All I will say on the subject is you're done working for him."

"You know who he is?" His interest has piqued.

Reed admits he does, but doesn't offer any other info. He holds no grudge against Sasha or Nic, but his business with Jake is incomplete. Reed asks Sasha if he would consider working for him in the future. "In full disclosure, I'm beside myself with envy knowing you and Nic were providing your services to Jake rather than for me. I have been a big admirer of you both for a very long time. If I hadn't been, Nic would not be here, and I would've found a way to separate he and Cara. I respected him and trusted her."

That's interesting. "And finding out my presence here?" Sasha sends out.

Reed confirms, "Water under the bridge, as they say. Cara and I have reconciled it. It's a non-issue at this point."

"So, what is it you want to talk about?" Sasha asks while reaching for the second shot and taking it in one gulp. Reed grabs his and downs it, making a slight face after he does. Sasha smiles, "It's not smooth like the vodka you're used to. Most vodka now is distilled wheat. This is still potato vodka. I won't drink the other shit."

Reed smirks at him. "We need to talk about something entirely different. Something only you can help me with. And I need your complete honesty and open mindedness. I think you will agree, as I lay it out, of its relevance."

Sasha studies Reed before he can respond. This first contact with Cara's best friend and former handler is not going as he anticipated. For all these years he has only known Reed in the third person. Although Cara didn't talk a lot about him, she did share some Reed stories. It's really Nic's constant complaining and whining about Reed that provided the most clues.

Sasha would try to take the higher ground with Nic. Fact is, Nic knew they were close before he married her. Why hang on to the jealousy? It's counterproductive and draining. And it certainly wasn't going to change the situation. It's obvious Cara adores her husband and only has eyes for him. Nic would admit he never questions her loyalty, he would just feel better if Reed wasn't handsome, successful, witty, single and unfortunately, not gay.

What Sasha found the most intriguing was how Nic would describe Reed when he was forced to spend time with him. He called him a goofball. Said Reed and Cara acted like silly and frivolous girls when they were together. Nic found it hard to believe the two of them were ever operatives, let alone the feared Duo they had the reputation of.

It was only in the last few years, when Reed's career became more public, Sasha was able to watch him on CSPAN. There was absolutely nothing silly about that coverage. The man could face a Senate hearing with steely determination. He was eloquent, intelligent, composed, and when he needed to be, biting. He could work the room like a pro. Sasha could finally see the truth behind the reputation.

He refocuses back on Reed and decides to take that higher ground. "Because Cara is very important to both of us, it would mean much to me if we could be friends. Please, appreciate I want to work towards that."

Reed nods to him seriously. He drops his head down for a moment. When he eyes meet Sasha's again, he drawls out, "That's a very mature, emotional statement, Sasha. Cara give you a vagina, too?" The son of a bitch actually winks at him. "Don't sweat it. I've had mine for 25 years."

He can't prevent the snort of laughter that comes out of him at Reed's self-deprecation. The look of defeat on Reed's face adds to the humor. Still laughing, he pours two more shots of vodka. This is the man Nic refuses to appreciate. The Reed who's an equal, who took control of this conversation by means of compliments and humor while still being formidable.

Up close and personal he can justify the hoopla over the man's looks. Reed is a very handsome man. He has a well-bred, tailored masculinity about him. Cara refers to Nic as 'gorgeous'. She calls him 'striking', which is better than Broody, and she uses the nickname 'dashing' for Reed. It's a very accurate description of the man, as well.

Handing Reed his shot glass, they both lurch back the contents before Reed's face composes. His jaw sets firmly and there's a vein to the left side of his forehead growing pronounced.

Finally, he leans further back in his chair and takes a deep breath. "I've never been in a serious relationship with a woman, besides Cara, but I know people say when you've been a couple for a long time you can finish each other's sentences." Reed inhales once again. "You ever notice how C and Nic don't finish each other's sentences? They actually blurt out the entire thought just as the other is having it?"

Sasha is completely confused by this sudden directional shift, but his gut is to protect Cara and Nic. "They are a very intimate couple, Reed. Always in sync with one another."

Reed shakes his head, like he took the wrong approach. "I know that. That's my whole point, here. Did it ever occur to you they are too in sync? Unnaturally close, too soon and too quickly?"

Sasha doesn't want to take this inquiry seriously, but he can see it's important to Reed. He thinks back to when Nic came to see him to ask for time off after Geneva. He was shocked by the request. Nic was not the type. He was a man that never dated, and rarely went out and got laid, despite women falling at his feet. And he only got laid at Sasha's urging. Then, suddenly, he's an emotional basket case over some woman, who he'd come to find out, later, was Agent Chase Bennett. Then, much later, again, he would discover Nic was a mess after just seeing her from a distance in both Kabul and Geneva.

Nic spends three weeks with her, was completely smitten, and ready to abandon ship, risking his career and possibly his life. It really was totally out of character for Nic. As much as Sasha thought Nic was being immature and naïve, the last years here with them have only reinforced that bond. They are truly an amazing couple. But, what is even more astonishing is his ass has ended up in Cleveland with them. Who in the hell would have predicted he would walk away from his post to live with Nic, his wife and their two children? "Okay, I'll bite." Sasha finally offers.

"The humming. Nic's humming. Do you hear it?" Reed blurts.

Sasha shrugs. "The Soundtrack of His Life? No, but do you know how many times I have fired a weapon?" He waves his hand by his ears, dismissively.

Reed leans right into Sasha. "He's not humming." Reed points to his own ear and gives the thumbs up.

Sasha's head tilts as he stares into Reed's eyes. He's attempting to process what Reed is implying. He sees the man's eyebrows rise. A light bulb comes on. Sasha's eyes go wide, his mouth drops open, and his hands fly to his face.

CHAPTER 27

"SO YOU'RE SAYING THAT DAD was a KGB agent for Russia and you were a CIA agent working for Uncle Reed like a hundred years ago?" Mia asks with total teenage angst.

"Mia, it wasn't a hundred years ago. It was 17 years ago we walked away from that, more or less." Nic responds trying to keep his composure.

Now Max chimes in, "And Uncle Sasha is not your blood brother, but another agent for the KGB that was like a brother to you? And you're not gangsta, at all?"

Nic is more frustrated, "If it makes you feel any better, Uncle Sasha and I are considered gangsta in Russia, big gangsta, shoot to kill gangsta."

"Cool," Max is more impressed.

Cara tries her hand, "Your dad and Sasha had to lie about being alive still to get away from a possible criminal charge, or 'extermination' order, so they can live here with me in the States."

Mia, catching on, asks, "Why would the people you worked for want you dead?"

Nic tries to patiently explain the things they used to do were very classified, and the information they retain is considered dangerous. If they ever decided to turn that knowledge against Russia, they could do tremendous damage. They could also use the intel, "That's what everyone calls military intelligence for short, against other countries, pitting one against another. There are secrets we possess many countries would not want touted."

Therefore, 17 years ago, if an agent was considered rogue, or trying to cut his ties with the group, many times that agent was given an

189

extermination order. In other words, better off dead than a dangerous threat to national security.

"Were all agents exterminated?" Max questions.

"No, it depended on their level of expertise and the security clearances they had. The more they knew, or the higher up they were, the bigger the threat." Nic continues, keeping his tenuous patience.

"You and Sasha were pretty good agents?" Max asks again.

Cara takes this one, "Guys, your father and Sasha weren't good agents; they were the best agents." She looks to him with indecision. "And they weren't considered Russia's best agents, they were considered two of the most dangerous operatives in the world."

Max and Mia posture at one another, thoughtfully. Mia decides to pose the next question, except it comes out more of a statement. "We think you guys are possibly exaggerating. I mean, Dad, you a dangerous agent? And Sasha?! He lets me paint and sparkle his clothes. We aren't trying to downplay this for you or anything, but can you see our point of view here? And don't even get us started on Mom. Mom as a CIA agent? Well, that's just not happening." Mia waves her hand by her mother in a dismissive gesture.

Nic is now holding his head in his hand and rubbing his forehead. The worry lines on his face are severely creased. "Cara, I want to jump the table with split second precision and grab Max in a choke hold while sending an upper cut to my daughter's jaw. It may actually prove something to them. Please stop me, because I'm highly considering it at the moment."

Cara places a reassuring hand on his arm. "Kids, I know this is a lot to take in, but can we move past the 'believable or not' part of the story, and get to why the FBI is around our house? Can we agree as a family your father's level of talent, and your mother's lack of talent, are not part of the issue here?"

Mia crosses her arms and huffs out, "Fine."

Max is unconvinced, "Can you really cross the table that quickly, Dad?"

Before Max has the words out his mouth completely, Nic has flown from the chair and gotten behind the twins with his hands on each of the necks. He's pulled their heads back, causing the chairs they're sitting on to tilt. Cara reacts with lighting speed and is across the table standing in front of the kids before Mia can even scream. As the shriek leaves her throat, Nic is placing kisses on the top of her head.

Max's eyes are wild and wide, looking at his mother. "Holy Shit!" he yells.

Nic releases them both, scolding Max, "Language, young man!"

Max argues, "Come on Dad, what the hell? You scared the crap out of us and we're impressed! And Mom, Jesus, you jumped that table like it wasn't even there, and so fast."

Nic places one hand on each child's head, "What do you think, Cara? Is this our new form of discipline?"

"I like it." Cara confirms as she walks around the table versus back over it.

"Can we get back to the issue at hand, now?" Nic asks while he walks back to his seat at the table. The twins nod affirmative, quickly, not wanting to incite him again. Maybe there is an upside to all of this after all. "So," He begins more calmly, "We think someone found out about how I married your mother and had two children. We think this someone believes the genetics that contributed to our talent as agents, has been doubled in both of you."

Max bursts out laughing, "Someone thinks Mia has any talent?"

Mia ignores her brother, "So...we're like the Spy Kids?" she asks with greater interest.

His wife moves in closer to him and peers. She's doing what he's doing; trying to recall this movie from the core dump of mindless kids' movies they've had to endure over the years. They both draw a blank, so Cara inquires, "Remind me again about this movie?"

"Mom, there's like three movies about them." Mia rambles on in one sentence about parents who were spies, and they have a fake uncle that watches over their children, and then the kids get kidnapped, but they have all these skills and they free themselves, and then they help their parents take down the bad guys.

Cara gawks at her daughter in horror, before she glares at him, and loses her shit, entirely. "Dear God! We're a total fucking cliché!" She is up out of her chair, pulling her hair and jumping up and down. "What the hell has happened? When did my life become an unmemorable kid's flick? Oh, I know when. When I fell in love with the TV movie about the handsome Russian agent!" She's now yelling, "We're like B grade movies! The kind that go straight to DVD! Fucking unbelievable! No wonder the kids think we're full of shit! I think we're full of shit!!" Meltdown in progress.

Nic is at Cara side trying to calm her down, but she's pushing at him to get away from her. The twins are horrified and frozen in their chairs. Nic tries, "Cara, you're scaring the kids, and frankly, you're scaring me."

"SCARED? WHY WOULD YOU BE SCARED? She lowers her voice to a low pitch shrill. "This is B grade, remember? THERE'S ALWAYS A HAPPY ENDING!"

"Baby I need you to breathe slowly. Slow, deep breaths, please." He looks to the twins sending Mia for some water and Max to Cara's bedside nightstand for a Xanax. Cara is now trembling. "Baby, I think you're going into that shock thing, again." He says, soothingly.

She snaps, "It's not shock, it's TOTAL INSANITY!"

"You haven't slept in over 48 hours, your mind is shutting down, that's all."

The twins are back with the water and pill. Nic tries to get Cara to take it, but she keeps pushing both away. She suddenly stops pushing, and grabs the water and pill and swallows. She's about to throw the glass at the wall, but he predicts it, and catches her hand in time to prevent it. He wraps his arms around her, pinning her arms to her sides.

"Cara mia, please, try to calm down. I know this is hard for you. You're blaming yourself for the position we're in. If you and I hadn't met, none of this would be happening, right?"

Clutching her firmly to his chest, he understands. If things had been different, she could've had a normal life. Maybe if she hadn't met Reed either, Cara could be some happy housewife and mother with a pleasant banking career in a nice small house with a white picket fence and 1.8 children. No drama, no missions, no guns, no killing, just debits and credits. She's questioning all of it. Why has she done this? Why has she taken this road? Was the path wrong? None of her friends have paths like this. They have normal lives; lives they don't make cheap, cliché movies about.

But aren't those other people's lives clichés, as well? Their unhappy marriages, their unfulfilling careers, their nasty children, they're all cliché to each other. These people she is comparing her life to. He can see it all in her wild eyes.

"Whose life would you rather have of all the people you know? Whose? Anyone? Look at me, Cara." Nic demands. She slowly tilts her head up to meet his eyes. "My path was always meant for you. I believe that, cheap

TV movie or not. And I believe Reed found you that day at UConn and your paths were meant to cross. Remember the thread?"

Cara said she followed the thread to Nic. He believes she's been following that thread her whole life. And maybe the thread knew she was meant for greater things. It by-passed the boring banking career and the boring husband. "The thread took you where you needed to be."

He spins her so she can see the twins. "These are our children, Cara. The thread wanted them, and more importantly, you love them more than anything in the world."

Her stiff body relaxes, and she begins to cry. "I'm so sorry" she mumbles to the kids.

Mia only shrugs, "No big deal. We all have meltdowns."

Max adds, "Maybe you're getting your period soon." Mia hammers him hard in the chest.

Cara's shoulders sag. "You still sure the thread wanted them?" She tries for a small smile. Nic releases his firm grip, but maintains her in his arms, and starts nuzzling her head.

"Jesus, now you've got to go and get lovey with each other? I'm out of here, but when are we eating?" Mia asks unconcerned by the event.

Nic assures his hungry daughter the Bishops will be there with Chinese food, soon.

"I'll be in my room. Call me when the food gets here." Mia states.

"Ditto on that." Max mumbles as he's walking out of the kitchen behind his sister.

Nic hangs on to his wife as he watches his children climb the stairs. Maybe the conversation didn't go as well as he hoped, but that was more communication from both his kids than he's heard in a month.

He carries Cara to their bedroom. He lights their gas fireplace before taking her to floor with him in front of it. Shifting, she gets comfortable sitting between his legs, her back to his chest so they can both face the fire. They sit in comfortable silence with his one arm wrapped around her waist and his hand stroking her hair.

Soon, he hears footsteps coming up the front stairwell. There are two sets, and neither sound irregular. The steps head to the kitchen. He can hear the weapons all being placed back into their special assigned areas. Shoes are left off.

"Um, is there anyone home? Anybody?"

Nic calls out to Sasha to say they're in the bedroom.

Sasha makes his way, with Reed following, to the open doorway of the bedroom. They both peer in. Sasha states politely, again, "Director Reed, this is the Master Suite."

Nic motions them to enter, but then stops them once they both get through the doorway. He scans them thoroughly, not realizing Cara's doing the same thing.

She throws her head back into Nic's chest, as if she's lost control of it, and slurs, "I win."

"Damn, Reed, I thought you'd at least take a swing at Sasha." Nic accuses.

"I knew they wouldn't fight, and no one would throw a punch." Cara slurs out, but more coherently than before. "It's like I said…Reed's going to have a girlfriend AND a boyfriend, now."

CHAPTER 28

REED IS WATCHING SASHA CRINGE at the notion, which is frankly insulting, because he would be an amazing boyfriend for Sasha. He gives the man a hard glare before waving his hands down his body at him. "Really, Broody? You think you can do better than all this?"

Cara busts out into giggles and waves her hand in the air, snapping her fingers at Sasha. "Sash, he's right. No better for you."

Reed stares at Cara unblinking for a moment, "I imagine the little talk with the kids didn't go well seeing we now have Xanax Cara with us?"

"I love Xanax Cara. She's funny." Sasha lets out while he gets down on the ground to their left to enjoy the fire and obviously contemplating a retort by imagining who would be better than Reed he could get. He's not coming up with anyone. "Damn, Vizzini, I hate when you're right, even hypothetically."

Reed decides he'll make it a love fest and sits to their right. Even though it's drug induced, he's pleased to see her laughing. He asks if they should put Xanax Cara to bed, but he heard there's food coming, and he thinks she should eat something as well. "Who wants to decide?"

"I was just thinking the same thing." Nic believes they should feed her something, and then she goes right to bed. Although he doesn't know how good company she's going to be during dinner. "Reed, are you going to behave with Jake? Cara can't take any more stress right now." Nic inquires casually, although she's still waving her arm around and snapping her fingers at nothing.

Grabbing her hand from the air and placing it on his leg, Reed admits, "I'll behave." Honestly, even he doesn't have the energy for more

195

confrontations. "I'm exhausted, you must be, too. You saved your wife from an assassin, and then all of our asses on the jet."

Nic waves at him like 'twas nothing. "Between the kids and Cara's total meltdown, I'm zapped now."

"You know I'm right here. I took a Xanax not a Valium. Not the same. I've driven your children to school on Xanax many a day." Cara pauses, "I'm suddenly feeling much better and more focused." She squeezes Reed's leg before leaning back against Nic and taking in the scene. "This is nice, though. Can we just sit here until those guys arrive?"

It really does feel more soothing with all of them, together, Reed observes. The intimate foursome in front of the fire, like old friends. Cara gives Reed a discreet wink and smiles at him. The wink, he's sure, is because he does really like Sasha. She knew he would, and he has forgiven her for being selfish.

Reed stretches out on the carpet on his side, almost in a fetal position, and gets comfortable. Sasha leans against the chaise lounge. Cara and Nic just stay in their original position except Nic leans back to place his weight on his hands and stretch his back in the process.

"This is nice, isn't it?" Nic asks almost rhetorically. "I am feeling more energized. Physically, I'm toast, but mentally, my mind is clearer."

Cara turns to her husband. "You think we couldn't have done this 15 years ago? We can only find this soothing, now, with the four of us? The thread."

Nic leans into her to kiss the top of her head, "Yes, cara mia, the thread brought us here. It wouldn't have worked 15 years ago."

Reed can feel the lasers, and shifts his eyes to catch Sasha staring intently at him. He only gives the man a subtle nod. When Reed turns his gaze back to Nic and Cara, he realizes Nic caught the tail end of that acknowledgement with a bewildered expression on his face. Soon enough, Cara and her husband will understand.

There's a flash of light igniting the bedroom, startling Sasha to open his eyes while simultaneously reaching behind him for his weapon. He sees Jinx standing in the doorway with her camera phone aimed at them.

"What the hell?" Jinx says calmly, "What did you guys do? Drink the Kool Aid? It looks like a suicide pact in here."

Sasha tries to articulate how they must have fallen asleep while they were waiting for the food. The others appear to be sleeping, still.

Just then, Reed reaches his arm up quickly, grabbing Jinx's leg, and bringing her down hard on top of him. She feigns a struggle, but is enjoying the contact. Reed flips her so she's wedged underneath him.

"I've missed you, Jinx," while he lands a huge kiss to her lips. "You're looking pretty hot. You still wanna have sex with me?"

Jinx pushes at Reed, "I always wanna have sex with hot guys."

Cara's eyes flutter open to add, "It's true. Any hot guy is Jinx's domain."

"Wait, do you want to have sex with me?" Sasha questions, perturbed this has never come up in conversation before.

"Always dream of it." Jinx admits.

"Will you tap me before Reed? I don't want his seconds. Besides, I think you won't want him after me." Sasha inquires, honestly interested in her answer.

Jinx thinks about this. She slowly looks from Reed to him, and then back to Reed. "No. Reed is first. I've wanted to get into his pants far longer."

Before Sasha can plead his case, Cara injects, "No, Nic, I didn't forbid it. I know what you're thinking. Remember Reed's rules, no cavorting with anyone on staff."

"Not that Jinx ever adhered to the rule." Reed adds while standing up, pulling Jinx up with him.

"How was I supposed to exist?" Jinx loudly protests, "Too many distractions in the office. I had to get them out of my system."

"I'm feeling left out, will you have sex with me?" Nic asks trying to sound hurt.

With a broad smile stretching across her face, Jinx admits, "Now Cara did forbid that."

Cara laughs at her friend and starts to rise slowly. She still looks exhausted and spent. Sasha watches Nic struggling to get to his feet. He can't be bothered. Sasha sits motionless in his position, too tired to even move.

It's then they hear a new voice join the conversation, "Nobody is having sex with my wife without getting past me, first. Although, the fact you're discussing it, is kind of a turn on."

They all snap their heads back to the doorway where Jake is standing with his arms on his hips looking menacing. He's wearing black cargo pants and a very tight white T-shirt giving his always tanned skin a darker tint than normal, and his tattoos are sharp and more vibrant against it. His height and body are taking up the entire doorway. The man has a way of sucking all of the oxygen out of a room.

"Dude, it's just conjecture, but happy to help your sex life in any way we can." Sasha muses to make sure to diffuse any tension. Now he's glad Jinx chose Reed, first. He'd rather Jake kick Reed's ass.

Jinx takes this opportunity to make introductions. She grabs her husband's hand and pulls him forward until he's standing in front of Reed. Jake is a good four inches taller than Reed, and has about 50 pounds more on him. "Director Connor Reed, I would like you to meet my husband, Jake Bishop."

Reed's face completely changes and becomes cold and hard. He narrows his eyes before bringing his arm up, hand out. Jake hesitates a moment before bringing his arm up.

Clasping his hand, Reed asks, "Is it 'Jake'? Or do you prefer the nickname 'Jack'?" Reed's one eyebrow is quirked up as he inquires. Ah, Formidable Reed is back.

Jake responds with slow words, obviously not intimidated. "It's Jake, and I could use some help putting the food out if you're up to it?"

"Lead the way," Reed offers pointing out the doorway, fearlessly.

Jinx adds she's set the table for the group, and Eli and Max are in Mia's room. The kids said call them when the food is served on plates. "Spoiled brats." She murmurs.

Jake nods his understanding as they walk away. Jinx quietly shuts the door to the bedroom, remaining inside. She turns back to them with a face of concern. Cara motions to Jinx to sit next to her on the bench in front of the bed. As Jinx seats herself, Nic sprawls out on the bed while he still hasn't moved a muscle on the floor.

"Start talking." Cara commands but places her hand on Jinx's arm. This, Sasha wants to hear. After all the commotion between Jinx and Jake, he needs to know what happened.

● ● ●

Jinx was hoping to put off this discussion. She leans into Cara and wraps an arm around Nic. "Nic, thank-you so much for saving my little buddy's life…twice. I can't believe you can fly a jet. Jake and Sasha admitted they can, too." All three sets of eyes are pinned on her. Sighing, she resigns, "Jake admitted a lot of things to me. Most of which I suspected." Their eyes become keener. "None of which I'll admit to you guys." The sad faces. "His story is not mine to tell. I'm sure when he's ready, he'll disclose it." After his confrontation with Reed, he may be forced to admit it.

"Did he know we were agents and we worked for Reed?" Cara whispers as if it's still a secret.

Jinx snorts out, "Jake had no clue! Can you believe he was ripping mad at *me* earlier? Said I betrayed him! The nerve! He lives a lie, and I'm the betrayer. Asshole."

Sasha giggles out, "Is that what all the screaming was about?"

"Yes!" Jinx hangs her head. So what if she always suspected her husband's career. That didn't mean she was supposed to fess up to hers. Like Cara, it was simple to live the lie. When she left the CIA, it was Reed who set up her interview in Cleveland. She signed an NDA with him, and her records were altered to show she worked for the Defense Department in a minimal capacity. This ensured her privacy, but kept her pension intact. Reed knew she was getting fried and wanted to start making more money. It was all exciting and interesting, but then the terrorism thing came, and it was just too much. It was hard not to get caught up in the sickness. Plus, she suspected it wasn't going to be much longer before Cara bailed, as well.

"Reed did that for me. He lined up my interview and told the hiring manager my true background. I scored an awesome job at triple my pay scale." Unlike Cara, Jinx didn't have a family to fall back on. The money was important. As much as she hated to leave Cara behind, Jinx was confident Reed would protect her. She certainly didn't expect Cara to show up on her doorstep only months later. The woman was an emotional wreck after what happened in Geneva.

"Ellie, you suspected Jake's career, but…his motives?" Cara inquires with as much finesse as she ever displays, even using her real name and not her nickname.

"I am not a dumb blonde. Jake is HOT, so I trusted myself to fuck a HOT guy and not succumb to pillow talk. And that's what I did, and did

I mention he was HOT? Hot enough to keep wanting him." She knows it was against her MO with men, but the idea of the secrets made it sultry, more erotic somehow. She knew Jake was fishing. She just wasn't sure whom he was looking to catch, or if he even was a threat. Of course, damn Reed with his old school mantras kept repeating in her head, 'Keep your friends close and your enemies closer.'

But then she got knocked up. That was not part of the fuck the hot, mysterious man plan. Jinx wanted the baby, with or without Jake. She was 32 years old, not a young woman by any standards. And that's when things started to change between her and Jake. He acted like he wanted to be a part of it all. He seemed to be really into her, besides just a good lay, besides a cover. Their relationship grew in a way she never expected. She wasn't comfortable telling Cara, who had made it clear she didn't approve of Jake.

"I'm sorry, but I didn't think you would understand, so I kept my feelings to myself. Until he dropped out of sight those last weeks of my pregnancy. I was a wreck. I had suspected his true career, and thought he was dead." Jake finally did show up in the middle of her labor and threw Cara and Nic out of her delivery room. He was incredibly apologetic, and he appeared haggard and contrite.

But what finally threw Jinx for a loop was when Nic and Sasha started getting really close to Jake. She knew they didn't go to Vegas on their first weekend guys getaway. "No way. You guys failed to come back smelling like smoke, sex, sin and depravity."

"That's what I thought, too!" Cara exclaims. "I knew they were lying."

"Smoke, sex, sin and depravity?" Nic muses, "That was our big mistake?"

"Absolutely", Cara confirms. "Think about when Jinx and I go, or I meet with my college girlfriends or Reed in Vegas?"

Nic ponders, "You come home exhausted, smelling like an ashtray, sweat, booze, broke and hung-over. Come to think of it, what the hell do you do there?"

"Our secret, we aren't sharing, but you guys didn't come back like that. If anything you came back exhilarated. All wrong." Cara gives them her disappointed face. "Not smart, boys."

There were more clues with each 'weekend getaway' the three guys did, and Jinx started to believe maybe this was all going to be fine. Nic obviously trusted Jake, and she respected Nic, immensely, so his opinion made an impact. "I stuck my head in the sand, went to Cara's Land of Denial, and let it all go. I love Jake, whoever he is." She peers at the closed door of the bedroom and admits, "Jake knows Reed. That's why he was so mad at me. He thinks Reed is going to do something...bad."

She stayed in the bedroom to give the two men time to, hopefully, just chat. She's somewhat confused by Reed's discretion, though. Why didn't he divulge who Jake really is? He's either having a charitable moment, or up to one of his brilliant manipulations. Withholding Jake's secret from these guys can swing either way. Her money is on Reed spinning something to his advantage.

Trying to change the subject, Jinx inquires, "By the suicide pact scene in here when I arrived, I can conclude Reed is settled in with the Sasha addition and none of you slept recently, either? I'm beat. Let's eat and all get some sleep."

They start to rise, but as they approach the door, Nic stops them. "What are we going to expect between Reed and Jake when we get out there?"

Jinx shrugs her shoulders, "Hope for the best and prepare for the worst." With this admission, Sasha checks for his weapon.

CHAPTER 29

AS SOON AS THEY OPEN the door, they hear voices and laughter from the kitchen on the other end of the house. They approach, cautiously, to find the kids are all seated and eating. They're talking and laughing with Jake and Reed. The men are seated next to each other at one end with the kids on each side of them.

Jake addresses the foursome entering the kitchen. "We were just about to send a search and rescue for you guys. Thought you might have formed that suicide pact after all. Better sit and start, the food is getting cold."

Without hesitating the four of them take the remaining seats and start passing trays of Chinese food between them. Cara notices Jinx must have placed wine glasses and bottles of Shiraz and Pinot Grigio on the table. Good old Jinx, she won't cook, but she sets a mean table and thinks of all the little things.

Cara passes on the wine bottles as they go by, opting for the ice water in front of her. She peers at Reed trying to surmise what happened between him and Jake. She's getting nothing from his face, but neither man appears injured. "What was so funny?" She decides to ask.

Before either man can speak, Mia pipes up, "We were talking about your code names. So lame, by the way, to have code names." She rolls her eyes. They have gathered the meaning behind Nic and Sasha's code names, but the kids are having difficulty rectifying Cara's. "Uncle Reed said we have to ask you if we want to know." Mia adds.

Cara freezes, water glass immobile hallway to her lips. Nic reaches for her leg under the table and whispers, "Don't go there if you can't handle it this evening." The whisper is loud enough for most of their end of the table to hear.

There's a loud, derisive snort from Jinx at his concern. "The kids are going to LOVE this story!" Then she yells Nic's fear across the table to Reed. Without waiting for Cara's approval, Jinx adds, "Shall I start and you finish, or vice versa?"

Reed's brows furrow at Cara with concern. She shrugs her shoulders to her boyfriend in defeat and points to the bottle of red wine, "Go for it, but I need to be drinking."

Nic kindly pours her some as Reed tells Jinx he wants to start the story.

"Before I begin," he turns to all three kids, "Everything you hear from us, earlier from your parents, or from now on, is strictly confidential. I trust you three with this information. You're not little kids anymore, and you have the right to know, but with that right comes responsibility. I expect the highest degree of discretion from you as I would any agents with this intel. Swear to it."

All three kids nod seriously, raising their right hands like it's a court of law. Nic and Jake smile at their reaction.

Reed continues, having made his point. "When I started a new team at the Agency, both of your moms were on my team. We engaged in some unique types of exercises to assist us with our fieldwork, but we also incorporated some standard training. Training like marksmanship, classes in weaponry and hardware. They did sleep deprivation training, lots of stuff similar to a military basic training camp.

"One of the facilities we had at Langley was a simulation room. These rooms, now, are tricked out with all the latest technology, and they don't even resemble the rooms from the late 80's. Back then, it was a mechanically driven series of diversions and obstacles. An agent would walk in, and objects would fly out at him or her. They would need to hit those targets within a certain degree of time to determine speed and accuracy."

Mia interrupts, as she's prone to do, "Like in the old movies? When the metal plated ugly mobster comes flying around a corner, and you have to hit it with a shot to bring it down before he gets off a bullet at you?"

"Yes, exactly like that!" Reed compliments. "Your Mom is pretty good with all of the other training, with certain parts she excels, but in the simulator, she's awful. She scores so low, a rookie can do better." Reed lifts his eyes in Sasha's direction.

● ● ●

Nic notices Cara is guzzling her wine, drinking under duress. Her head is averted from everyone. He places his hand on her leg under the table. She raises her eyes to him, smiling for his support. When Nic turns to her to smile back, he notices Sasha gives that glance to Reed, again. Like earlier. What's up with those two?

Reed continues his story admitting Cara is anything but a quitter, "She kept going into the simulator to try and get better scores, sometimes late into the evening. And just when she was improving, I would change the program completely, because I suspected she was improving by memorizing the movements. Then her scores came crashing down again."

Cara glares at Reed from the memory of when he did that. Reed winks at her and continues with the story.

"She tried to change how she entered the simulator. C decided the sounds were a diversion to her, choosing to run through it with headphones on playing music, instead. This was years before IPods. All we had back then were Sony Walkmans with cassettes tapes. The player was bigger, and heavier, and she kept it in the pocket of her cargos.

"C did show improvement with this method. I changed the program again, and she continued to score in the same range. I surmised she was on to something that worked for her. I wanted to be a supportive handler; I suggested she might do better if she plugged her cassette of music into the simulator speakers, versus carrying around the bulking cassette player and wearing the big headphones. Her scores might improve if she's more handsfree."

While Reed is telling the story, Nic notices the kids are on the edge of their seats, and then he looks to Jake and Sasha and realizes they are as well. He can hear Cara regulate her breathing in an effort to stay calm.

"After directly connecting her cassette into the simulator speakers, her scores did improve. She was still considered below average in the simulator, but her scores were on the charts at least. But she kept working at it, and then one day, late in the afternoon, we were all in the team room when the paging system went off." Reed motions to hand the baton over to Jinx.

Jinx has to gain composure because she's already losing it. "Next thing we knew, blaring out the paging system, throughout the entire facility at Langley, is The Reflex by Duran Duran, and in that moment I knew. I yelled to Reed, 'Bennett's in the simulator!'" Jinx is struggling to breathe out the rest of the story between laughing. "Cara had a huge crush on Simon LeBon, who's the lead singer, and she loved all of Duran Duran's music. But she especially loved The Reflex.

"Apparently, Cara must have screwed up the connection in the simulator and had her music piped into the wrong speakers. Reed went running to the simulator, but the entire song was over by the time he got there and disconnected the player." Jinx is wiping tears from her eyes. "Appreciate this. There were high level meetings and work happening all over the facility. There was going to be hell to pay!" Jinx yells through her mirth.

"I didn't have a choice!" Reed jumps back in, "The Deputy Director wanted answers. I had to tell him the truth. He demanded both of us in his office immediately."

Cara has both of her hands covering her face. They are trembling. Nic isn't sure if she is laughing or crying. Before he can further inspect, Reed continues, "The man was enraged when we walked in. Before either of us could apologize, he yelled to Cara to get on one knee. He pulled a huge sword out of a sheath he had hanging on a wall, and walked over to point it at her.

"I'm freaking out, thinking he's going to hurt her, but suddenly, he taps her shoulders, then her head." With an English accent, Reed quotes, "'I dub thee Sir Reflex from here on in', and then he bursts out laughing at her!"

Everyone loses it except for he and Cara. She is mortified. Her face turning completely red. Nic doesn't feel an ounce of concern for her. His mind is too appalled by the story. "That's it? That's why everyone called you the Reflex? Because of a badly versed song from an 80's pop band?" Nic spits out.

Apparently, this sends everyone into more laughter because he is so distressed by the revelation. But really? The actual song is the moniker?

Sasha is trying to speak through his delight over the tale. "And to think all along we thought it was your speed or agility that warranted the name, and instead it was a mishap over your failings in a simulator!"

Again, more laughter ensues, until Reed puts his hand up to get some composure back, "She just couldn't shake that name ever again."

Mia gets up with the other two kids and she runs to Sasha to whisper in his ear before they take off. Sasha's laughing even harder, and Nic knows what's coming.

"Okay, stop already, will you?" The kids aren't there, so Cara takes the opportunity to confess, "You can see why when I heard the music playing a few days ago it totally freaked me out. It's not like it was public knowledge beyond Langley about this story. Even now, I find it ironic that Vlad thought to use it. It hit too close to home. I mean the moniker IS the song."

"It was the reason I took the threat so seriously when you emailed me." Reed confesses back. "And I did, and still am, looking at possible connections." He turns to Sasha, "You guys really didn't know any of this? Vlad had no way of knowing from his employment with you?"

Sasha turns serious when he advises, "We should be exploring known associates of Vlad. It is very viable Vlad knew the story from someone who may have been connected with the Agency during that time period. He knew to bait Cara with the song."

Reed agrees and informs them he has analysts on it. He lets Sasha know he will send him what he has so far on the investigation and asks him to add any known associates of Vlad he hasn't considered.

Nic is watching this exchange between handlers like he isn't even there. Like this isn't his wife and kids under threat. It's taken less than a few hours for Reed and Sasha to become BFF's and trusted colleagues. What the Hell? The two of them agree to meet at 10:00 AM tomorrow to discuss the investigation and bring everyone up to speed, deciding everyone is too tired tonight to be worthwhile.

Before Nic can process how he feels about his exclusion, there's commotion in the great room as the three kids return from their trip to the music room. Mia walks into the kitchen and hands Sasha a guitar and him a wireless microphone. She whispers in his ear. Nic grabs his daughter by the chin and kisses her nose. Mia gives her mother a wicked grin as she strides back into the great room to the baby grand piano.

Cara is completely humiliated. Her children think she's a joke and her husband, the music snob, is disillusioned with her. Why, oh why did this story have to come up tonight? Of the four of them she is the only one with a ridiculous moniker. Reed received his because everyone saw him as the "White Knight." She called him that at the Agency, but it stuck because both the men and women who worked there saw him as either too honorable to engage in any sexual harassment, or too respected for being the man who saves all damsels in distress. Neither is necessarily true, but it was how he was perceived. Her stupid code name is another example of women needing to work harder to get any respect.

Before she has a chance to wallow, Carter enters the house with two empty plates and some silverware. Cara assumes Jake and Reed must have served them food, but told them to eat outside. Poor things.

She looks pleadingly to Reed while Nic and Sasha make their way to the living room, "Reed, can't they eat with us in here? It's pretty rude, and I am Sicilian, and this is my house. People EAT here. It's ingrained in my DNA. Speaking of manners, have you and they been shown to your rooms?"

Jake answers her, "I did when you guys were in the bedroom. Carter, and what is it you call him, 'far guard'?"

Cara nods and smiles while Jake informs her everyone is all settled in their rooms, and he took Reed on a tour of the house when they fetched the kids for dinner.

"By the way, sweetheart, beautiful house. Nic designed the house and you decorated the interiors?" Reed compliments. It's his first time visiting since they owned their new home. "I'm very impressed; some more amazing designs from you. You really are very talented, but Nic has a great eye for architecture, as well."

She and Nic have both done so much traveling, and seen so many places all over the world; they always utilize that knowledge when they work. Without actually discussing it openly, they both wanted to glean something positive from their pasts. "Architecturally and decoratively, we have seen some of the most beautiful places in the world, despite being there for more nefarious reasons. We took a lot of that into consideration with the design of our home."

Jake asks not understanding, "Are you saying as you were being chased through the Hermitage, you would stop and admire the frescoes in each room?"

Reed looks to Cara in full understanding, but she replies, "Something like that, yes." She gets up to meet Carter at the sink. "Carter, please help yourself to anything in the house. You are my guest here, and should be afforded full access. Do not eat outside anymore. Understand? And tell your nameless friend, too."

Carter nods graciously, and then asks, "What are they doing in the living room?"

"THEY are setting up to mock me, my children and Mean Man. Stay for the entertainment portion of this evening, please."

Carter peers into the living room and wanders in. Ignoring everyone, she clears dishes as the others get up to help. By the time they have the table cleared, leftovers put away, and dishwasher loaded, they hear the all too familiar sounds. The three kids singing the backgrounds...

"Ta, nah, nah, nah

Ta, nah, nah, nah"

Then Nic's voice, sounding better than Simon LeBon could ever dream of, belting out the first verses of The Reflex.

Reed tries to drag Cara into the living room, but she's resisting. He finally picks her up and throws her over his shoulder. Jake, not wanting to be outdone, grabs Jinx and throws her over his shoulder. The girls clasp hands in an effort to prevent the boys from making any progress, but they fail and end up sitting on the floor in the living room.

Mia is at the piano and Sasha on acoustic guitar. Elijah is playing an electric bass guitar while Max has dragged up some drum pieces and cymbals. And look who has joined in? There's Carter with a saxophone. Great, even he has other talents.

The music is familiar, but they have re-arranged it to make it sound more contemporary. It's like a combination of a Lady Gaga and an Usher song. Her family is so frigging talented.

Nic winks at Cara as he hits the full out chorus.

Reed leans into her. "Holy shit, they're great! I had no idea they were this good!"

Cara inclines back into his ear, "They are. They make me proud."

Nic wired the entire house to plug and play with full Bose speaker system throughout. It's their outlet, the music, but they could tour, they're that good. Looking at her children, now, they are ecstatic. She always tries to be encouraging, even if it's at her own expense.

All Reed can say is, "Amazing."

Nic launches into the second chorus, crooning it out for full effect. He even throws his hips around like a rock star.

Sasha does a little guitar solo next, fingers flying over the strings like a pro. Just when he's done, Carter launches into a sax solo. He waves the instrument towards Mia when he's complete. Her fingers fly across the baby grand like a concert pianist. She earns a round of applause from the four on the floor, and then she nods to Elijah who starts plucking out bass riffs worthy of a jazz musician. Again, he earns applause and some hoots and hollers from Jake and Jinx. Nic hands the mic to Max and replaces him at the drums. Max starts rapping the next chorus section.

Cara looks at Reed's face and the expression of awe on it is priceless. Max is spectacular. He's rapped the entire section but added some of his own digs at his mother in the verses. It is so like her son to be the showman. She is beaming. Suddenly her face changes as she looks around the room and she feels one of those seizures coming on. This is it. THIS is her family. She has had the great fortune of growing up in an amazing family, but then she acquires what most people never receive, a second, wonderfully amazing family. How could she have questioned it, earlier? Why did she freak out and think she was starring in a B rated movie? It just can't be true.

"Don't do that."

What? Cara looks to Reed. *Was I just biting my lip? Reed hates it when I do that. Reed isn't paying me any attention, though. That's weird; I thought I heard someone speak. I'm losing it. Bedtime for Bonzo when this mockery is over.*

They wrap up the song and all stand for the bow and applause. Using the microphone still, Nic states, "Well, I decided the lyrics are truly bad, but I have to admit, some of them are applicable to you, cara mia."

"I don't want to know which ones, please, but Bravo, Bravo to all of you." Cara says with great admiration and pride. "Do I get to go to bed now?"

"No, Sasha has one for all of us. I promised the kids one more, then bed for the adults." Nic sets up the stand for the microphone in front of

Sasha. He comes over to Cara and bows in front of her, "May I have this dance, my lady? Or should I say, Sir Reflex?"

Cara launches herself at him in an effort to knock him over, but fails, and only lands in his arms. Mia has moved off the piano and is seated with her cello. Elijah replaces her, and Carter takes the electric bass. Sasha switches to an electric guitar.

Mia starts on her cello with a haunting extended intro to Secrets by One Republic. Nic brings Cara into his arms to dance with her. Jinx and Jake follow suit in each other arms. Switching over to one of the overstuffed chairs, Reed gets comfortable to watch the impromptu band. Sasha starts his first verse and he sounds so soulful. His voice is beautiful.

The lyrics are resonating around the room; the melody is poignant and evocative, yet cleansing. They hit the full chorus with instruments getting louder. Sasha's face changes so every line on it appears etched in pain.

Cara notices Reed is watching him sing. *I wonder if he senses Sasha's anguish.*

"You want to help him now, don't you?" Nic whispers, pulling her eyes from Reed and Sasha to focus on her husband. "Sasha loves this song, and it's appropriate for this evening. The kids like playing this one with him, but it's his voice that transforms it. Full of pain."

"I was just thinking that, too."

"How are you, baby?"

"Ready for bed and a new start tomorrow."

CHAPTER 30

CARA PROMISED JINX SHE WOULD run the front nine of the golf course at 8:00 AM. It sounded like a good idea the night before, to exercise, but when the alarm goes off, she isn't convinced. She fell right to sleep last night, not even recalling if Nic was out the bathroom yet. As she looks around the bed, she notices her husband isn't even there. She gets up and readies herself for a, hopefully slow, jog.

When Cara enters the kitchen, Nic is cooking full out breakfast. Carter is seated at the table eating scrambled eggs. Nic has sausage, bacon and hash browns served already. A soiled plate sits in front of Reed while he works his tablet beside it with a cup of coffee. Jinx is already over and is seated with only coffee next to him.

"Order up." Nic serves Far Guard three eggs over easy.

Cara gets a large mug and prepares a cup of coffee before going over and sitting next to Carter. He looks up at her from his plate filled with everything Nic had served. "Mean Man makes a mean breakfast." Reed and Jinx both inhale sharply and start laughing at their simultaneous gesture. Carter gazes at them confused, "What?"

"Agent Carter, no one, and I mean NO ONE speaks to Agent Bennett before her first cup of coffee is complete in the morning. If she was armed, she would've shot you by now." Reed advises.

Nic pipes in from the range top, "That used to be true, Reed, and for the most part, it's what she prefers, but I've had to break that horse."

Cara scowls. Nic believes she can't shoot the children or him when they speak to her prior to caffeine. He's unreasonable like that.

"You and Jinx skipping breakfast or you want something? I'm only here till 9:00 AM," Nic warns.

She would hurl it during the run. Maybe Jinx will take pity on her and get them back here by nine.

"Which speaking of, hurry up with that coffee and let's go." Jinx pushes.

It's a rare beautiful morning for late April in Northeast Ohio. The daffodils and crocus are blooming. The sun is peeking its way out. The golf course has been cleaned and landscaped from the winter abuse. The weather is a perfect 55 degrees for a leisurely jog.

"Jesus, Jinx, my lungs are frigging burning. Slow down, bitch. You know you're like two inches taller than me. That stride of yours is killing me."

Jinx glares back at her over her shoulder. "Stop bitching and start breathing, slut. Besides, we're almost back to your house." She hadn't notice, she can't see. The sweat has poured into her eyes.

Two of the FBI agents have taken the run with Jinx and Cara as protection. Sasha and Nic had insisted. They have kept the girls flanked. The second agent is directly behind Cara as she lags.

About 50 yards from the house, Cara gives up and walks the remaining distance while chatting up the FBI agent. They are deep in conversation when she suddenly hears Jinx screaming, "Oh NO, NO, NO…HELL NO, NOT HAPPENING!"

Cara breaks out into a sprint with concern. As she rounds the corner up the driveway, she sees the cause for alarm. Cara stops dead, halfway up, shaking her head back and forth unable to verbalize. Jinx has her hands on her hips. Beyond her are five gorgeous men wearing nothing but shorts or track pants, and sneakers.

Jinx turns to engage Cara, "This is not acceptable. AT ALL. Nic preening in front of Starbucks is one thing, but this!" She's pointing at them wildly, "THIS is completely intolerable!"

Cara pulls her shirt up exposing her not so tight abs and chest, but she has to in an effort to use it to wipe the sweat from her face. She takes her time walking the rest of the way up the driveway, taking in the view. Very calmly, for effect, she states, "Is it your intention to run the course together, gentlemen?"

Cara's Nic and Sasha know better than to answer her, but Reed doesn't understand the concern. "Yes, what's the issue?"

Jinx jumps at him "You can't go out there together and shirtless! The women of this neighborhood will faint! Have you no clue what you all look like? This is Cleveland. Men don't look like you here – let alone five of them together! You look like a Chippendales act!"

Nic mans' up and speaks directly to his wife, "Cara, you know I don't like to wear a shirt when I run. The fabric hurts my nipples when I start to sweat." It comes out more of a whine, though.

"Yeah, honey, you know I have sensitive nipples," Jake adds flexing his pecs for effect after he says it, and then placing his hands over them, protectively.

Jinx drops her hands from her hips and starts stomping on the cement with one foot. Cara looks them all over one more time and heaves a big sigh. She knows they will lose this battle.

She places a calming hand on Jinx's arm, "Fine, but I hope one of you is carrying."

Carter raises his hand. Cara gets closer to inspect his shorts and identifies where the weapon is. She turns to the group requesting, "Please don't give any of the older women on the course a heart attack. It's Women's League morning."

The men head down the driveway when Cara catches Sasha's hairy arm and looks down past his, covered in hair like a gorilla, chest to his shorts, "I see you're packing a weapon as well."

Sasha gives her a rare ear-to-ear grin. "No, but I've had some women refer to it that way."

"EEEEWWW!" Cara screams as she chases Sasha down the driveway trying to punch him.

CHAPTER 31

CARA ARRIVES LATE TO THE party at 10:09. She was held up from her shower serving breakfast to the kids, who overslept Nic's cut off time and wanted to eat. Apparently, they cannot locate cereal and milk on their own. She has gone casual with jeans and a light sweater. She put the Olaf boots back on because she loves how they feel, even after only wearing them once. She blew out her hair, but skipped any fuss straightening it. She even managed a little make-up.

As she makes the corner into the living room, she sees additional seating has been added to accommodate everyone. Headcount shows the kids are missing and Sasha and Nic. Reed has on jeans but with a striped collared shirt and a blue blazer. Her boyfriend looks like he's going to the club for dinner after the meeting. Jinx, who utilized Mia's bathroom to shower and get dressed, has on a fitted long black skirt and a blouse. Cara decides she's underdressed for this meeting. *I should go change.*

Just then Nic turns the corner and comes in giving her a little peck on the cheek, "You look lovely, baby. You're wearing some makeup. Oh, and you smell nice."

She gives him a little smile, resolved to remain as dressed.

Sasha comes up from the lower level wearing a T-shirt that says 'BAZINGA' on it. Painted footprints adorn his jeans.

Cara stops him as he passes by, "I know the jeans yesterday were homage to that show Supernatural you watch with the kids, but what's this?" pointing to his legs.

"These are my Just Dance pants."

Reed tilts his head and winces. "Don't you have Call of Duty jeans? I think that would've been more appropriate."

"Mia and I don't play that together, the boys and I do. They don't decorate, though." Sasha says very seriously by means of explanation. "Where are the chosen ones by the way?"

Nic leans into the back stairwell and yells up to the kids.

As the teenagers arrive, everyone gets seated, but Reed is still standing. Cara runs to her favorite chair to take a seat, but can't get comfortable. She stands back up and looks at the cushion. Feeling it with her hands, she doesn't locate any issues. She sits back down but is still bothered. Rising once again, she pulls the cushion off to look underneath it. Her suspicion is one of the kids hid some contraband below. It's clean, though. She repositions the cushion but does not sit. Instead, she stands stiffly looking at the chair.

Her discomfort is not the lovely upholstered armchair. The tension in the room is filling. Something is wrong. Cara is scrutinizing in all directions. *There's a threat. I know it. It's that prickles on the neck thing happening.* Slowly looking around her, she rests her gaze out the wall of windows facing the backyard. It's not out there. The tension and threat to do harm is in the room with her.

Cara turns to her children, who are seated on the couch with their backs to the glass wall. Sitting with Eli, all of them appear bored. She shifts her eyes to Jinx and Jake. Jinx is reprimanding her husband to use a coaster on Cara's side table for his coffee. Nic and Sasha are seated in the two leather club chairs across from them in deep discussion. No one is paying any attention to her or noticing the problem.

Her scrutiny finally rests on Reed. He's still standing, and right next to her. His eyes locked on her. Cara peers into those eyes and feels great peril coming back at her. The threat is emanating from him. Her head tilts in confusion. Reed has his ice face on, and it's directed right at her. She is dumbfounded. Reed has given her mad, raging, frustrated and betrayed faces, but she has never seen him look at her like this. He has his ready to kill you face on. Without taking his stare from her, Reed slowly reaches inside his jacket.

All of sudden Cara lunges towards him, grabbing his wrist with both her hands. "Stop."

"Stop what?" Reed asks quietly.

She backs away slightly, but then he gets his hand further into his jacket. She firms the grip on his wrist. "NO, STOP!"

Nic sees the confrontation and gets up to head towards her and Reed, but Sasha jumps out in front of him preventing any progress.

Still locked in a battle over his wrist, Reed calmly inquires, "C, what's the matter?" but his face and eyes are cruel. His pale baby blue eyes have turned frigid.

Staring intently into those glaciers with astonishment and determination, Cara states firmly, "I need you to take your hand out of your jacket, NOW!"

Reed, still with that forbidding glare, "But I'm just getting my phone, C."

She shakes her head, but nothing changes the threat she's feeling from Reed. "You're lying. Your phone is not in your jacket."

"C, let go of my wrist, now, before I have to hurt you."

Nic tries to push pass Sasha, but Sasha grabs him hard, and Nic's confusion prevents him from fighting back.

Cara is completely panicked. This is all wrong. Reed wants to hurt her. She's sure of it. "No, you ARE trying to hurt me. Why do you want to hurt me? TELL ME!"

Reed grabs Cara so quickly, she doesn't see it coming. He has restrained both of her arms and is shaking her. Nic is flipping his head back and forth between the confrontation and Sasha in bewilderment. Sasha only takes a more defensive hold around him.

Cara is close to hysterics. Reed is in her face now. Those awful eyes on her. *I feel his hatred. I don't understand. He loves me.*

Reed yells into her face, "TELL ME WHAT'S IN MY JACKET IF IT'S NOT MY PHONE! TELL ME!"

"YOU HAVE A GUN!"

Reed shakes her harder, "OF COURSE I HAVE A GUN HOLSTERED IN THERE!"

A sudden jolt of pain spears through her brain. It's dizzying, but she can see a clear picture of what he has. "No, no, not that gun!" Cara pleadingly whispers back at him.

"WHAT DO I HAVE IN HERE, CARA!?" Reed demands.

It just comes blurting out of Cara's mouth, unchecked and uncensored, from somewhere she has no idea of. "You have Sasha's gun!"

CHAPTER 32

WITH CARA'S DECLARATION, REED RELEASES his firm hold but gently runs his hands down her arms, massaging where he gripped her. Sasha releases Nic and all eyes are on he and Cara. Reed opens his jacket and deliberately pulls out a vintage Makarov PM pistol. He walks towards Sasha and hands it to him. Nic is staring at the gun with recognition, because it is from Sasha's collection. He looks up at Cara, tilting his head.

Cara is standing by herself, trembling, one hand on her forehead. Her eyes shift to Nic, who's frozen in his spot. Reed slowly approaches to stand in front of her. His heart bursts with love, devotion and sympathy for her. "I am so sorry, my sweetheart, but it had to be done. We couldn't figure out a better way to make it happen. And we can't move forward anymore without it." Reed says as gently as possible. Cara looks up at him with tears in her eyes, unable to speak.

Nic tries to finally move, and finds Sasha stepping out in front of him, again. He places a hand on Nic's shoulder, "Nicolae, please, we must see this through. Trust me." Sasha says as soothingly as he can.

Reed can only gaze at Cara. "C, sweetheart, this is my fault. I was your handler, and I was so remiss. I just didn't see it. It was all there for me, and I didn't put it together. Maybe, I didn't want to see it. Again, I am so sorry." He tells her with all of the guilt and resignation he feels.

Cara questions him with a shaky voice, "What did I just do?"

Stroking her hair, he admits, "You did what you've been able to do since I met you, sweetheart. It was all there."

Cara always knew what to do. She always could predict everyone's next move. She was amazing in the field, yet she couldn't get through a simulation. Reed thought she was a natural, but her intuition was too sharp. He should have seen it, but chose not to. When he looks back, he thinks himself a fool. And then his brain just clicked into place on the plane ride back from Berlin. He had a moment of illumination.

When she started singing the song Nic was humming. It was then. The illumination was blinding. She kept asking if he remembered about Nic's humming, and of course he had, but Nic wasn't humming. He was sitting right next to Nic, and Cara was across the table, at least four more feet away. And he knows for a fact her hearing is not as keen as his.

"You don't hear Nic humming, C; you hear in the music in his head." Cara is backing away from him, rigidly, tears running down her face. "You hear a lot of stuff in everyone's head, C. I would endeavor to predict you feel what's in their heart, as well." He is almost pedantic in his delivery. "You're not a natural, my dangerous, little sweetheart. You're a bit of a cheater."

With this accusation, Nic tries to get past Sasha, but again, he restrains him. Cara is only focused on Reed as he continues his slow revelation.

It all reconciles when Reed thinks back to Kabul. Why was Kabul a failure? Why didn't Cara feel or 'hear' those men coming into the alley with her? There were six of them. Something went wrong in her sonar. Then, there's Geneva; she was a mess. First time Reed had ever seen it. "You were so fucked up and out of sorts in Geneva, it spilled over to me," he confesses.

But the pinnacle was yesterday morning. Reed listened to the tapes of her conversation with Vlad. She was doing great. She had him talking, and giving up information, and then suddenly, Cara shut down. Training gone. Sonar gone. She jammed. She went off to seizure land. "What do those three only times you fell apart on a mission have as a common denominator, C?"

Cara's gaze shifts to take in her husband. Nic brings his eyes to hers, but nothing is on his face.

Reed continues his accusations. "I berated you over Nic, your fascination, your obsession, your complete failure to see any reason whatsoever. You have NEVER been that way. What made Nic different? True Love? That's for Hollywood and romance novels. No one gets that from just seeing one another across a dusty Afghani alley."

At this admission, Jinx and Jake rise from their seats. Jinx can't stop herself, she interrupts Reed's monologue. "It isn't, Cara. It's not normal what you and Nic have, I'm sorry. Reed's right. You two are just something else, sometimes. Like too in sync. Unnatural for a couple. And the chemistry still after 17 years together?"

He needed to confirm his suspicion. Cara is not what she appears. She is more than that. The clues were everywhere. He didn't bother to recognize them. "Somehow, your brain isn't processing it, but you're reading people's minds. And you're not alone." He delivers with zeal, wanting effect.

Reed starts to back away from Cara as she begins to sway. *Can this even be true?!* She sees movement to her right and notices Jake coming closer to her. She turns her head to glance at him and…*He's so scary. Why does he always have that awful menacing look?*

That's the only look he has. In her mind, it's as clear as if he spoke.

She spins her head to Nic so hard; it causes her to become unbalanced. *Nic?*

Baby?

Cara goes down, knees crumpling beneath her at the sound of her husband's voice in her mind. Jake manages to catch her before she hits the ground. Nic's still frozen in his spot, just staring wild-eyed at her. He's as shocked by what's happened as she.

Cara mia!

I'm okay, I'm okay. She sends that thought out to him with some strength.

WHAT THE HELL IS HAPPENING? She can not only hear him, but also feel his fear and confusion. Nic reaches her, scoops her out of Jake's arms, and takes her falling to his knees. The children are horrified. The entire room is petrified in time with everyone gawking at her and Nic.

Nic turns angrily to Sasha and Reed, "This is what you two talked about last night, isn't it!?"

To Be Continued

Ready to find out what Cara, Nic and the gang are going to learn from their new-found talent? Will they be able to solve the mystery of who is after Cara so badly they hired an assassin and tried to bring a plane down? Are the Andre children talented beyond measure and the true targets? What about Jake? Who is he, really? And what truly happened between Reed and Cara in Geneva in her hotel room?

Read on to The Reflex, Part II for the answers.

Hope you enjoyed the first book in The Reflex series!

CPSIA information can be obtained
at www.ICGtesting.com
Printed in the USA
LVHW101635091122
732727LV00002B/69